Love Protects

A novel by

Julia David

Field Runner Press

ISBN 978-0-9991134-5-5

Published by Field Runner Press

Field Runner Press

Redding, Ca.

Printed in the United States of America

Leaving Lennhurst Asylum Series

"And His fame went throughout all Syria; and they brought unto Him all sick people; that were taken with divers diseases and torments, and those which were possessed with devils, and those which were *lunatic*, and those that had the palsy; and He healed them." Matthew 4:24 KJV

Love Covers
Love Flies
Love Protects

Other Historical Romance Books by Julia David

Mighty One Series
Available on Amazon and Kindle Ebook
Burgundy Gloves
Broken Chain
Black Coat

Escape to an Era where True Love Prevails

Visit: www.juliadwrites.com for behind the scenes, photos, videos, newsletters, release dates, and fun giveaways.

Dedicated to Ethan, Leon and Wells. All mighty first-born older brothers.

"Sing, O barren woman, thou that didst not bear;
break forth into singing, and cry aloud,
thou that didst not travail with child:
for more are the children of the desolate
than the children of the married wife, saith the LORD."
Isaiah 54:1 KJV

1

Centerville, Kentucky
Winter of 1867

ENJOYING THE COLD morning silence, Mrs. Anna Plugg leisurely stretched her stiff neck and shoulders, trying to find another few minutes of comfort in her warm bed. Laundry day with Tallie, the housemaid, didn't usually leave her so sore. But Tallie had talked and fretted on and on about her son, Otis, yesterday which left Anna doing most of the heavy lifting and wringing of the household wash. A deep yawn overtook her as she willed her mind to drift back to sleep. Any second without Mr. Plugg in the bed was a pure reprieve. Considering he had been out late on one of his many rides, she wondered what would have him up so early this morning.

With one open eye, she peeked around the room and noticed the well-stoked fire, and his clothes flung here and there. Something loud clamored downstairs. Was he in the kitchen pestering Tallie for his breakfast? As long as he didn't want anything from her a few minutes more of sleep could be hers. Another strange sound echoed up the staircase and diverted her thoughts of morning freedom.

The sound startled her—as if there hadn't been any bizarre noises growing up at the Lennhurst Asylum and School for

Disabled Children. She'd lived all her life on alert, why couldn't she drift back to sleep with a few strange noises? What was he doing?

Muffled sounds. Surely that was someone suffering. Was he hurting Tallie? What could she have possibly done this early to set him off? As one of his many slaves, Tallie had learned early how to tip-toe around him. Another sound. A door slamming or something dropping?

"Oh, for heaven's sake," Anna grumbled, throwing off her covers and reaching for her winter robe. She dropped down the stairs in hopes of finding Tallie preparing a warm breakfast. Turning the corner, she glanced around. The kitchen was empty. No rattling pots and pans, just a strange ruckus coming from the pantry.

Anna looked out the window hopeful Mr. Plugg was gone for the day. Seeing nothing through the frosty pane, she turned slowly, willing the nervous tics starting to well up to still, but her head suddenly jerked down. Knowing she was helpless against the ailment that jerked her chin from her early days of living at Lennhurst, she remembered the kindly doctor from Lennhurst who patted her on the back and assured her it was nothing fatal. Dr. Powell had much more severe cases to tend then her. Something creaked, bringing her back to the moment.

Stepping over to the pantry, she brushed her blondish-brown hair from her face and clenched her fist before she laid her hand on the knob. She'd heard these same sounds before, many a painful night, in her own ear. Her stomach lurched, and her body began to sway. A fierce trembling radiated down through her arm to her hand. Gritting her teeth tight until her jaw hurt, she jerked the door open.

Tallie screamed and tried to push Mr. Plugg off her half-naked body. Alfred Plugg twisted his head and nailed Anna with his bright red rage. "Get out!" he snarled, as Tallie struggled out of his grip.

Anna turned and bolted upstairs. Flinging the bedroom door closed, she knew she had only minutes before he would pound up the stairs and take her by the neck. She quickly dropped her robe and nightgown and threw on her day dress and grabbed her shawl off the peg. Barely able to breathe through the shock and dizziness, she pulled on her stockings and boots and wrapped her body in the warm shawl.

There was only one way to get out before he was upon her. She'd rehearsed this before. She could do it. Glancing down the empty staircase, she quickly entered the room Mr. Plugg's sons used when in town and closed the door.

She pulled on the frosted windowpane, and it thankfully rose. Flipping a leg out, she reached for the branches of the barren tree that reached toward the house. A cold snippet of wind tried to take her breath away and blow the loose strands of hair into her eyes. She clutched each frozen branch, borrowing its strength to lower herself to the yard. Leaning against the frosted brown-sided house, she tried to steady her pounding pulse.

Now what? The neighbors were all tucked indoors on such a cold morning. The pond that backed up to the large houses looked frozen solid. How long would she last shivering in the cold?

Tallie, what about poor Tallie? She covered her mouth and felt her chin bouncing under her fingers. Mr. Plugg had purchased Tallie years before his first wife died. The middle-aged servant was strong as nails. Anna recalled the scene in the pantry. Tallie's shocked face was creased with sweat, and her eyes flashed with anger. Did she try to resist him to no avail? The act made her stomach recoil, and she groaned.

Her white breath swirled around her oval-shaped face as her panicked gaze flitted from one neighbor's house to the next. How long would she have to wait for him to calm down this time? Her teeth began to chatter. She should probably walk the three blocks into town. He would never hurt her in front of the townspeople.

Pushing off from the protection of the house, she took two steps into the yard. The only thing moving this frigid morning was a neighbor's dog when he looked up from his protective stance in front of a small, green barn.

Dread and panic rose up her back as her feet crunched the frosty grass.

"Get in the house now!" Alfred Plugg sneered baring yellow teeth, walking towards her.

"I will not." Anna's green eyes narrowed with defiance. Backing across the slope of their property, she kept a protective distance from his grasp. "You have committed adultery with Tallie." She tried to steady her chattering teeth and involuntary head tics. "I want a di—divorce."

"Ha!" His face was still bright red and his lips tightly drawn in a thin white line. "She is my property." He growled. "I can do whatever I want with her." He grimaced and put his hand to his round chest.

"President Lincoln freed the slaves." She sucked in the icy air. "She is not your property, and you cannot just force yourself on her." Anna kept stepping backward and found herself at the edge of the frozen pond; she edged back closer. "I *will* get a divorce."

"No, you won't, you ungrateful castoff," he swallowed hard. "No one will listen to you," he shook his head, squinting, trying to find his breath. "Imbecile." He spit the words out, "Defective murderer from an insane asylum."

Anna used his apparent distress to step carefully onto the thick ice covering the pond's surface.

"You'll do as I—" he clutched his collar.

She moved further out on the ice, her body shaking from the cold. "You have always despised me, hurt me." She noticed the beads of sweat forming on his blotchy bald hairline. *How could that be? How could he sweat in this numbing cold?*

"Get off that ice. Now." His eyes rolled back in his head.

Anna hesitated. How many times had he falsified a need, just to be able to grab her quickly then used his large girth to overpower her? "You are an adulterer. Tallie and I will take refuge somewhere until…"

His hands seized his chest, and he ground out a strange, curdled groan. He stepped forward with bulging eyes and reached out for her to steady him. Anna moved quickly away from his grasp, and his body wavered and then toppled like a tree in the forest straight onto the ice, his face striking the hard surface.

"Oh, dear God," Anna bent over as the blood poured from his face onto the white frosty ice. She tried to pull his obese frame onto his back, but he was limp and too heavy. "Alfred, can you hear me?" She heaved with all her might but couldn't turn him over. She looked back at the house wondering if Tallie would come help. And then she heard the sound. The ice was cracking beneath them.

"Alfred, get up! I can't—" She tried tugging on his jacket to move his large frame back toward solid ground. They were only a few feet out from the yard. Clenching her teeth, she bent down to his legs and strained to lift and pull them to the safety of the shore. Her feet slipped out from under her, and she landed on her backside with a hard thud. A large crack in the ice started under his left arm and continued across under his shoulders. As she rose to try to pull again, the ice creaked and separated around him. His face and chest sank into the shallow, icy water.

"Help!" she cried out. "Someone help!" The freezing water seeped into her boots and soaked the shawl that had fallen from her shoulders. Trying again, she waded in up to her knees and yanked his legs backward. All her effort was in vain; she watched in shock as his entire head and torso now submerged under water. She grabbed the back of his jacket. It was of no use. He was too heavy for her alone.

"Tallie!" She screamed. Wobbling on frozen feet and legs, she ran through the back door into the kitchen. "Tallie, I need you now!" She searched around quickly, finding no sight of her.

She ran back outside and past the barn to pound on the neighbor's back door, calling out, "Please...please...help." Over her quaking and numbness, she kept thinking *his sons are going to k-k-kill me.*

2

SHIVERING UNCONTROLLABLY NEXT to the sheriff's small woodstove, Anna willed her head to stop jerking to no avail. Nervously turning her shawl in front of the stove, her tics surged through her shaking body. Maybe the others would mistake her incessant head dropping as a sign of her chilled state.

"So, I'm writin' this down. Did I hear you right? You and Alfred argued, from where you snuck out of the house and walked out onto the thin ice of the pond." The sheriff looked up from his paper with cynical eyes. "Most folk can argue in the house or yard. Not many argue out on the ice." His southern drawl accentuated his belief her story was ridiculous.

Her head dropped, not in agreement or shame, but he went on. "Then Alfred turned red, then white, clutched his chest and fell." He smirked, rolling his tongue inside his cheek. "I just rode with him last night, and he didn't seem stricken then." He let out a long breath. "So you couldn't catch him, and he was likely knocked out by the fall, then the ice cracked, and you couldn't pull him out alone. Is that the gist of it?" He dropped his paper on his desk.

"Yes, sir." Her head tics made it impossible to look him in the eye. She stepped away from the burning heat of the woodstove.

"I already sent Don to the Plugg plantation to tell them boys."

Anna's head shot up. "They…I can't…where will I go?"

"Back to your house in town," his brows creased. "Don will tell them. It took four of us to get him from the water to the wagon. We couldn't lay him out at the house in town or take him to the plantation. While we had the manpower we had to take him on to the mortician. They can see him there." The older, beefy sheriff had missed her point entirely.

"I can stay at—at the house?" she murmured.

The sheriff frowned; he'd lost all patience with her. "Yes, I'm sure the boys will have respect for you and ah…" he swung his hand in the air finding the words, "help you with what you need." He shooed her, "You can go."

Anna clenched the damp, knitted shawl closer and walked from the sheriff's office to the frosty sidewalk of Centerville, Kentucky. She stopped and had to find her bearings. There wasn't one pulse of grief in her being. Shock, but no sorrow. Had Tallie heard her call and chosen to stay hidden?

Keeping her head low, she noticed the few people out in the bitter cold. Two men on horses crossed in front of her. A woman with a scarf wrapped around her hurried into the mercantile. A little boy in a ratty jacket sat on the corner of the sidewalk. How could everyday life in Centerville look so untouched? Everything in her world just got turned upside down. Or maybe after four, long years of being Mrs. Anna Plugg it just got turned right side up?

She took slow and quiet steps towards the mercantile. For the first time in a year, she didn't have to hide her entrance. Mrs. Hart was the only caring soul in this town. When Mr. Plugg found out she'd been sewing baby gowns and selling them there, he refused her to do any business, calling her a common peddler, a constant shame to his good name. But today she was free, free with no need to watch her back and sneak in the mercantile's side door. Shivering from the cold creeping past her damp shawl, she passed the little boy who was now running back and forth then hanging onto the wooden rails outside the store.

She entered the large, glass-windowed door and felt the warmth and smells of the lovely store. Her heart found solace when she viewed the table of baby things that held her beautiful gowns with the special tatting she'd sewn around the collars and edges of each little cuff. The absolution it gave her heart was worth every stitch. The pain of never placing one on her own babe was quieted by how many other little ones would have the beautiful handiwork. The bit of coin in her pocket gave her a sense that she did have value for something. Mr. Plugg had belittled all her other confidences, especially berating her for her barrenness, but this simple task she wouldn't let him take.

She heard a muffled squeal and looked out the side window. The little boy was squeezing his hand and crying with pain. Anna looked around the store. No mothers missing their children and no Mr. Plugg to explain herself to. She turned and walked back out the door and met the child's watery, brown eyes.

"Can I help you?" She noticed his dirty toes peeked out from the open-ended leather shoes.

"Oww...oww…" he cried, lifting the wound up for her to see.

Noticing the large wooden sliver embedded under his fingernail, she met his dirty, tear-streaked face. "I know just what to do." Before he could open his mouth to protest, she pointed to the side. "What is in the dog's mouth?" As soon as his eyes averted, she yanked on the little piece of wood. His face whirled around with open mouth, but no sound came out.

"It's gone." She smiled and rubbed his dark matted hair.

He sniffed and squeezed his injury. One little drop of blood surfaced from the under the fingernail. He quickly shoved the dirty finger into his mouth and looked up at her with soft, swollen eyes.

"What is your name, brave boy?"

"Milo," he mumbled.

"Can you wait another minute, Milo," she asked, looking around, wondering if he was out and about on his own. "I have to pick up some socks from the store, and I have an extra pair that is too small for me. Maybe you would take the socks?"

His eyes widened, and he nodded.

Anna reentered the store and grabbed the thickest wool socks she could find. Her love of children always took over, and she smiled lovingly as she placed the socks on the counter.

"Oh, Mrs. Plugg, ma'am." Mr. Hart stopped and stared at the socks then at her. "We heard about the tragedy befallin' Mr. Plugg."

Anna quickly looked down and lost the pinch of joy she was feeling.

"Mrs. Hart had a trip to Lexington planned. But as soon as I heard, I went through some of the warm skirts and blouses in black. I'm sorry we don't have any mourning dresses in stock. Would you prefer to order a dress?"

"No, no." Her shoulders tensed. "Whatever you have will be fine. May I purchase these for a little boy outside?"

Mr. Hart looked toward the window, confused. "Yes, Ma'am."

Anna eyed the peppermint sticks standing in a large glass jar and thought against it. She didn't know how a grieving widow should act. "Can you put it on our account? Or I could pay from my sewing money." Suddenly aware that she had no idea how Mr. Plugg received money and paid for things. Would her abrasive step-sons see to her care? That was hard to imagine.

"Let's see what we owe you," he said. "Mrs. Hart keeps a little ledger for the local vendors." He flipped the page and pulled out a dollar from the cash register. "Minus the socks and your mourning clothes, we owe you a dollar for last month's sales."

Anna wanted to smile as he placed it in her hand. A dollar of earnings felt wonderful, and Alfred Plugg was never the wiser. More relief flooded her being. Never again would she be yoked with someone so dispiriting and cruel. Maybe the curse of God could be lifted from her life. She pressed her smile into a thin line and nodded to Mr. Hart. "I will be right back for the skirt and blouse."

Anna hurried to the side of the store where the boy Milo waited. She wondered if his mother or father would appear and refuse her charity. After seeing no one near, she sat with him on the step of the sidewalk.

"These are the socks I was telling you about." She lifted his little foot and pulled off the ratty shoe. Looking side to side and still not seeing anyone, she slipped the sock on and quickly pushed his shoe back in place. "Does that feel warm?" She smiled at him, receiving a little sweet smile back. "Poor little toes." She rubbed them quickly with her hands before she slipped the other sock on and replaced his worn shoe. "Now they can have a—"

"What are you doing?"

Anna dropped Milo's foot and jumped up. A man, unshaven, with loose, dark hair and dark, probing eyes looked down at her from the sidewalk.

"I'm sorry, sir." She flinched and stepped back. "I—I—he had a little sliver from the railing, and I didn't see anyone." She spoke to the ground then turned to step back into the mercantile. "I meant no offense." She finally took a quick look back at his stoic features. "Your son is very brave." She nodded and turned to walk away.

"And she brought me new socks," Milo said excitedly.

Anna grimaced, she had hoped those socks would be their little secret. With her palm gripping the ice-cold knob, she pushed open the glass-framed door.

"He's not my son," the man grumbled, as he stalked away.

Anna took one quick, careful glance back. Young, sweet Milo skipped along merrily behind the dark, sullen, man who had worry lines along his smooth brow that made him seem much older than her at first glance. His shoulders were broad, and his hands were work-worn, which spoke of someone used to hard labor. His face, though, had an unexpected coloring she could not place.

3

ANNA STARED AT the ground until she entered the kitchen door of the brown house by the pond. Thankful to avoid seeing where Mr. Plugg died, she added some sticks and stoked the large kitchen stove. Laying her shawl over the chair, she listened and felt the stillness of the house. Tallie was still nowhere to be seen or heard. She put her bundled black skirt and blouse on the table. Anna and Tallie were both given a new work dress and apron every Christmas. Another set of clothing seemed unneeded. If black were to symbolize mourning, she would be an imposter.

She turned in the kitchen and grabbed a biscuit from the basket. It was well past the noon hour and in all the commotion she hadn't eaten. She walked back to Tallie's sleeping porch. Her few things were still hanging from the peg above her simple straw mattress. Would she have risked running to the plantation to her son?

Poor Tallie, she'd had four sons—all taken from her and sold except her last one, Otis. As a little one, he'd napped under a tobacco wagon while Tallie had worked in the fields. Years ago, that wagon rolled right over his leg and without any doctors to care for him, the leg healed crooked. Anna shook her head.

Avoiding bitterness, Tallie said she was thankful the Pluggs had let him help in the barn. How often did she hear Mr. Plugg remind Tallie one way or the other how undeserving she was of his kindness? He thought a housemaid was receiving his supreme generosity by keeping her crippled Negro son on his plantation. How could the man think he was benevolent? Every square inch of his mind was sicker than the demented folks at Lennhurst Asylum.

Anna stepped in and touched Tallie's work apron. "Please come back," she whispered. "We are the only two that understand this day of liberation." Anna dropped her hand from the rough stained cotton. *You may never feel free, but I don't, and won't, hold any annoyance towards you. I know you were in that closet against your will, so I have no grievance against you for that.*

She sighed. How many nights had Tallie made her a poultice for her own tender black and blue bruises? She would never be vexed with a woman who'd shown more mercy than even her own flesh and blood family. Would the Plugg brothers insist on Tallie going back to the big house on the plantation?

The thought of Floyd and Bernard Plugg made the last bite of biscuit clog in her throat. Both of them were older than her years and as round and mean as their father. Never had they shown a drop of respect. Poking and swiping at her body until she threated to tell their father of their nasty insinuations. She walked back to the warmth of the stove and started some coffee.

What had the sheriff said? They would 'help her'? She chewed on her bottom lip. They would be enraged. Her heartbeat spiked. If only Tallie was here; that woman knew how to scare a rat from its nest.

Taking the warm coffee to her soft chair in the front room, Anna set it down on the side table and listened again. Without Tallie busying around the two-story home, it was eerily quiet. She grabbed a knitted throw and curled up in her brown chair. Rubbing the back of her neck, she tried to release the tension her tics caused. An irritated snort escaped, something was amiss. She pushed the throw off her legs and stood up and pushed Mr. Plugg's chair around until it faced the wall. When Tallie returned, she could use it and put it anywhere she pleased. Now Anna could try and relax. Her head sank into the back of her own chair, tucking the throw close. She closed her eyes.

What about returning to Lennhurst? I was an excellent nurse's aide, and they were sad to see me go. What would I do without living daily in fear and hesitation? Kentucky to Pennsylvania seemed like a daunting trip. She straightened up and pulled the dollar from her skirt pocket and opened her sewing cabinet next to her chair. It looked like every other sewing cabinet until she pried a little piece of the side panel loose. It was the perfect hiding spot for her few dollars and the current baby gown she'd been crafting.

Someone knocked on the front door, and her heart leaped to her throat. Pulling in a breath, she knew the Plugg brothers would never knock. She flattened her thin wild hair behind her ears and peeked through the side window. It was the neighbor from this morning.

Anna opened the door and nodded to the middle-aged woman on the front step. "Mrs. Holden."

"I feel so, so terrible for poor Mr. Plugg." Her eyes blinked quickly. "All day I've been in tears thinking maybe my Conrad could have pulled him out. But he was such an...an oversized man." Her voice dipped, and the dish wobbled in her hands.

"There was nothing anyone could do." Anna reached out as Mrs. Holden passed the warm bowl. "I believe he had a heart seizure of some kind before he fell."

"I would have brought you something earlier." Mrs. Holden was onto another thought. "But my ole sass-a-frass gal can't move any faster than a slug." The woman spied over Anna's shoulder. "And you've got your gal to keep up house and home, with just you now?"

"Yes." Anna could only hope. "Thank you so much for the dish." She forged a smile. "It's very thoughtful." She prayed she would be on her way.

"Now what are you to do?" Mrs. Holden continued. "Poor young thing. You're slight and plain in a soft, pale sort of way. Much too young to be a widow, I suppose if they close up this fine house, you could live on that big plantation of Mr. Plugg's."

Anna felt her head twitch. "I have so much to think about, but I do appreciate this neighborly gesture."

"Or your family? Will you go back to your family?" Mrs. Holden seemed to need answers forgetting her dead husband was pulled from the pond not even five hours ago.

"No, not my family." Should she tell her nosey neighbor, her own family insisted she leave the safety of an insane asylum and marry the devil himself? She cleared her throat as more tics came on. "Thank you again." Anna clenched her jaw and closed the door before Mrs. Holden could ask another ridiculous question. She leaned against the door, gripping the dish. She didn't mean to be rude.

Later in the afternoon, before the sunset, she pulled all Mr. Plugg's personal things out into a pile. Tomorrow she could wake up in peace and not have to look at one reminder of him. Scooting an old trunk from another room, she opened it and began to drop his things inside. Lifting a pair of pants, she noticed dried blood stains on the pant leg. Underneath his bulky jacket was a strange hood of some kind. Two eye holes had been cut out. The two items alone made a chill run up her spine, but his large canvas bag taunted her to look inside. Carefully opening it, she saw a large coil of thick rope, a hammer, and some large nails. A small stack of handwritten flyers lay next to the rope.

Black Code Meeting.

Law abiding Kentucky citizens welcome.

Rounding up all freedman under the vagrant law.

No business, no wages, no land. Slaves in their place. Or ELSE.

Anna felt her skin crawl and quickly dropped the paper and bag in the trunk. Sitting back on the bed, she contemplated how to burn it all.

Glancing over to her new items, she huffed and frowned at the black clothing. It did feel like someone asking her to put on a costume of sorts. She so rarely went out; maybe she would wear it for town only. Anna blew out a sigh and fingered the simple black fabric. She'd been melancholy and tired all day.

If facing the Plugg brothers wasn't enough, Mrs. Holden's notion of moving home had upset her. She would wire her mother the news tomorrow, but highly doubted Mother would extend an invitation to come home. Her stepfather had made it clear after the accident where he believed Anna belonged. For years she wanted to resent her mother for not choosing her over her new husband. Anna released a long breath. But if anyone understood the restrictions of a domineering husband, Anna did. It was hard for her to stay angry for long. And her mother had the other four children to raise. Anna looked back to the unmade bed and reached for Mr. Plugg's pillow. Pinching it by the corner and holding it out in front of her, she stood and dropped it into the trunk. Pushing the lid to slam shut, she grabbed the old trunk and pulled it by the handle out into the hallway.

She opened the door to the room that had provided her morning escape route, pulled the trunk in letting it land on the hardwood floor with a loud thump.

She gazed out the darkened window. How many times had she rehearsed how she would escape the thick grip of Mr. Plugg's violent hands? Why had she had the nerve to run from him today, to trust the barren, thin tree to hold her? And then to back step onto a slippery, icy pond? Because even though she'd done nothing wrong, he would have found a way to blame and accuse her, sealing his justification of his harsh punishment. Poor Tallie, if only they could talk and clear the air. She heard the door open downstairs. *Oh, thank goodness, she'd returned.*

4

RENEWED WITH A hopeful wind of energy, Anna dropped down the stairs and abruptly froze. Two large bulky frames glared at her with disdain. She looked past them, her heart sinking to her feet. Tallie was nowhere to be seen.

Bernard pushed the open door wider. "Get out! You murderer!"

Anna backed up a step. "Your father had a heart seizure." Her tics started in as she gripped the rail of the staircase. "I've told everything to the sheriff." Her lungs constricted. She needed air.

"We've just come from there." Floyd hissed. "Eyewitnesses said you pushed him into the frozen water and held him under. We've filed charges for the murder of our daddy." Floyd put his foot on the first step. "We know all about your murderin' ways," he snarled. "First your baby brother and now our father."

Anna had seen this rage before. She took another step backward. There was a hammer in a trunk, not far—

"You'll never live in this house again. Get out now!" Bernard pushed Floyd forward as his girth encompassed the stairs. Being faster than she could anticipate, he grabbed her by the arm.

She tried to fight against the vice grip, but he jerked her down to face Bernard. Bernard gripped her other upper arm, and they lifted her off her feet, heaving her out the door.

Anna felt the sharp pain of gravel and dirt dig into her hands and arms as her body skidded to a stop. She jumped up quickly and brushed off her dress, glancing to see if that was all there was to tonight's degradation. The door slammed closed. Maybe she should be thankful a toss out the door was her only affliction. Tucking her cold, stinging hands under her armpits, she looked around. Why had she put that dollar in her sewing kit? She could have purchased a room at the hotel, but now it was dark. Who would possibly take her in?

Walking the four blocks to the sheriff's office, she knocked on the door and entered. A deputy stood and watched her with a sunken, annoyed expression.

"Sir, I tried to tell—" she stopped and swallowed, her tics were nodding rapidly, competing with the shivers in her body, "the sheriff earlier, the Plugg brothers would blame me and…" Her whole body rattled with the cold, and she hovered back near the pot belly stove. "They pushed me from my home. I didn't have a moment to gather a coat or—"

"She can come in here with me!" a loud, slurred voice echoed from down the hall. "I'll keep ya warm darlin'."

The short, balding deputy shook his head. "The sheriff already spoke to them boys, and then he went on home." He nodded down the hallway. "I've got my hands full here. I think it best you take a night with a friend or relative."

Anna held her mouth open, pressuring her chin and head to stillness. "Mr. Plugg allowed me no friendships," she ground out. "And I have not one relative in this entire state."

"Come on, Donny, put her in here with me," came another drunken comment from the hall, "I'll be her new pappy. She done purty enough."

Anna drifted toward the door. Staying here was out of the question.

The deputy opened the door. "Go on down to the church. The preacher brings food and Bibles here a couple of times a week. He can figure something out."

Anna was out the door and a few steps down the sidewalk when she spun back. "The Plugg brothers can't possibly press charges against—"

Her question was cut off when the sheriff's office door slammed shut.

Anna stared long at the mercantile closed sign. Mrs. Hart was a good woman, but Anna had no idea where she lived and didn't Mr. Hart say she was out of town? She blew out a cloud of breath into the icy air. How long till she'd freeze to death outside? Tallie had talked about the thirty-minute walk to the plantation. But without knowing the trails and secret paths, she'd likely get lost and *then* freeze to death. Maybe the Plugg brothers had already left? Could she sneak back into the house? Her last shard of good sense told her she'd probably fare better with the drunk in his cell.

One long block of cold steps later, she took in a deep breath and knocked on the little house behind the church. A flickering light was seen through the lacy curtains. Anna noticed there was a tear in her skirt from the fall and tried to hide it in the folds of fabric when the door opened, and a tall man with a long neck looked down on her.

"Yes, Miss?"

Anna tucked loose strands of hair behind her ear. "I'm so sorry to bother you, sir, um, Reverend. I am Mrs. Anna Plugg. I usually reside in the brown house around the pond loop."

"Yes, I've heard. Mrs. Holden, your neighbor, told us of the tragedy." His tone held no sympathy.

"I have come into an unfortunate conflict with my stepsons tonight. In their anger and grief, they have removed me from my home." She paused, wondering if he was the reverend, he looked irritated by her.

Her head tics instantly ceased, and a lucid thought flooded her being. *Dying in the woods is what you should do.* The darkness of night seemed to engulf her with clarity. "I—I've decided, I don't want to ask for help." Shivers rattled her body as she moved back off the low step. "I'm so sorry, sir, for bothering you." She turned. It would be painless to fall asleep against the frozen ground. No one would find her body. Would God in his mercy allow her into heaven?

"Mrs. Plugg. Wait." He followed her out of his warm home. "See there, the back door of the church?"

Anna stopped and looked over her shoulder.

"I never lock that door. The ladies had a quilting time a few hours earlier. It might still be warm. There is a box of charity items. Use what you can for the hard pews."

Anna turned slowly.

"Can you be gone by sunrise?" he asked.

"Yes, sir," she said despondently.

"Good night then." He turned like he'd been caught breaking a rule and closed his door.

Anna stood still and dazed for the longest time. She realized she'd been doing that a lot today. Idle time was the devil's tool, wasn't that what Tallie always said. She rubbed her cold fingers over her lips and contemplated the door to the church.

Mr. Plugg had convinced her no one would befriend a young woman from an insane asylum. And God *had* spoken his mind by her four years of barrenness. She didn't begrudge the Creator. If He knew all things, then certainly God knew she had despised her old husband. Her hardened heart was deserving of the curse of a closed womb.

Looking back up the shadowy street, she chewed her lip. She'd always been fearful of being alone in the dark. At least in the church, maybe God would have a leftover miracle laying around. She shook her head and stepped to the back door. What a cold, unrepentant sinner she was. A miracle for an unchurched crazy woman? How full of strange notions she was tonight.

5

WILLIAM GIBBS HELD his breath and tried to find a calm tone. He exhaled, scooping his last bite of porridge into little Maribelle's bowl.

"No tears, honey, here you can have my last bite." He forced a half smile.

"I don't want *yours.*" The loud sobs began, and she pushed the bowl toward him.

Will stood and scraped her bowl clean, dumping the bite into his mouth. "Maribell, please, I have to get to the barn," he said around the bite. His younger brother Nathan had already been working for over an hour, and he needed to—

"I want socks!" Maribelle burst out, red-faced. "Milo got socks. I want socks." She dropped her matted-haired head, the dark strands of her hair splaying out on the table. "It's not fair," she sniveled, pounding her little fist on the wood.

Will looked over to Milo's happy but hooded eyes. Milo licked the last of his porridge from his bowl. He'd been like a child with a penny prize since the woman in town bought him those socks.

"Milo, you've worn them for two days. Could you share and let Maribelle wear them today?" Before Will could get Milo to look at him, he saw the same pale-to-red crushing expression. Large tears now overflowed from his little brother's round face.

He stood back, watching his two little siblings cry for lack of—just about everything. With their mother passing a year ago, and the little ones' father no longer trusted around Della, parenthood fell to Will. The family's resources were as meager as his ability to stop their crying, provide for, or bring any security to his siblings.

"I don't want *his*." Maribelle sobbed. "I want my own socks!"

Before he could hush the two criers, his worst fear arose from her straw pallet next to the rock fireplace.

"Alla na na! Eeekk!" Della began to rock and clap. At sixteen, the girl was passing pretty, but the defective mind and matted hair marred it. Pulling her hair into her mouth to chew on, she screeched in between chewing. Will knew how to read her. She was hungry. He scraped the bottom of the pan and placed a scoop in a bowl and handed it to her. She dug her fingers in and ate the mush before she took another full breath. She held the bowl out like she did every morning.

"That's all." He took it from her hand and handed her a small cup of milk. The whining and rocking would go on for about twenty minutes, and then she would settle down. On a good day, she'd chew on her fingernails and fell back asleep.

"Milo." Fresh guilt assaulted Will for making a small child responsible for two difficult sisters. Maribelle at four, almost five, he could control and communicate with, but the damaged one at sixteen was more than any boy could handle. Milo was removing his socks with tears still streaking down his face.

"Milo, keep your new socks on. Maribelle, listen to me." He went over and knelt next to her. He brushed his dark hair from his face, and his expression softened as he studied her sweet but dirty face. "I have to get out to the barn because when Nathan and I work then we have money, and with the money, I can buy you your own socks."

Her mouth hung open, and hollow, wet, brown eyes pierced his heart. Anger and self-pity fought for dominance in him this morning. He stood and raked his hair out of his eyes. "Milo, bang the pan with a spoon if you need us. I will send Nathan back as soon as I can." He flung the door open and shut it quickly behind him.

The giant, tobacco barn loomed across the expanse of the Ford land. He pounded across the damp ground. The hard freeze seemed to have lessened. Maybe today they could get the rest of the seed started in the soil.

Could they possibly get ten thousand hills in this year? He shoved his hands in his pockets. Nathan and Della's father had shown him everything he knew about growing tobacco. He had learned how to use the bedding troughs in the barn to start the seedlings, and how to build hills in the fields for the small, tender plants, and when and how to transplant them to the fields. The land had just the right nutrients for tobacco and should yield a decent crop, but the land belonged to the Ford family. Even with a full crop, he owed half of the profit to the note the Fords owed the bank.

He never understood how, after his step-father's death, Nathan would not get the full inheritance of the land. His younger brother would be eighteen next month. Surely he would come into his full portion of the land. Not one Ford relative had ever stepped onto the soil. They didn't care if it produced or not.

He looked over to a small grove of trees. About once a month his elderly grandfather, Chief Red Gibbs Many Feathers, would just appear—Will's one last legacy to his mixed Indian heritage.

He rolled his lips and blew out a breath of relief the old chief wasn't lingering under the bare branches. His steps speeded up to a trot. This would be the wrong day for his grandfather to fault him for not being part of the needy, scattered tribe. Will kept telling him since his mother's death the greater need was to care for his siblings. His grandfather would never enter their home nor speak his mother's name or to any of the other children. He had no ear for anything Will was up against. His grandfather only told him of the lovely pure Chickasaw woman who would be his bride as soon as he took his rightful place.

Every visit from the old man presented more pressure for Will to return to his culture, his identity. His grandfather would never understand. Celia had been a good mother but white. He'd never known his Indian father. As miserable as each day felt, he'd no desire to abandon all this to Nathan. A Chickasaw bride would only want to stay with her own people. No woman in her right mind would come to join *his people*—a family by three different fathers who lived so wretchedly. Just as he reached the large barn door ready to focus on all that needed to be done, he heard the echo of a banging pot coming from behind him.

ANNA OPENED THE door to the wood stove, her only source of light and heat, in the back corner of the First Congregational Church of God. She sat and crossed her legs in front of it. The flickering shadows of light danced on the back of the large, dark-stained pews lining each side of the square building.

The first night she'd grabbed an old coat from the charity box and slept on the hard bench in the fifth row. The second night she made a place on the floor closer to the stove. The large pew back had felt safe but blocked most of the heat. Hearing a steady pitter-patter of rain on the church roof, she would likely do the same tonight. Her stomach growled, and she dug the last of her crackers from her pocket.

She sighed, of all weeks for Mrs. Hart to be out of town, she felt so foolish telling Mr. Hart a story of why she hadn't yet worn the black mourning clothes. Putting a few small food items on the Plugg account felt like stealing. No one was coming to pay it. The way Mr. Hart eyed her; he must have known something was wrong.

The sheriff was a piece of no good effort. He claimed he understood why the Plugg brothers had taken the furniture and bolted the house up. One night he was assuring her the mean-spirited sons would be of help—the next night he was excusing their eviction of her.

"Their shock is overwhelming," the sheriff had said, his tone as unconvincing as his platitudes. Reassuring her the brothers would likely drop the charges against her should've made her feel better, but since the whole town looked at her like a ragged leper, no doubt the accusations had sped through the gossips, she felt worse, not better. Tomorrow she would have to speak to the pastor. She needed a job—maybe as a caretaker for an elderly woman with room and board.

The back door opened slowly, and Anna scooted against the church wall, looking for a place to hide.

"Mrs. Plugg?"

Anna stood and tried to straighten her dirty clothes. "Hello, Reverend." She swallowed hard. "I didn't ask permission the last two nights. I'm sorry. I…I…thought I could get back in my home. But—"

The tall, lanky man in a faded gray suit, walked over quickly and shut the wood stove door. "You can see a light flickering from the street."

"Oh, I'm so sorry," she said, dropping her head to the side.

"You understand I cannot allow you to stay here," he squinted at her.

"I—I—was hoping to speak to you tomorrow. I don't know what to do. I need to get a job of some sorts. I'm a wonderful nurse's aide."

"Is that so?" A woman's stern voice spoke behind them.

They both looked back to see a woman in the shadows with a dark brown dress draped over her thick body.

"Reginald Horworth, how long has this been going on?" she snapped.

His shoulders dropped. "Mrs. Plugg, this is my wife, Mrs. Horworth." Before Anna could curtsy to the woman with the severe frown, she spoke, "I know who she is. But why is she here, Reginald?"

"It seems her husband has left her destitute." He lit a candle on a side table.

She released a barbed snicker, "And is *that* much of a surprise?"

Anna looked at the reverend and back at the reverend's wife. Did they know Alfred? She waited, feeling for one moment maybe they would find pity for her.

"Well, she needs to be out tonight." Mrs. Horworth walked closer and scrutinized Anna up and down.

"I …I was just telling her that." The reverend sighed, rolling his eyes at the interruption.

"We are the house of God, not a hotel of God," Mrs. Horworth cut Anna another sour frown.

Anna's thread of hope dropped at the harsh tone the reverend's wife oozed, and the rain picked the same moment to pepper the roof. "I would be happy to go to a hotel, but the only money I have is locked in my house, and I cannot get it." Her own exhausted indignation was rising, "or long gone to the plantation with my other belongings. Likely I will never see my mother's silver spoon set again. They were her wedding gift to me." Anna stepped toward the reverend's wife, and the cross woman huffed a sigh.

"And did I mention, his body was already taken to be buried, without one person informing me?" Anna announced.

Mrs. Horworth jutted her chin out. "Humph, a bit difficult while you're hiding in a church building."

"House of God," Anna mimicked back at her.

"All right, all right, then…" the Reverend stepped up between them. "For tonight, with the rain—"

All three looked to the sound of pounding at the front door.

"Oh, dear Lord, now what," the reverend rolled his eyes.

6

"WE'RE SORRY FOR the late intrusion, Reverend," Will and Nathan stepped across the church threshold, "but we saw the light on and—"

Will stopped and cleared his throat. Two other women stood in the middle of the church, even in the shadows, neither looked like the night had been especially kind to them. "My sister has been missing," he continued, "the older one, the retarded one." He pulled his wide-brimmed hat off, and water trickled on the hardwood floor.

"We've searched for hours. Now with the rain, we can't find any tracks." Nathan heaved a tired sigh.

The reverend looked over to his wife, whose nostrils flared.

"Has she done this before?" the younger, thinner woman asked, breaking the tense moment.

Will looked at his brother. "Yes, twice." He turned his hat in his hand.

"And how did you find her?" she asked. Will wondered if he'd met this woman somewhere before. She seemed familiar.

"We didn't. She just showed up back at the doorstep. She can't talk right and so we never, um, know."

"Someone is taking her and bringing her back." Anna stepped closer. "How old is she?"

"Sixteen." Will tried to comprehend what the thin woman had just suggested. Suddenly, he remembered those soft, green eyes. The woman who'd bought Milo socks now nodded her understanding.

"This recent widow is looking for employment." The older woman with the square jaw stepped forward. "You are the family whose mother passed about a year ago?"

"That's right," Will said, taking his eyes from Anna.

"It seems to me you could use some help with supervision." She pursed her lips.

Will didn't like her judgmental tone nor the fact that she was completely right. He glanced back at the young woman who now looked at the floor.

"I—we—" Will looked back to Nathan. "Don't have the means to hire anyone right now."

"What about for room and board? Her supervision for a trade." Mrs. Horworth asked. The reverend cleared his throat. Anna glanced up quickly.

"We only have a one-room cabin, ma'am. My siblings sleep in a small loft. There is no room to offer." Will felt anxious, even though this young woman seemed to possess the insight to his dilemma, he needed to find Della and get her home. He could only pray his sister hadn't caught her death on a night like this. He tried to ignore his one possible notion of her whereabouts.

"I have worked with the disturbed," Anna spoke up. "I was a nurse's aide at Lennhurst Asylum. I think I could help her and you have another brother? Yes? Milo?" Anna chewed on her bottom lip.

"And another sister." Nathan offered. "It would be of great help to have someone stay with them while we work the fields."

Will looked back at his moppy-haired brother and the dark circles under his blue eyes. They had no money to pay for a caretaker. No extra food to go around. No woman would ever want to work in their miserable cabin. "I'm sorry, your help would be wonderful, but we must go."

"Wait." Mrs. Horworth stern voice made him turn from the entrance. "This woman has been staying here without my permission. My husband often forgets his place." She twisted a frown. "Before you entered, I was about to show her the door. Now that the war has ended, leaving many widowed and in such hard times, a couple could get married under worse circumstances. A wife will cost you nothing, sir. And you," she drilled Anna with her eyes, "will have the security of a home and children to raise. That is a full blessing for any woman. You may call it a beneficial arrangement of sorts, free to only help each other if that's all you want."

Thankfully, the helpful young woman was staring at the ground again. What would she think of his quick assessment of her? Why wasn't she taking her leave from this place? Had she really nowhere to go in all of Centerville?

Reverend Horworth turned to his wife. "Let's give them a minute." He pointed to the back of the church. "Why don't you two go back there and discuss this without us and our meddling?"

Anna opened her mouth to speak and shut it quickly as she followed the young man with damp, dark hair and a strong frame down the center aisle. She guessed him to be about her age.

"What is your name?" he asked, turning to face her.

"Anna." She blinked, trying to see him in the dim light. His face was calm, lacking the creases of age and anger. She shook her head. "That cruel woman is going to throw me out into the rain. But you don't have to marry me. I will think of something."

"I am William. Will…Will Gibbs."

Anna sighed, wondering why she didn't ask him his name. "And your little *brother* is Milo." The corner of her smile lifted.

"Yes, Milo is seven, and Maribelle is four." Silence fueled the awkward moment. "The reverend's wife said to raise the children would be a blessing."

Her eyes met his in soft response. He was handsome in a quiet, agreeable way.

"That's not true for us." He blew out a light breath. "Maribelle cries over everything. Someone told us once Della has a demon. There are no comforts for anyone in our small cabin. You have to know there are *no* blessings."

Anna almost felt an amusement in his confession. Dare she tell him about her time at Lennhurst Asylum and School for Disabled Children? "I understand. No blessings. And I often talk to myself." She looked at the ground. "And have small head spasms that will overtake me at times. I've tried to control them, but I can't."

His chest rose and fell while taking in deep breaths. Was it the shock of her words, or was he weighing this idea? After what she'd lived with the last four years, had she taken time to decide for herself?

"All I ask from you is to help care for my siblings," he said flatly. "My sister is exceedingly difficult. I would be willing to try this as an arrangement. It would not surprise me if you wanted to move out in a week. I would bare you no malice."

She could move on as she wanted? Is that what she heard? "I have no fear of your sister, sir." Anna waited, neither of them wanting to admit their willingness to try this strange agreement.

He nodded once with strained, tight lips and looked back to where the others waited. "The reverend will marry us tonight?"

Anna subdued a groan, her rebellious chin and head involuntarily jerked down. She knew William Gibbs would take that as a yes. He started back down the aisle.

"Wait." She grabbed his wet jacket, and he turned to her stricken face. "You must tell me, sir, with the fear of God's truth in the *house* of God."

He glanced down at her, his head tilted slightly, listening.

"Do you believe in striking women, children, the Negros?"

His brows creased under the long strands of dark hair hanging near his eyes. She released the grip on his arm as he replied, "No, ma'am, I don't raise a hand to anyone defenseless." He fiddled with his hat and asked, "Is there anything else?"

"No, sir." She closed her eyes and released her held breath. Opening them, she followed him down the aisle. He was the complete opposite height and build of Mr. Plugg.

"Oh, and also I'm barren." It slipped out before she could catch it.

He came to a sudden halt and looked slowly over his shoulder. He blinked wide-eyed as she pressed her lips together. Turning in silence, he pushed on his temple while he finished walking down the narrow church aisle.

7

ANNA GIBBS STOOD under the short church overhang watching the dark rain pelt poor Nathan Gibbs as he jumped up onto the wagon bench. Will stood taller, near her, looking her over with a frown. Slipping his coat off, he laid it on her shoulders and dropped his hat on her head.

"You're next," he nodded to the bench where Nathan held his hand out.

Pushing the broad-brimmed hat up where she could see, she stepped out into the heavy rain and reached for Nathan's hand. He pulled her close next to him as Will rocked the bench and sat, squeezing her in between the two brothers. He slapped the reins, and the wagon rolled forward.

"Where do you live?" she asked Will, watching the rain soak his hair and dark blue flannel shirt.

"Just south of town. We grow tobacco." Will swiped the rain from his eyes.

Her heart froze. The Plugg plantation grew cotton and tobacco. "Do you have slaves? I mean freedmen?"

"No." He shook his head. "Just Nathan and I."

Anna turned and gave Nathan a small nervous smile. His hat kept the rain off his face, and she noticed his light hair and skin, the opposite of his brother, Mr. Gibbs.

"The reverend said your name was Anna Plugg during the," Will rubbed his neck, "the ceremony."

"We know of your late husband," Nathan said. "Just from the tobacco auction," he murmured, "and that he has one of the largest crops in Kentucky. We are sorry for you being a widow now."

Will tapped the reins again, looking side to side, possibly for a sign of where Della could have gone.

"I guess I'm no longer a widow," she whispered.

Will raked his hand across his forehead to slick back his wet hair. "Humph," he grunted, shaking his head.

Nathan laughed and said, "No, I guess you aren't."

Anna was plenty warm pressed tightly between the thick arms of these two young men, yet a chill covered her body. "What would you like me to do—for the most help?" Her eyes glanced toward Will.

Will rocked on the bench still looking left to right. "I don't expect you to do it all. The little ones can carry their chores. Our mother was abed months before she passed. She would give Milo directions; he's smart and wants to help," Will paused and lifted a crooked smile, "well, most of the time."

Anna felt her own nervous caution squeeze in her gut. He seemed kind, looked friendly. But with Mr. Plugg, everyone had told her what a lucky young woman she was to have an older gentleman with land and security. No one had warned her about his mean side. Would Mr. Gibbs find out about her past and despise her for her shameful youth?

"I suppose you had a housemaid and a cook?" Nathan broke into her thoughts.

"Yes, her name was…I mean is Tallie."

"Can you garden?" Nathan asked.

Anna wanted to smile. Unlike Will Gibbs, this brother asked all the right questions. "Yes. And I can sew." Anna took in a deep breath, now seemed like as good as time as any. "If it's all right with you, Mr. Gibbs, I often sew a few baby things. Mrs. Hart sells them at the mercantile." She glanced at Will. "When I have any spare time."

"Sounds fine to me," Nathan said.

"Okay." Anna looked between them. "I see there are two Mr. Gibbs." She sighed.

"I am the only Gibbs," Will spoke up. "Nathan and Della's last name is Ford. Milo and Maribelle's father was Mr. Vernon Lack. He is still alive but not allowed near our land."

"Oh, I see. Was he cruel to them?"

Will rolled his lips in a thin line, still looking left to right. "No, he loves them very much." Will's elbow brushed close to her chest as he handed the reins over to Nathan and jumped down. Anna blinked, startled at his near miss. Damp and cold, the wet air invade her side.

Will pulled an old wooden gate across the road and Nathan tapped the horse forward. Will closed it, then grabbed the bench and swung back up. Anna wanted to know why the children couldn't be near their own father. And she now understood the predicament—their mother had been married three times. Will's jaw was set as they pulled up in front of a small log-sided cabin. Maybe enough was enough for tonight.

Will jumped down and opened the cabin door and leaned back out. "She's in here. Della is." He sighed, shaking his head. "Sound asleep." He pushed his wet hair over to the side.

Even in the dark, Anna could see the discomfort on his face. He walked back around to the wagon and held his arms out for her. Anna stood nervously and reached out to his shoulders. "I'm so glad she's safe," Anna said as Will easily held her weight and lowered her to the ground. "Thank you for the use of your coat and hat."

"I'll take the wagon," Nathan said as it rolled by.

Anna walked to the door and stepped in out of the rain. Closing the door quietly, Will stood inches behind her as she tried to take in her new home. He moved around her and turned the knob on the flickering lantern sitting on the table.

Carefully removing Mr. Gibbs's hat, she stilled and almost missed his outstretched hand removing the coat from her shoulders. She watched him hang his hat and coat on a peg near the door, and then scanned the square room. The place was small.

Very, very small. Maybe the size of the entire kitchen of the Plugg house on the pond. An old threadbare gray blanket with sagging holes hung on her left. Her eyes drifted to the floor. Was there wood under the layer of dirt? Or was the cabin built on an earthen floor?

She gave Mr. Gibbs an awkward smile. "It's warm."

He lifted the lantern off the table. "We don't use the fireplace. I'm sure it was put in before the iron stove." Anna looked where he nodded and saw Della asleep, curled in a ball next to the rock fireplace.

Anna stared at the rough handmade table in the center of the cabin. She took in the little dry sink under the window, the small open cupboard that held a few meager food items, and the tiny shelf next to the sink, she supposed, was for food preparation. The room was cramped but efficient.

Will held the lantern over the stove and added a few small logs. "This will keep everything warm and cook a fair bit in the morning."

She nodded slowly and looked up, seeing two little bare feet hanging over the edge of the small loft. Next to those were the familiar feet held by the socks she'd bought. Something began to squeeze her chest and mist in her eyes. Could she really do this? Why had she sounded so confident minutes ago? Hadn't all her days just been a mixture of increasing pain and hopelessness? She remembered her own little brother, Elias, from Lennhusrt.

He wasn't really her blood brother, but as an orphan, he'd had no one to care for him. He took to her quickly until there was the heart-breaking goodbye when she had to leave Lennhurst. Swallowing around the knot in her throat, she looked around again. These children weren't really her—

"Did you hear me tell the reverend's wife, there was no room?" Will interrupted her worrisome thoughts.

She nodded to him and held her hand against her cheek. "I see a bed through the blanket. You and Nathan share that?"

He nodded, shivering, and warming his hands over the cook stove. He was probably wet to the bone. Nathan came in and quietly shut the door. Somehow the cabin got even smaller.

"Not much to see, eh?" Nathan hung his coat and hat and slid off his boots.

Anna walked around the table and knelt next to Della. She didn't see any bruises or marks on her; just a wad of damp, tangled hair and the usual pox-cheeks many teens had. Did the brothers want to know her experience of what happened to the insane young females at Lennhurst? She pulled Della's blanket over the teen's thin shoulder. Likely not.

"You can have the bed," Will nodded to the left.

"Where will you two sleep?" Anna had already seen the dirt floor. It had no free area for two reasonably large young men.

"We'll figure it out," Will looked away. "Do you need something dry to wear?"

Anna stepped over Della and looked through the gray, shredded blanket. "The bed has a blanket, and I will be fine. You, Mr. Gibbs, please get whatever you need." She stepped back as he entered the small area and grabbed a shirt and pair of pants.

For the next few minutes, the three of them looked back and forth at each other as if there was a pie suddenly missing from the window sill.

"This is peculiar and shocking." Nathan rubbed his jaw. "Will, you agreed to marry a stranger. What were you thinking?" Nathan's eyes grew curiously wide, and he covered his mouth, suppressing a snicker.

"Please, Miss." Will's face held no humor, and he pointed to the bed behind the blanket. "Tomorrow will be long and difficult. Nathan and I are trying to plant seed tomorrow."

"Yes, thank you… for the bed." She bowed quickly, covering her chin tics with her hand. Stepping behind the thin blanket, she sat on the bed and unlaced the long line of boot laces. Her hem and small patches of her tattered skirt were wet. She looked back through the thin blanket and chewed the corner of her lip. At least she wasn't frightened by them, she realized, which softened the tension a bit. Fingering the old crumpled bedding, it looked in need of a good wash.

Hearing the ruffling of Will's wet clothes being removed, she was keenly aware they had been pronounced husband and wife but were really strangers. A long window on the right side of the bed with a latch at halfway seized her attention. If he tried anything in the night, it could be an easy escape. Her heartbeat spiked. Although she'd felt a kindly feeling when Will gave up his hat and coat, he was just polite this first night. They certainly did not know each other. Nathan's words echoed. What had *she* been thinking?

The light went down and dropped the little cabin into darkness. She sat back against the rough-hued log walls and pulled the blanket up around her flinching chin. How could she find sleep with this strange family? At least it was a bed. She took a few calming breaths. She remembered the plaque on the church wall above where she'd last slept. *The House of God*, she smirked. *Who remembered us in our low state; for His mercy endureth forever? And hath redeemed us from our enemies; for his mercy endureth forever.* Or something like that. She lowered her head onto her knees.

8

W ILL CREPT AROUND the gray, new morning light seeping through the cabin windows. Sleeping while leaning over on the table had left a stitch in his back. He tried to stretch his neck side to side as he reached for the coffee pot. Was he talking to a young woman in here last night? His hand froze over the water pump. Did he dream he'd left here looking for Della and came back home with a wife?

Nathan's long legs curled around Milo and Maribelle in the loft. Della slept in her usual place. He stepped forward to the worn blanket wall. *There she was,* he rubbed his whiskery chin. A low pop came from the remaining fire in the cook stove.

The strange woman leaned like a ball on top of the two pillows at the top of the bed. Her bed, his bed. He sighed. He really had gotten married. His breathing seemed to come in short spurts, and he turned to face the small cabin. It had been his only choice. Without Vernon Lack or his mother, the little ones were—were one accident away from something bad every day. And Della—he had no choice. They needed someone mightier than Milo needed to watch her. Every time he or Nathan were taken from the farming, it set the planting back.

Hadn't he said just yesterday, no one would ever want to live like this? His breathing returned to normal. Although this very woman had training as a nurse or something close to it, she didn't look that sturdy. He peeked over the blanket. She was still curled in a ball.

He noticed the morning light accented the dirt and disarray of the room, his jaw clenched. Sleeping against the cabin wall, she was probably afraid of the filth. Knowing their supplies were pitifully low, he hoped she didn't eat much. He'd never been one to pray to the English God, but it seemed to comfort his mother. *God of heaven, could you find forbearance for us as heathens. Grant us favor for the crops and for this woman to stay as long as we need. Amen*

Nathan bent low and began to back down the ladder. Milo sat up and rubbed his eyes. "Did she come back?" He whispered, looking at Will.

"Yeah," Nathan answered, heading out the door under the loft.

Will knew in a few minutes Della would awake, and everyone would be hungry. He imagined Anna would want to be fair warned. Pulling the blanket door to the side, he walked up to the top of the bed and tapped her arm.

"Miss, Miss."

She opened her eyes and clutched the blanket.

"Will Yam," Maribelle yelled from the loft.

"Everyone is waking." A little white feather stuck from the side of her messy hair, and he reached for it.

She jerked back and protected her face with her arms.

Will pulled his hand back quickly. "I'm sorry I frightened you. I…I…you have a feather from the mattress in your hair."

Her eyes were like green saucers, and she swallowed hard. Pushing with her feet, she flattened her backside against the wall. With a stunned expression, she brushed her hand down her hair. "I'm sorry." She swung her legs around to stand. "I'd lost my bearings of where I was, Mr. Gibbs." Heat rushed to her face. "Did I oversleep?"

Maribelle swung into the cramped bedroom. "Will Yam, I haf to go to da outhouse." She stopped cold and grabbed Will's leg. "Who is dat?"

"This is Anna. Anna, this is my sister, Maribelle."

Anna's green eyes softened, and she offered the little, moppy-haired girl a smile.

"I can take you Bellie." Milo walked in and froze. "Hey, that's the lady from the store. This is her, Bellie…the one who gave me the socks." Maribelle eyes narrowed, and a little red and pink tongue stuck out from the once angelic child.

Anna looked down to Maribelle's dirty bare feet and suppressed a smile. "Socks for Maribelle would be in order next," she whispered, glancing at Will.

"Please take Maribelle, Milo, and I will help Anna start breakfast." The two children scurried out, and Will watched her. "Are you all right? I was hoping to wake you before all of them woke up. Give you a head start of sorts."

"I'll be fine." Anna shuddered. "Please show me where you keep the supplies. How do the children prefer their eggs?" She took in a deep breath and walked from the small room.

"We just have porridge every morning. We do have a cow and Milo will bring in the fresh milk. We have a few old chickens, but very few eggs." She nodded to Nathan as he stood over the sink, rinsing out a pan.

"We don't have time to do many dishes." Nathan nodded at Anna. "They're just used for the same thing every day." Nathan pulled the dirty bowls out onto the counter. Will showed her the sack of ground buckwheat and oats. "We are low on most supplies. I can try to get a few things later today."

Her eyes glanced across the messy kitchen counter. "I'm good at making do," she offered, turning to watch Milo and Maribelle enter the cabin. Will added the hot water to the mush and took a pitcher of milk from Milo. Stepping back with barely any room to move, she held her chin still with her palm and scanned the small cabin in the daylight. "Della sleeps late? The noise does not bother her?"

Nathan shook his head, setting cups of milk out for Milo and Maribelle. "I guess when she's been out late, she can."

Anna walked around the table and watched her sleep. "Is she deaf?"

Will stopped stirring the cooking porridge and looked back at Anna. "I don't know. Our mother never said." It seemed like a reasonable question, yet he'd never met a deaf person. Did they all behave as she did? "When my mother was alive—Della was different." He spooned the scoops into the bowls. "Some of her words sound like words." Now Anna was watching Maribelle stare at her as he set the bowls on the table.

"Pease pudding hot, pease pudding cold." She leaned toward Maribelle.

"Pease pudding in the pot nine days old.

"Some like it hot, some like it cold.

"Some like it in the pot nine days old," Anna quoted to the sleepy-eyed children.

Milo and Maribelle watched her while spooning in their mush. With a mouth full, Milo smiled, "Say it again."

Anna slowly came down between them, rubbing Maribelle's back.

"Make my porridge hot or make my porridge cold. But don't make my porridge nine days old." Anna made a silly sour face and received a small smile from Maribelle. Will watched Anna's eyes narrow while she separated a bit of Maribelle's tangled hair out of her face. Lifting some strands, she dropped the hair quickly and straightened up. Her gaze bore into his eyes.

"I will need a razor and comb," she said matter of factly.

Will handed her a bowl. "I have both, but what are you going to do with a razor." He sucked in a breath, realizing he could not leave this stranger, no matter how motherly she seemed, alone with the children."

"Maribelle and probably Milo have lice." She took a small bite. "The nits are unmovable from the hair shaft. The only remedy is to shave all the hair off. I will need to boil their clothes and bed linens. All the hay up there will need to be replaced. Where did your mother do the large washing?"

"I pick them from her hair," Milo added.

"And then he eats them," Maribelle giggled.

Will rubbed his forehead and bit his bottom lip. "You can shave Milo, but not my sisters."

"Della is always digging at her head," Nathan added glancing at Will. "Might do her some good to be free of the bugs."

"I know what I'm doing, Mr. Gibbs." Anna walked the four steps to leave her empty bowl in the sink. "I will leave a layer of hair on top. Most people won't be able to tell it is shaved underneath. If you could take Milo with you for the morning, we ladies will bathe and wash, and then if he could come back for the noon meal, I will start on him."

"We are going to eat at noon?" Milo's eyes widened.

Will blew out a breath. "I can get Milo off fishing, and we usually eat *after* the workday. I'll set up the stand for the black pot with a fire outside for the wash. We usually bathe out in the creek."

"Who is we?" she hesitated, gazing at his sheepish expression.

Will knew he'd let many things go, and now they all seemed to come calling this one morning.

"Nathan and I have no problem with the cold water. But the others don't like it."

"I'll be out in the barn." Nathan smiled at her and grabbed his coat."

Della moaned, and they turned to see her rise from her pallet. Thankfully his slight new wife was a few inches taller than his ragged sister.

"Good morning, Della." Anna smiled at her.

Della looked at Will and stuck her hair in her mouth. He handed her a bowl.

Anna walked to the counter and poured some milk. "Would you like milk?" Della never looked up from shoveling the mush in her mouth.

"If you tap her, it helps." Milo offered. "We usually just give it to her."

Will and Anna exchanged anxious glances.

"How long is she going to be here?" Maribelle asked, pointing a round short finger at Anna.

Will turned to the bare breakfast pan, his empty stomach already hurt. "I've had enough questions for the morning. Milo, get your shoes on if you're going fishing." He turned to Anna. "Are you sure you don't want him to stay?"

"I will be fine." She straightened up. "And what would you like me to prepare to go with the fish?"

Will shook his head and closed his eyes. "No more questions please. I will start the fire for washing outside." He went to the door and grabbed his jacket, then paused by the door. Pressing his lips into a thin line, he looked back at her then walked behind the old blanket coming out with a comb and razor. He set them on the counter and rubbed his chin. Staring at her, he tried to read her intentions, but it was too difficult to see past her fair skin and sun-lightened hair that fell around her shoulders. Was she as kind as she looked? As confident as she sounded? Della grunted and slammed her empty bowl against the table.

"If you are going to leave, or…or change your mind about helping here, please just walk straight out from the cabin." He set his hat on his head. "You can't miss the tobacco barn. Just tell me if you're leaving." He hesitated, wanting to say something else. "That's all I need." He rocked his determined chin to the side with a serious frown and nodded once at her. Without another word, he walked out.

9

T HROUGH THE WINDOW over the dirty sink, Anna spied the large barn across the field. *That's all I need.* Now Anna had heard that twice from him. Someone to care for the children and to give him notice of her leaving. Certainly, he needed food. Pushing the empty pan under the warm water, it did not go unnoticed that he hadn't eaten. And no noon meal? She hunted around the small kitchen cupboard. A small bag of flour, no lard, spices or sugar to be found.

Feeling the children's eyes on her, she pulled in a deep breath. "Old Mother Hubbard went to the cupboard," Anna pretended to open it's missing door and make a shocking face, making Maribelle smile and Della watch as she quickly peeked in and out, "to get her poor doggie a bone. When she got there," her voice rose with drama, "the cupboard was bare, so the poor, little doggie had none." She accentuated a frown.

Maribelle clapped. "I like that one, do it again!"

"As soon as we get your bedding washed." Anna held out her hand to take Maribelle to the ladder.

"Maribelle, Maribelle, so sweet and kind. Brings out the wash to hang on the line." Maribelle handed her down the sheets and pillows. "Milo, Milo, bring us some fish. So tonight we can," she helped Maribelle back down the ladder.

"Put it on a dish!" Maribelle finished.

"Yes, yes! That's how it is done. Where are your other clothes? We must put these you're wearing in hot water."

"This is all I have." Maribelle pulled Della's stained bedding from the floor. "Della can wear something of my Mama's, but my things are too small."

Anna tapped her fingers on the table. Thinking about the fabric she had at the brown house. "Does Nathan or Will have another shirt?"

"Yes." Her little body jumped, and she ran behind the blanket.

Anna smiled and said, "First, put the wash on to boil, and then we remove infested hair. Della will cooperate like… tea with a bear." She shook her head at the truth in her newest rhyme.

FUNNY SHE HADN'T thought of Tallie all day. Figuring out how to use the bare necessities of this cabin stretched her past all the days of working side by side with hard working Tallie. Only another woman could stand back and appreciate the miracles that had taken place.

Using her sing-song nursery rhymes to entertain Maribelle through the bath and partial head shaving went well enough. She even found a loose ribbon from an old dress in the wardrobe to tie a little wisp of hair back at the nape of her neck. The child was clipped and clean, and not even one tear was shed.

Della was another story. One thing she'd learned at Lennhurst was every person, even the lunatics, had a currency. Bribery was her best tool. But the only thing Della liked was the idea of wearing one of her mother's old dresses. Anna had pointed to the warm bath water and then the dress. The girl had a certain understanding, though she dropped all her clothes before Anna could guarantee her modesty. She understood the dress would be hers to wear after her skin was clean, and the nit-filled hair was gone.

Anna flipped the drying bedding in front of the cook stove and looked long at the barren kitchen area. The pond house was stocked with beans, potatoes, rice, and even frozen meat in the cellar. Had the Plugg brothers taken it all? She watched Mirabelle show Della her clean fingers and toes. The big house at the plantation had a pantry as large as this cabin filled with barrels and gunny sacks full of supplies. Mr. Plugg reminded her often that she, being mentally disturbed, could never run that large household as his late wife had.

What if the pond house food was still there? What if she could retrieve her own clothes and warm things? She could provide the girls some socks. Certainly, Will would be… fine with that. She peered out the window for the second time. The large barn loomed far off in the distance. "Hummm," she said, contemplating an idea. She pulled her hair behind her ear. He'd said to let her know if she was going anywhere. So far, he didn't seem overly demanding.

That afternoon Milo had returned with four small trout and a proud smile. She had fresh, warm water waiting for him as he agreed to take the bucket behind the curtain to bathe. He tossed all his dirty clothes out, and Anna had set them in the water boiling outside. Maribelle's faded green dress had dried, and she found another large shirt for Milo to wear while his things stewed.

"Milo, are you all right in here if I go to the barn for fresh hay?" Anna asked through the curtain.

"I'm fine," he answered amid sounds of water sloshing from the small bucket.

Anna bit the corner of her smile. Many a time she'd had to wrestle her brother, Elias, into the bath. He never did like the water. Once outside, Anna used a stick to pull Milo's steaming hot things out of the water and set them on the washboard to cool. The barn was through a simple gate on the right, and she found an old canvas to load fresh hay upon.

The cow and horse were unimpressed with her efforts, and she stopped and touched the saddle hanging on a sawhorse. Could she take the horse into town herself? Would Mr. Gibbs approve or want to take her? She knew by his serious face, he would *not* agree to her breaking into her old house. She huffed out a breath, a scoop of porridge and four small fish weren't going to sustain six hungry bellies for long.

A branch snapped outside the back of the barn, and Anna stepped back to hide. *Probably just an animal.* She tried to calm her racing thoughts. Would the Plugg brothers come to harass her more? She listened. It did sound like someone running away. She carefully peeked through the crack in the planks of the barn wood. Something large bolted behind a tree. From the height, it could be a man, maybe with a dark hat on. Was it just Nathan or Will? She blinked and looked again. It was gone.

A scream wrenched through the air. Maribelle! She jumped over her pile of hay and ran toward the small girl screaming at the cabin doorstep.

"Oh, dear God." Anna knelt and grasped her arms. "Did you get burned? She panted, looking over the tear-streaked face and back to the hot water.

"My ribbon!" Maribelle sobbed. "Della took my ribbon and is eating it!"

Anna relaxed her hold on the child and rolled her eyes. "All this hubbub for a ribbon?" Anna ran her fingers through the small clean wisps left on the child's head. It had been a long day. She pulled Maribelle into a warm hug. The child clung to her neck, and Anna put her hand down to push them off from the ground. Her hand touched something furry and squishy.

"Ack." Rising, she flung her hand back. Five dead squirrels were laying in front of the cabin door. She pulled Maribelle off her chest.

"Where did these come from?" She huffed, setting the child on the ground. Hadn't she just walked out this very door only twenty minutes ago? Had she stepped over them?

"Was someone here at the door, Maribelle?" Anna looked left to right.

The girl shrugged. "Can you get my ribbon back?

Anna chewed on her lip, looking long around the yard and barn. "Let's go in and ask Milo about these squirrels."

BY THE TIME Will and Nathan had come in to wash, their eyes glowed to see what was cooking in a large fry pan. As if the smell of fish and the fried squirrel wasn't enough, Will looked long around the cabin at his sibling's new haircuts. Though Anna thought they had improved in scent and appearance, she couldn't read his approval or disapproval. Anna continued to fry some makeshift flapjacks to round out the meal.

"Which one of you brought the squirrels to the door?" She asked as she put a portion in everyone's bowl. "I was only in the barn for a moment getting new hay for the loft and Della. I almost stepped on them."

Milo, who'd told her earlier he'd seen no one, stared at her wide-eyed. She handed him his bowl, and he looked about to cry.

Nathan forked another piece of squirrel meat, and Will looked long at each of his younger siblings. A strange silence hung over the table.

"Who was here, Milo?" Will questioned sternly.

10

WILL STOOD RUBBING his jaw and flashed dark, serious eyes at his siblings. "Anna, could you join me outside so I can talk to you alone?" He set his bowl down and stepped to the door.

Nodding, she stood quietly and placed her bowl in the basin.

"Please let her stay!" Maribelle cried out, jumping from her spot at the table. Grabbing Will's leg, she leaned her distraught face up at him. "I will be good, I promise," she whined and shook his leg. Will scooped her up, and she buried her face on his shoulder. "I don't want her to go. Please, Will Yam." She murmured in his ear.

"I will give Bellie my new socks." Milo squeaked, round brown eyes filling with tears. "There was enough food tonight for everyone," he reasoned, trying to read Will's motives. Della banged her empty bowl on the table, and Milo took it quickly from her hand.

Unnerved by the desperation in the younger one's outburst, he glanced at this peculiar, fair-haired young woman quickly and looked away. In one day, she had already changed the little one's appearance and gained their attachment. Something conflicted, twisting in his gut. "Just give us a minute to talk," Will said, as he placed Maribelle on her feet.

He held the door open and held out his coat for Anna. She slipped it on, and they walked to the low coals of the heating water. The pot gave off enough heat to counter the frigid, night air.

"Did you see anyone today?" Will asked, his gaze on her. "As you can guess, neither Nathan nor I left the squirrels."

"When I was in the barn," she only looked at him for a second, choosing her words carefully. "I thought I heard something, but I could only look through the planks of wood. My guess is it was a man, maybe with a dark hat. But since I don't know your neighbors or any of your relations, I thought maybe it was just you or Nathan."

Will looked down kicking around the dirt at his feet. "I think it was Milo and Maribelle's father."

Since Anna had spent most of her life expecting trouble around every corner, this news didn't seem so bad.

"You never told me why he isn't welcome here." She tucked her hands in his jacket pockets.

Will rolled his lips, and a vein in his neck bulged. "He can't be trusted." There was more left unsaid in the silence. "With Della," he finally admitted after a long pause, "He can't be around her." He looked up to see Anna nod her understanding.

"You need to protect her," she asked cautiously, "from him?"

Will raked his fingers through his loose hair. "That's right. He thinks he can…leave food…and…"

"Does he take her while you're gone?"

Her question made his jaw lock with resentment. She hadn't known this family for even two days, and already she'd uncovered the depravity, the shame.

"You might as well know." He rubbed the back of his neck. "I am half Chickasaw. My mother chose to marry an Indian. Her father was an old French-Indian trader. It was just the two of them, and to her there was nothing wrong with her choice until my father died in a battle at Ridge River." Will grew silent for a moment.

"The tribe was told to move to a reservation, and she and I went onto Danville. She served tables at the saloon until she met

Mr. Ford. He seemed to overlook her past, and they moved to this land and started tobacco farming. Nathan and Della were born in this cabin." Will cleared his throat. "He was a good man. He taught me about farming, then the war broke out." He rubbed his hands near the steaming water. "I wish I could tell you he died in battle, but it was typhoid that got him. The Ford's came to kick us off the land, but somehow my mother convinced them she and I could keep the crops going." He blew out a hard breath. "Nathan's been working sun up to sun down since he was ten or so." He glanced at her shadowy face, and she seemed to hang on his words. "Then my ma married Vernon Lack. Milo came along. She lost two babies after that, then Maribelle came without a midwife. My mother caught an infection of some kind. The doctor called it the birthin' fever. She tried month after month to get well. Sometimes we thought it was gone, but then she'd be in bed with the fever again.

"She sent me back to what was left of the Chickasaw people. I met my grandfather for the first time, and he sent a healer woman to our cabin. Our mother hung on a few more months." He rubbed his hands together near the hot pot and then shoved them in his pockets. "I think the care of another woman was a comfort to her at the end."

"What was your mother's name?" Anna whispered.

"Celia."

Will watched some feathery clouds cross over the moon. "I like to picture her in peace. In heaven." The silence was soothing. They didn't often talk about their mother; it seemed to upset the little ones. It was strange to open his private life to a woman that was his wife, yet he knew nothing about her.

"And you, you had no family to take you in?" He glanced at her sideways.

Anna shook her head.

"No mother or father?" Will asked.

"Well, yes, I have a mother and stepfather. My father died when I was young." She pulled his jacket tighter around her and offered no more information.

"And no one could come to you in your time of sorrow?" he questioned.

"Oh, sir." Her countenance soured. "I have no sorrow for my husband's death." Her head began to twitch. "I was told to marry him because no one would ever have me. I am not close to... I don't really... I didn't grow up at home."

MR. PLUGG ENJOYED using any of her information against her. Of course, her stepfather had told Alfred Plugg his version of what happened. The details were never a bother at Lennhurst, only with her family. Should she tell Will the details? The truth? She owed him nothing, and he said she could leave in a week if she wanted. Anna's chest relaxed, and her breathing slowed.

"When I was around five," Anna felt the strong desire to tell someone the truth. "My mother and stepfather had a new baby. A boy. He was named Hubert after my stepfather. We lived in a lovely two-story home with servants, and when my mother was pregnant, my step-father insisted we have a nanny." She lifted a rueful grin to his watchful dark eyes.

"The nursery was upstairs with beautiful cream and blue curtains. The baby had a large bassinet with a shelf above that held the diapers, pins, and powder. Nanny had taken away a particularly smelly diaper and told me to get the powder off the shelf. The baby was tired and screaming. I scooted over a little stool and reached for the talc. Somehow it bobbled from my hand and fell onto the baby's face. The little thing was covered in powder and inhaled a deep breath of it. The baby couldn't cough or get free of the powder," Anna's voice sank along with her chin.

"When Nanny came back in, I was trying to get him to move, but his face was turning blue." Her head ticked down twice. "Nanny pushed me to the floor and began to bang on the baby's back. She screamed for me to get my mother. By the time we came back, the nanny was in a hysterical state. She pointed to me and said I'd poured the talc on the baby; that she saw me do it. You can imagine the shock I felt at her words. The baby died that morning. I knew it was my mistake, and I felt their deep despair and loathing of me. Then my stepfather announced I could no longer live at home. He could not live with someone so demented who would injure their future children. So I was sent to Lennhurst Asylum and School for Disabled Children."

Will blinked. "For how long did you have to stay there?"

"Until I was taken away to marry Mr. Plugg. My marriage was the worst four years of my life. I know God cursed me for such an evil rebellion I harbored against that man. I always believed if I could just have my own little babe to love…" Her words trailed off as she stared into the distance. She looked back at him leaning against a tree. "But I understand why it was not to be."

"I thought you said you were a nurse's aide?" Will's brows lowered.

Anna knew this information would likely taint his ability for her to help his family. She could see the distrust in his eyes. "I don't remember when it happened. I guess around ten or eleven when the nurses let me have free reign. In fact, they asked me many times to calm the bad children." She stopped. He still seemed to be interested in her past. His face had relaxed.

"They weren't really bad. They were just frightened. I remember being dropped off there. I—think that's when the tics started." She rubbed her cheeks and covered her mouth. "The smells of cleaning fluids and vomit, and sounds of people moaning, children crying. I cried myself to sleep many nights. So I would hold the children and rock the unwanted like I wished someone had done for me, and they would calm down. It made the nurses' jobs easier, so they took me under their wing, I guess you could say and allowed me to help—the very thing I love to do. I found acceptance in an insane asylum, the one benefit my family would not afford me."

His mouth hung ajar. After a moment, he said, "I don't know if I'm amazed or worried." He lifted a small grin. "Milo and Maribelle have obviously experienced your… gift."

"Gift." Anna felt the word drop warmth into her vacant heart. Since leaving Lennhurst, no one had seen anything in her. "Thank you for saying that, Mr. Gibbs."

He dropped his chin and scratched it. Looking at her through his thick, dark lashes, his eyes held soft appeal. He asked, "So you are going to make it through the week here?"

"Yes." She smiled. "How are you going to explain me to the children?"

He pulled his long hair back behind his ear and blew out a breath. Looking slowly around the dusky yard, he rubbed his hands up and down his shirt sleeves.

Anna chewed on her bottom lip, watching him struggle.

"I know you needed shelter, not another marriage." He shook his head and sighed, "It *is* very strange what we did."

"Yes, it is," Anna murmured. Now that they'd exchanged the most hidden things and he had not shamed her, it seemed uncomfortable to consider they were husband and wife. Should she tell him now she would never welcome his touch or want to perform her marital obligations? The thought alone made her stomach coil, no matter how kind he appeared. "You asked for help with the children when we spoke at the church."

"Yes, I did," he said quickly.

"I will only take care of your home and siblings. And, I apologize for today and not checking further to see who was here." His brooding silence caused her to force the words out. "You may tell them I am your wife." Sucking in the crisp evening air, she swallowed the nerves down. "I realize the one bed is needed for two people. But this marriage will only be in words." Her chin ticed, and her blood froze, anticipating his ire. Her shoulders drew up, responding to her tension that he would lash out just as Mr. Plugg would have.

He tipped his head and scuffed the dirt with one shoe. Staring at the ground, he said, "Of course."

Anna stilled, feeling the very air calm. That was all, was the man truthful?

11

THE LANTERN FLAME flickered low, and the children were all abed when they reentered. Anna had asked him to go to sleep while she sat at the table to take apart an old dress of Maribelle's. He stood behind the curtain and stared at the bed. A stab of consciousness hit his gut. Why would she agree to raise children that were not hers? How could he abide by her never-ending work to clean and care for the cabin and take on the heavy burdens of his forlorn life?

Didn't people do all this for love of their own? Wasn't there something better she wanted? He'd seen the large houses around the pond in Centerville. She likely had fine furniture with rugs and an array of food. *Yes, food, that didn't need to be meagerly portioned out.* His stomach twisted with its usual emptiness. But she made it clear there was no love between her and Mr. Plugg.

He sat on the bed and pulled off his boots. Remembering his mother tonight must have done something to his mood. Mr. Ford had loved her, he supposed. They'd often laugh and share a kiss. He laid down on the bed and faced the window. What a strange feeling swirled inside him. Even Vernon Lack appeared kind and helpful, and neither man had ever laid a hand of anger on his mother. After just a few seconds of reflection, he knew he wanted to be that kind of husband.

Pain, something besides hunger, pinched in his gut. He'd never really imagined this moment of lying in his own bed, married yet contemplating his future loneliness. When he didn't know of her past life, the decision made sense. Her work for a place to live. But now he'd almost begun to find a comradery with her.

He knew shame. It was a companion while facing town folk. Living in the shadows of being a half-breed. His mother having three husbands. Some people had no compassion when faced with other people's different backgrounds.

This soft-faced woman with eyes the color of freshly budding leaves also knew of family shame and rejection. No words were spoken of comparison, but did she feel what he'd felt all of his days? Maybe of all people, they could understand each other? She'd never judge him for his differences, and he could just be himself.

Knowing he'd nothing to offer, how did he meet the only person that didn't seem bothered by their lowly state? He never took the time to think of what he wanted. But her soft, round eyes and ten, tan freckles on her nose were petitioning for his attention. He needed to quit these thoughts now, or sleep would never come. He must remember she could leave at any moment, and though the children would be heartbroken, he was too old to expect nursery rhymes and happy endings. He pulled his pillow tight under his neck and thought of the farm work that needed doing tomorrow.

Will never felt Anna come to bed, and now as the morning light entered the small room, he knew she must have slept hunched at the table. He knew first hand it was a pitiful excuse for sleep. He rolled over and closed his eyes. The cabin was plenty warm, either she'd stoked the stove or Nathan had already risen and headed out to the barn. It was so peaceful, maybe just a few more minutes of shut-eye.

"Will Yam!" Maribelle's shriek wrenched him from the bed.

"What, child," he growled, throwing back the curtain and scanning the cabin and missing his new wife.

"She's gone! I don't want her to be gone." Maribelle flopped on the table, pounding her fists into the wood.

"Stop now." He grabbed her thin arms. "She's just probably out—" A piece of paper on the table caught his eye.

Mr. Gibbs. I have taken the horse to town. I need some of my personal things. I will be back shortly. Will looked closer, she'd underlined *'will be back.'*

"Maribelle, this is from her. She says she is coming back." He stood to make the coffee, trying to make sense of the note and calm his own concern. Why would she go to town this early without asking him? One minute he thought he was getting to know her, the next this. Certainly, he would have taken her. Was the note a ruse, had she stolen their horse? He huffed and looked back at Maribelle's bottom lip still hanging out.

Nathan sat hunch-backed on the top of the ladder. Rubbing his eyes, he asked, "How did you two like the bed?" He slid down the ladder and stretched side to side. Will watched him and wanted to apologize knowing his brother had been removed from the only place of comfort in all the four walls.

"Anna is gone to town," Maribelle sniffed.

"Can you make the mush?" Will didn't give Nathan time to ask more questions. "I'm going after her."

ANNA TIED THE compliant horse to the very tree she prayed would aid her entrance to the brown house. Looking down from her first long step up to a thin branch, the same old dog watched her without as much as a yawn. She tried and failed to ignore the blue-green pond. The ice had melted, and all the signs of Mr. Plugg's death were gone.

Taking another step and a deep breath, she reached the second story window that had once helped her escape from this prison. The window lifted. *Glory to all that is good and right.*

She flipped her dirty skirt layers inside with her legs. The house was ice cold, a good sign no one was living there. Quickly she ran into her old room. Her things lay scattered on the floor. The bed frame and mattress were gone, a lone pillow lay in the corner. She didn't care that it might have belonged to Mr. Plugg. She emptied out the pillow and began to shove her work dress, good purple blouse, nightgown, pantaloons, and stockings in the case. Her black clothes from the mercantile had been thrown in the fireplace. "Good riddance," she panted, looking around the floor.

Under the water table, she found soap, her comb, and towel. Her heart beat with a fury, and she had to leave before anyone saw her. She dragged the pillowcase to the stairs and left it as she ran down the stairs.

The kitchen and living room were as chaotic as the bedroom. Groaning out loud, she searched for her mother's spoons, but her sewing box and the spoons were nowhere to be seen.

She flung open the pantry door, the hideous last place she had seen poor Tallie. Mostly empty, she found some bags left at the bottom and pulled them out. Chickpeas and hominy, the things Mr. Plugg never liked. Half a bag of cornmeal was next to those. Gathering the bags, she remembered the honey Tallie liked on her cornbread. Turning the corner to Tallie's sleeping porch, she eyed the servant's little cupboard. She opened it and found the honey pot and various spices along with a few of Tallie's other things.

"Lord, forgive me," she whispered as she grabbed Tallie's blanket off the straw tic and pulled everything from the cupboard into the center of the blanket. Knowing the front and back doors were barred, she hoisted the blanket of supplies up the stairs and grabbed the pillowcase. Trying to steady her shaking hands, she held the window sill as she carefully lowered the pillowcase next to the horse. The blanket-wrapped supplies were heavy, and she stepped out on the thin limb and pulled them through the window. Letting them down as far as she could, she dropped the bundle, praying the honeypot hadn't broken. Pulling the window shut, she lowered herself down and felt the ground beneath her feet. The cellar was the last stop, and she could be gone before anyone saw her.

Studying the other houses that faced the pond, she spied a man two houses down enter his barn. Likely gathering eggs, he walked with a basket back to his back door without seeing her or the tan horse. Whirling toward the cellar, she tried to steady her nerves, but her heart constricted her throat.

She had started out before the sun rose. Now the sun was spreading its rays across the morning, so now was not the time to sneak around. She could come back when it was dark. She'd never saddled a horse before and now understood the benefits of having something to tie her things to. Shouldering the weight, she pulled the supplies onto her back and held the case with her teeth. Pulling the horse close, she lifted her foot back onto the high branch and raised herself up and onto the center of the horse. Stuffing the pillowcase under Will's jacket, she pulled the supplies in front. Taking a deep rattling breath, she kicked the horse away from the house.

Pure relief flooded her being as she entered the small barn next to the Ford's little cabin. She'd done it. She'd made it from Centerville with no one the wiser. Allowing the bags to slip off the horse, she pulled her leg around and jumped down. "Thank you for your help." Anna patted the long neck of the horse and pulled the bridle off.

"Where have you been?"

The voice behind her caused her body to jump in panic. She turned to see Will standing with a locked jaw in the barn's open doors. Her mouth went dry, and she remembered how her excuses just made Mr. Plugg more hostile.

"I was in Centerville. Did you see my note? I'm sorry I didn't…" she backed up looking for another way to get out. He stepped closer, and she hid behind the bulk of the horse.

"Why are you hiding, Anna? What have you done?" his voice seemed composed and seemed to hold no anger, but hadn't she learned anything from Mr. Plugg's thick hands. A pitchfork was only a length away so she grabbed it.

"Stay away from me." She growled, the pitchfork pulsating towards Will.

"Mrs. Plu—I mean," he squinted, holding his hands up. "I just asked a simple question. Can you tell me where you have been? You went to get your things?"

"I don't owe you anything, Mr. Gibbs. Yes, I went to get my things and a few more." She felt her face burn red, and blinked back watery eyes.

"All right." He opened up his hands. "Can you put that down?" he pointed to the wicked- looking pitchfork. He shook his head. "I'm just confused because I was under the impression you couldn't get back into your home."

"I have my ways." She glared at him, her knuckles white from squeezing her weapon of choice.

He opened his mouth to speak then shut it staring at her. After a moment, he rocked his jaw from side to side, "Then why were you living at the church?" His strained tone spoke more like anger than confusion. She'd seen this trickery before. Eyeing him like a hawk, her breathing quickened, and the tense silence grew longer.

"If you refuse to give me the satisfaction of an answer, I will leave you then." His eyes narrowed before he turned and left. She peered from the corner of the cow barn as he walked long and purposely out to the large two-story tobacco storehouse. Just as the pounding of her heart slowed, her tics began in her head and jerked throughout her body. Not until he was inside the large barn for some time did she have the breath and strength to enter the tiny cabin.

12

NATHAN WALKED IN from work at dusk and closed the door. Anna's chin began to tic. Her anxiety had built all day about sharing this small area with Will. Now, looking past Nathan, she wondered why he was alone.

"Why is your head bumping up and down?" Maribelle asked.

"Bellie," Milo barked, "it's not polite to ask people about their conditions."

"Oh." Maribelle squinted. "I think my mama had a condition. Is that why she died Milo?"

"What is all this!" Nathan's voice filled the cabin. "Something smells good."

"Cornbread and chickpea soup." Anna held his bowl out. "And I have butter and honey."

Nathan beamed the largest smile Anna had seen from him. He looked wide-eyed into the full bowl and back to her. "Don't tell Will, but I think I love you." He laughed, sitting down. Della reached for his bowl, but he turned his back to her and began to scoop the food into his mouth without stopping for a breath.

Reaching across the table, Anna handed Della another piece of cornbread. "Is Will coming along soon?"

"I doubt it." Nathan never looked up. "His grandfather had a few rabbits. They sit around the fire and eat, talk some."

"His Indian grandfather?" Anna asked.

"Yep," Milo piped up. "You should see him. He's got long white hair down his back and feathers and beads all over him. He wears a bearskin coat. Someday when we are all big, Will's going to go be an Indian."

"No, he's not." Nathan looked over at the stove.

Anna reached for his empty bowl and gave him another scoop.

"He's married to Anna now," Nathan said between bites. "He's not going to marry an Indian woman."

Anna felt Milo and Maribelle look her over. "You married Will?" Milo squeaked.

"Now you're our Mama?" Maribelle whole face brightened.

"No, Maribelle." Nathan shook his head, chewing. "That makes Anna your sister-in-law." He let out a loud burp. "Blazes, that was good!"

Anna watched Milo and Maribelle look her over, and something occurred to her. She went behind the blanket and came back out. "I almost forgot. Some socks for Maribelle."

She held them out, and Maribelle's jaw dropped before she hid her face in her crossed arms.

"These are for you." Anna gently rubbed her back, wondering if the poor child was completely overwhelmed. "You were such a good helper today. We churned butter, and ground corn, and cleaned the floor."

Her little hand escaped from under her face and pulled the socks in close.

"Say thank you Bellie." Milo nudged her.

"Thank you." Maribelle murmured into the wood, never looking up. Anna watched as Della licked the cornbread crumbs from the table. At least the table was clean.

"If you want to give *me* a gift, not that you haven't already," Nathan smiled at her. "Could you cut my hair? It's been a long while."

"Yes, of course." Anna liked the lanky teen. It had been some time since anyone smiled or was happy with her. Certainly, after this morning when she'd broken off the benevolence of William Gibbs there wouldn't be much from that quarter. Even today, she'd taught Della to use signs for yes and no and won a measure of cooperation from the demanding teen. These mismatched four seemed to accept her, need her, and it unknotted something deep within her being.

"Thank you for this fine meal, Sister Anna." Milo smiled at her. "To celebrate you being in the family, I'll do the dishes for you." He stood and gathered the bowls.

"Are you sure you are only seven?" Anna pinched his cheek. "I will pour the warm water, and you can dry."

WILL HAD DONE the right thing and told his grandfather of his marriage. He knew the stoic face this man could wear. He'd let him down—far down. Again. Telling him, he would always carry the honor of the Chickasaw people yielded little response either. But it was impossible to convince the man who'd watched his own people be spread far and wide, that Will's allegiance would make a difference. He'd ask the weathered man to come and meet his new…his... Anna. But his grandfather only frowned and shook his head.

Will sighed, pulling his coat close as he marched across the dark night. The coat smelled different. It smelled like Anna. The cabin, the children, everything smelled clean. The shock of her missing this morning, her sneaking away, had jolted him.

How could he be angry? She wanted her own comforts from home. Then why not ask him to take her? Why did she look so guilty, so scared? Her pale face this morning had been a pitiful picture. She was frightened of him.

He's stewed on it only half the morning before he remembered her strange question the night at the church: *Do you believe in striking women?* The way she covered her face when he reached for the feather, and to think she thought he would punish or hurt her. She didn't have to say why she despised Mr. Plugg. It was clearly said without words. The man had mistreated her.

But tonight they would talk, and they would sleep in the same bed. He would try and show her he was a peaceable man; building one day at a time on this new trust. They needed a barrel of that between them for this marriage thing to work.

He walked in quietly in case the children were sleeping and heard laughter. Anna stood close behind Nathan at the table, fingers in his hair. Will felt something spike fast in him as he hung his jacket and set the extra rabbit down. He turned to silence and wide eyes.

"Please don't stop on my account." He rolled his lips tight from frowning. Stepping to the basin to wash, he took stock. It looked like she was giving Nathan a haircut. He tossed a couple of sticks into the stove and tried to calm his rapid heartbeat. It was hard to cut hair without standing close and touching the person.

"How did it go with your grandfather?" Nathan asked. Will glanced to Milo and Maribelle asleep in the loft then Della asleep on the floor.

"Well enough, I guess. I asked him to come and meet Anna." Will locked eyes on her, and she quickly looked back to what she was doing.

"Why would you do that?" she said softly, curiosity etched her face for a moment. Something in his gut flipped. He liked her voice. She spoke plain and clear, no southern drawl like everyone else. And he really liked the tone that wasn't raging with a pitchfork ready to impale him.

"I told him about you and that we'd married." The clean dress she was wearing, arrested his attention—plain green with a wide bell skirt and a little white collar.

"What else did you tell him?" she asked.

The scissors stopped, and he wondered about his brother's safety. "Nothing personal, just that we had married."

Her face relaxed, and she finished trimming around Nathan's left ear. She held a mirror up for Nathan, and when Nathan took it, Will could swear their hands were overlapping.

"Is it short enough?" She asked.

"Yes. It feels much better. And no bugs?" He turned to smile up at her.

"I promise, I saw no bugs." She smiled back and carefully took the towel full of sandy hair from his shoulders. Nathan stood and brushed off his shirt.

"Will could be next." Nathan offered.

"No." They both said in unison. Will squinted at her, he could say no, but she was as eager to respond as he was. Was there an unfixable reproach between them? He needed her more now than he'd ever expected, but making amends with such an erratic woman?

How?

13

A FTER NATHAN CLIMBED the thin steps of the ladder into the loft, Will rubbed his neck and pulled his fingers through his own dark scraggly locks.

"Are you hungry? Anna asked, pulling a towel off a bowl of biscuits and cornbread. "I found the old butter churn outside. We girls made butter."

This cabin was far too small for six people. He could feel her womanly presence and kind voice invading him. "No, no, I'm fine. Thank you." What was wrong with him? Why did he feel a sweat rising on his skin? He cleared his throat. If he could disappoint a grandfather with decades of tradition and expectations, he could ignore the small space and speak frankly to her. "I want to talk to you about this morning."

Anna put the rabbit in a bowl with a cloth over it. "All right."

"Can you sit at the table?" he asked, watching her chew on her bottom lip. She turned and carefully sat down. He sat and watched her fiddle with the cuff on her dress.

"I'm not cross or anything," he said. "I guess I assumed you couldn't live at your old house."

"I can't," she said, not looking at him.

"How did you get your things today?"

"I broke into my own home. I had to climb a tree and—" she pursed her lips together. "It should still be my home. A widow shouldn't be thrown out like a full chamber pot. After all that I–" she stopped, looking up at the loft and shook her head.

WILL FELT UNEASY. How foolish of him marrying her not knowing anything about her. What was he thinking? She had a complicated past beyond what he could safely rely on.

"The Plugg brothers had no right to lock me out," her voice lowered along with her gaze. "The sheriff said—oh, it doesn't matter." She shook her head and pressed her hands together. "There were things I needed."

He wished she would look at him. "I understand that." He tried to sound understanding, "But you could have waited for me," he paused, "I would have taken you."

"I assumed I wouldn't be considered a criminal for taking my own things, but if you or Nathan were there, I...I..." she sighed and said, "it's that I just don't trust those brothers. So I just wanted to go myself." She closed her eyes and put her elbows on the table, resting her face on her hands.

Will didn't want her asking Nathan; he should be the one. He reached over to touch her shoulder but pulled his hand back, changing his mind.

"I had a gal that helped me. Her name is Tallie." Anna spoke slowly into her fingers. "I took everything from her cupboard. I guess I did steal." She squeezed her cheeks together. "Mr. Plugg thought the Negros had no right to own anything. Have anything. Tallie wasn't even allowed her own children. I hope she would forgive me for taking her honey." She huffed. "She was dear to me."

"Do you know where she might have gone?" Will asked.

"I assume back to the Plugg plantation. Her one son, Otis, works in the barns there."

"And the family didn't want to give you a room there?" Will watched her swing her head slowly back and forth in her hands.

"They think I killed their father." She whispered.

"What?" Will's back straightened. "Why would they think that?

"Because of what happened that morning. We had argued." Her voice was barely audible. "I had snuck out to get away from him—"

"Wait," Will stopped her. "What was the argument about?"

Anna rubbed her eyes, then her temples. "I found him with Tallie…committing adultery."

Will looked away, wide-eyed.

"I said I wanted a divorce and he just laughed at me. Said he could do anything he wanted with Tallie." Her face was drawn and pallid when she turned a pained expression toward him finally. "That's not true. Is it? I thought President Lincoln freed the slaves, but not according to Mr. Plugg."

"It's true for many of the states. But things are a little slower here in Kentucky. We will have to follow suit."

They both looked over as Della turned to her other side.

"I also think he had a heart seizure of some kind. He was sweating and red, and then pale, clutching his chest. When he fell, it was straight onto the ice. He never caught himself. Then the ice broke, and he started to sink." She shook her head, looking at Will. "I was useless to pull him out. After he was long gone, it took four men to lift him from the water."

"Did anyone see this happen? Many backyards and outbuildings face the pond."

"No one ever came forward. The sheriff never asked me about killing him, but the Plugg brothers accused me."

Will inhaled sharply, "I'm sure it was just blame from their anger and shock."

"I think Mrs. Hart at the mercantile would have helped me. It was just bad timing." She bit on her bottom lip. "Her being out of town and all. I didn't feel right asking her husband for anything."

Will nodded, trying to let the bizarre information sink in. "You look worn out. Go to bed, and I will wait till you are asleep before I come in."

Anna stood and looked like she wanted to say something. She walked to the curtain and turned back to him. "The more we share these confidences, I feel something changing between us. It's something I see in your eyes, or maybe I'm just being silly." She hesitated, looking at the ground before she met his quiet expression. "I need to feel safe at night, Mr. Gibbs. Am I going to be able to sleep…um…without interruption?" Her chin dipped quickly.

Will felt the heat in his cheeks rise instantly. "I need…I want only my side of the bed. I warned you this place was small. I will only occupy my half. If you want something from me, you'll have to come find me there." He lifted a small smile breaking the tension in the air.

"I won't be coming to visit anytime soon," she grinned before she stepped behind the curtain.

Will rose and pondered those last words. The jar of honey beckoned him close. He opened it and stuck his pinky finger down in the thick sweetness. His need for her to care for this cabin and the children was like his need for water. He stuck his finger in his mouth and tried to keep the sugary goodness lingering on his tongue.

She saw something in his eyes, hmmm. Were all women mind readers? She was strange and interesting. Pretty but plain. Smart but naive. Mr. Plugg sounded like a pig. She should have gotten a divorce long ago. But who would help her? Who would have taken her in with her background? He glanced at the jar and couldn't help himself. He took one more swipe and savored the sweet momentary escape. They'd had nothing sweet in so long. That's all it was.

He'd had no conversations with a woman his age. No social time. Nothing feminine had held his interest. Of course, he looked like a stupid goon bird seeing a female for the first time. He turned and stepped close to the curtain. She lay sleeping in her full dress, and a blanket tucked around her. He determined that he would never press her for husbandly affections.

He sighed as he turned the lamp down. Then why was his pulse spiking as he sat on his corner of the bed taking off his boots, suspenders, and shirt? What if he accidentally bumped her in the middle of sleeping? He tried to lay carefully, like a stiff piece of wood facing the window. But his breathing wouldn't cooperate. His chest rising and falling was keeping him awake. Clenching his pillow, he was thankful to be without covers. This small cabin bedroom had a soft, female body laying right next to his, making the bed tinier and far too warm.

14

WHAT A STRANGE new rhythm developed from one week to the next, Anna thought, as she hung the clothes out on the line. Without the predictability of knowing when Mr. Plugg was at home or gone, she hadn't realized what a tenseness she'd carried. But now each day felt just like the others. She and Will had developed a routine of one person going to bed before the other. One would wait at the table one night, and then the other would wait the next. Mornings were hard to control who would rise first. Wanting to make sure Will had breakfast before going out to the fields, Anna often could feel him leave the bed and would try to rise quickly. She held Milo's wet shirt over the line and stared out to the cool but sunny day.

On Sunday he'd told her to stay abed, he would feed everyone. *It was a luxury, to be sure.* Yet within a few minutes, she missed being in the middle of the morning chatter. Holding up Maribelle's remade dress, she flipped it hard to shake out the wrinkles and tossed it over the line. Yes, her tenseness was gone. Her tics had hardly made an appearance in these last weeks.

Funny, she'd only thought of having her own babies. Her own children would be the only thing to love in a loveless home. Never had she thought she could *take over* a family. She laughed softly, hanging a towel.

Wasn't that what she did at Lennhurst? Blond, fuzzy-haired Elias, and the birthday game with the trinket each year. Poor little Patience and her lonely eyes. Any little child that needed her, she took on as her family.

A thought hit against her heart. She knew God had closed her womb because she'd despised her husband. Michal, in the Bible, had despised her husband, King David, and was struck barren. The minister at Lennhurst had fiercely taught that one Sunday. But maybe God was showing her some mercy. The faces of Reverend Horworth and his wife entered her thoughts. They had no mercy for her, but they were God's appointed ones. She shook away the cross face and voice of Mrs. Horworth as she pinned Milo's socks by the toe.

She had shown Milo mercy with these silly socks, and maybe, just maybe, mercy was coming back to her. Will had said this family had no blessings. Anna could understand that with loss of their mother and then Mr. Lack's removal, it had made everything more difficult. But to her, they were each a true blessing.

No one was going to give her a pot full of joy, so she would consent to being joyful on her own. God's goodness and blessings were hers to have, at least today. She gazed to the feathery blue and white sky, the fresh air filling her lungs.

Nathan had killed a turkey last week, and it had fed them many nights. The children were still wide-eyed and thankful for all the bowls full of her invented recipes. Besides the few dresses Anna had remade for the girls, Celia Lack's wardrobe left little to discover. Clothes, a white apron, an extra blanket, and a little Bible were all she had owned. Tucked in the pages of her Bible were snippets of papers with her prayers written out. In between teaching Milo and Maribelle their letters and numbers, Anna enjoyed reading a verse or wondering about the woman who'd had three husbands and birthed these five children.

Then Della—how that one had changed. Certainly, she was delayed and immature, but she didn't seem to be insane. With a little taste of honey for a reward, Della had learned over twenty signs to communicate what she wanted. Anna shook her head, smiling. It was entertaining after dinner to watch the others try to learn the simple signs and come up with their own.

Milo and Maribelle chased each other around the barn with stick horses dragging along the hard ground, their giggles ruffling the fresh air. She gathered the empty laundry basket and headed back into the cabin. With three quick glances around the tiny interior, she noticed Della wasn't inside. Her first instinct was to check the honey. It was still sitting on the top shelf, so Anna knew she'd not snuck off with her favorite treat. Likely the teen was gone to the outhouse. She glanced out the window as Milo ran by now carrying the stick over his head. She stepped to the door and leaned out.

"Milo! Do *not* swing that stick at Maribelle. Milo!" She tried to get his attention as he ran on. "Maribelle." The little girl stopped running, face red from playing. "Did you see Della outside?" Maribelle shrugged and ran after Milo.

"Why is everyone running from me today?" She stepped out and past the pot of water simmering on the hob. It was useless to call after Della. Anna was sure her greatest malady was being deaf. She circled back around the empty outhouse and felt her belly tighten. She'd only been hanging laundry a few minutes. Will had said Della never strayed far-unless—"

Milo and Maribelle scampered in between some barren trees. "Children! Come now!" Anna started to march toward them and broke out into a run. "Where is Della?" She yelled before she could reach them. Maribelle hunched down and covered her arms over her head. Milo turned and put something in his pocket.

"Milo, what do you have?" She grabbed his arm, and he pinched his pocket closed. Anna looked at Maribelle, wondering why she was hiding in such a fashion. "What is going on? Did someone take Della?" She jerked his hand from his pocket and reached in, pulling out a sticky peppermint. "Ha!" She knew instantly. Someone was using her clever tricks.

"Which way did they go?" She grabbed Milo's shoulder. "You must tell me now, Milo. If you do, you will not be in trouble." She tried to steady her words. He jerked his head from side to side, and she could feel his body tremble.

Finally, his gaze settled behind the barn. Of course! Right where she'd seen a man weeks ago. "Get Maribelle in the house and don't leave." He seemed frozen in place. "Do it now, and you can have your peppermint." Running around the side of the barn, she had no time to see if he would comply. Running, gripping her thick skirts in one hand, she stormed the dense brush.

"I know what you are doing!" she yelled at the empty woodland. Something protective swept through her as she slowed to a walk, looking back and forth. If he was anything like Mr. Plugg, she was running into a snake pit at this very moment. Will hadn't said what height or weight of man Vernon—

"What do you know of my family?" A thin, sunken man stepped from behind a large tree. His clothes were tattered, and his eyes hollow. Anna sidestepped until she could see Della sitting in the brus, licking a candy stick. A rush of relief flowed from her.

"I know enough, Mr. Lack." Anna knew to keep a fair distance from him. "There is a reason you bribe these children with candy. There is a reason Will does not want you near them."

"They are not just any children. They are *my* children." His voice rumbled with defeat. "I would never hurt them." He frowned. "You mustn't listen to Will, Miss. Della had fallen against the rock fireplace. I was only trying to see what kind of scrapes she had. She was the one who pulled her skirt up and sat on my lap. I would never ask such a thing. Will walked in as I was looking at the scrapes. That's all. But he treated me as if I was a demon of some kind. I would never hurt any of them." His eyes reminded Anna of the old hound at the plantation. "Now they don't have enough food or help. I have to sneak around like some criminal just to care for my own. You'll never know, ma'am, how hard it was to lose my lovin' Celia and then my whole family. I need to care for my children."

Della stood and began to pull and rummage his pockets. She rose on her toes and kissed him on the cheek.

"See that, ma'am. She knows I would never hurt her." He patted the top of Della's head. Anna felt her stomach roll. This man was a fool to the moon to think she didn't understand what evil men were capable of.

"If you care for your children at all, you will put her away and send her to me." Her brows creased. "Now! This very moment." She reached her hand toward them.

He swallowed hard. "Of course," he pulled Della forward as Anna signed for her to come.

"Now you must say something to Will," he pleaded. "He needs my help to get the seed planted, the harvest. Maybe you two need to go live as young couples should. All I ask is for another chance to be with my family. I love Milo and Maribelle with all my heart. I have a soddy not far from here. I won't ever come into the house if Will doesn't want me to."

Anna barely focused on his words as she quickly grabbed Della's sticky hand. She knew not to aggravate him. "I will tell him." She nodded once and stepped backward, her heart pounding. She hadn't noticed a knife or gun on his person. In one more gift of God's mercy, Della came along peacefully while Mr. Vernon Lack did not follow.

15

JUST BEFORE DUSK, Will stopped at the black pot of warm water steaming outside the cabin. He'd taken a new interest in washing the dirt and grime off each night. Anna still slept tucked in her dress and blanket in their bed. He shook his head at their strange arrangement as he scrubbed his face and neck. Tonight, Nathan had agreed to hunt until dark. Now with the reliability of food left for him or the smile on Anna's face, Nathan didn't seem to mind. Will walked in and noticed it was unusually quiet.

"How is everyone?" Will waited. Anna wouldn't turn from the kitchen counter. Milo and Maribelle looked tired. Della played with the yarn on the ragdoll Anna had made her.

"There is a bit of turkey stock and dumplings for tonight." Anna set two bowls in front of the little ones. Something was weighing on her shoulders. The way she moved was different.

"No one has yet answered my question." He sat and watched each one with narrow eyes. He cupped Maribelle's chin before she sipped from her spoon, but she jerked away from his touch.

"We got her back. We did. Don't be mad, Will Yam." Maribelle said wide-eyed.

Will shot Anna a stern glare. She shook her head and scooped a bowl for Della.

"What happened, Anna?"

"Let's talk after supper." She set his bowl before him.

"No, we'll talk now." He pushed the bowl away and stood. "Outside." Opening the door for her, he tried to settle his pounding pulse.

Once clear of the closed door, she turned on her heel and faced him. "It was Mr. Lack as you had suspected." She blew out a breath. "He brings treats for the children and they...they..."

Will felt his face burning red.

"Don't be angry." Her chin dipped quickly. "I do the same thing. That is why Della has settled down. I bribe her to be kind or helpful or learn a new sign." Anna brushed a loose strand of hair behind her ear.

"And that is to *help* her." He stalked around the black pot. "She's settled down because she can communicate with us. That's completely different than his motives." Anger laced his voice. "Was he here in the cabin?"

"No!" she boomed. "I confronted him in the woods behind the barn. I never got near him. I just heard him out and then asked him to turn her over, and he did."

"That simple," he said sarcastically, brushing his dark hair back from his eyes.

"I said I would talk to you about him rejoining the family." Anna chewed her bottom lip.

"Really. So quite the tea time you two had." Will pressed his lips in a thin line.

Anna stilled and crossed her arms across her chest. "I don't believe he should be anywhere near the children. He naïvely thought I would swallow his explanations. But I don't. He picked the wrong messenger. I am distrustful of men to the bone."

Will stared long at her, brushing his fingers under his chin stubble. Somehow her words probably meant to sting Vernon Lack but had turned and stung him.

After a strange frozen moment, Will shook his head. "I don't know what to do, and I can't protect her and—"

"You're doing everything you can." She stepped closer to him. "I...I...am not perfect. One minute I was hanging laundry, the next minute she was gone." She touched his sleeve. "*I* was neglectful. I should have been watching closer."

Will covered her hand with his then brought it up and squeezed it. "This wasn't your fault. You know that Nathan and I lost track of her more than once." Still holding her hand in the air, he entwined his fingers in with hers pressing their palms together. "And you got her back. I…think…" suddenly he lost his words. He'd never really touched her before, and her hand meshing with his was making his blood rush like a white water river. Why did he have an urge to jerk her forward into his arms? He stole a glance at her rounded green eyes. She was so pretty.

"I ran out of daylight." Nathan's voice came up from the left, and they quickly dropped hands. "Needin' another outside talk?" Nathan walked up to the hot pot with a rifle slung over the top of his shoulder. "Sorry, Anna, nothing worth eating tonight."

She shook her head and opened her mouth and then looked down to fidget with her skirt. Will wondered what she was thinking. Did she feel what he just felt?

Nathan watched their serious expressions and said, "My guess is something's wrong."

Will found his focus. "Vernon was here today. He had Della with him, and Anna chased them down." Will rubbed his hand over his jaw. "Thankfully, Della went with Anna. He told Anna he wants to rejoin the family."

"Why wouldn't he?" Nathan snorted. "Now we are all clean and fed. The children are learning lessons, and Della is doing better. None of that happened after Ma died. He was good for nothin'."

"He said he would work the land and live in his soddy," Anna added.

Will and Nathan looked at each other. "If I'd seen what you saw, I'd have kicked him out too." Nathan sighed and ran his fingers through his hair, "But what if it wasn't really what it looked like? We could use the help."

Will finally looked away and wearily back at them. "Let's go inside. I'm hungry."

IN THE MIDDLE of the night, with his shoulder burning from sleeping in one position, Will rolled onto his back. Anna was so close. He could hear little pants and half words coming from her. She said she talks to herself, yet he'd never heard her do that by day. Just as he was drifting back to sleep, her whole body jerked, and she cried out.

"Anna." He rolled up on his elbow and tried to see if she'd awakened.

"Oh, Lord," she whispered, flinging the blanket off. "It was only a dream." She rested her arm over her forehead. "I'm sorry. I must have awakened you."

"Bad dream?" He laid back, their arms almost touching.

"I was being chased." She turned back to her side, away from him.

"Was it me?"

"No." She leaned back toward him. "It wasn't you. Just a bad dream."

"Anna." He whispered.

"Hmmm." She turned back to her back pushing her hands down her dress.

"I want to tell you that, well… tell you that I find myself surprised every day by you." Funny how the darkness turned him into someone daring. "I should have told you, but my grandfather had an arranged marriage planned for me with a woman from the tribe." He looked over and hoped she wouldn't be asleep so quickly after a bad dream. "He's a very difficult man to rebel against. It did occur to me the night we were at the church that if I married you, then I wouldn't have to bear the burden of being part of the tribe. It was selfish on my part to have your help and also to use you for keeping me from that obligation."

She found the blanket and covered her legs. "I know." She yawned. "The children told me."

"Humph." *Of course*. He sucked in a tired breath. "I'm just shocked at what a difference you've made. Nathan said it better, but we—"

She turned toward him and wrapped her hands around his thick upper arm. Her face nuzzled into his arm and shoulder. "Umm hum."

Will froze with the bold display, was this not *his* side of the bed?

16

A NNA'S EYES FLEW open. She set her mind to rise before the sun peeked across the land, but the shock of awakening facing Will almost sent her reeling. Something about a bad dream and his grandfather, she cautiously peeled herself off his arm and moved gently from the bed. Finding her warm shawl in the pre-dawn, she tied it in a knot around her shoulders and tiptoed from the cabin. Without anything from Nathan's hunting this week, most of the supplies were gone. She would try the pond house cellar for salted meat and, if that worked, she could be home before sunrise. Pulling the horse from the barn, she stopped. She forgot to leave a note. Stepping up on the wood chopping stump, she swung up on the horse. No matter, if she hurried, she could return before the household awoke.

Tethering the horse to the same skinny tree along the side of the brown house, Anna looked around. She wouldn't have time to gather her mother's spoons or search for her sewing box. Stepping on the cold, crunching ground, she hastened to the flat cellar doors that loomed off the ground. Thank goodness, no bolts, or chains through the long handles. Heaving the heavy door to the side, the handle slipped from her hands and landed with a loud thud.

Goodness, she groaned, all she could see in the cellar was pitch black. Knowing from memory the narrow stairs were there, she clung to the side and tried to safely find each step. A month ago there was a side of pig chopped into three hams and a lamb roast that was from the plantation. Her feet hit the dirt floor, and she reached back and forth in the dark. "They should be here somewhere," she mumbled, stretching deeper inside until she hit the back earthen wall. Disappointment flooded in. As round as all the Plugg men were, how stupid was she to think they would leave meat unattended. She found the steep stairs and reached one more time into a corner until she hit the frozen dirt. A twinkle of black sky to gray was above her as the sun began to peak up from the east.

Just as she was stepping up the first step, the large thick cellar door slammed above her and knocked her onto her backside. She scooted back until she hit the dirt wall and clutched her chest. That was no wind. Something or someone pushed closed the doors above her. Should she cry out? Was it friend or foe? Anna shoved her knuckle in her mouth and waited. After what seemed like a long time, enough for the cracks of sunlight to appear through the door slats, she rose and stood under the cellar doors. Pushing with all her might was of no use. Someone had shoved something heavy between the handles of the two doors, trapping her in the cold empty meat cellar.

WILL FINISHED THE breakfast dishes and looked at Della still sleeping in her corner. "Milo, listen to me. This morning is like what we used to do." He tried to sound more optimistic than he was. "You watch the girls. Nathan will be in the barn, and you can bang the pan if you need him."

"Where are you going?" Milo asked with brows creased.

"I'm going to find Anna."

"Yeah!" Maribelle clapped. "Maybe she went to get me a candy."

Will jerked his jacket from the peg. "Milo." His brother looked worried. "I'm coming back as soon as I can. Please, just help with the girls. And don't," how did Will tell him to stay away from his own father? "Don't let anyone out of the cabin."

Milo never agreed but glared at Will. What would he do if they chose Vernon Lack over him? What if he came home to find them all gone? The brisk morning air hit him as he walked out.

Why was Anna doing this? Last time he got to the barn she was there. But not this morning. Today, their only horse was missing. It would be a long run to town.

AFTER AN HOUR of jumping and swaying side to side to stay warm, Anna sat on the steps of the damp cellar and curled into a tight ball. The cold and darkness were making her feel tired and blurry. She felt alone and unprotected. Those feelings pulled her thoughts back to Lennhurst Asylum where she was left a defenseless child, alone and unprotected.

What if it was Maribelle who had made a horrific mistake?

Stewing with that thought, she tucked her layered skirts around her legs. What if Maribelle had dropped the powder and killed her own baby? Would Anna send Maribelle away? As bad as she'd longed for a baby? Maybe…No, she couldn't. Her grief would be deep, but she wouldn't cast her out. Anna had just been a careless child, not a damaged chair to be thrown into the burn pile. Then why did broken Anna find herself back in another dark prison? She shivered with the cold.

Fear not for I am with you. Where did that thought come from? Anna lifted her head, listening. Celia. It was one of those Bible verses Celia had written out.

Had Celia been afraid of dying? So many of her written prayers were for her children. Had she been afraid for her children's future? Had God answered her prayer?

Celia's children were all alive and thriving. Anna rubbed her eyes and looked up, seeing the sliver of sunshine through the cellar door. "God are You really with me, this unlovable Anna? Do You come into the darkest of places?" Her heart cried out, *How do I feel your mercy one moment and abandonment the next?*

She sighed as her thoughts drifted back to when she'd been a child at Lennhurst. Every day she'd felt abandoned until she started helping here and there. The crazed people tolerated the little girl who helped them eat or combed their hair. So many were crippled limbs sitting in a ball but would allow her to rub oil onto their boney skin.

Moving and standing up, she found her confidence slowly returning. It was the same with her new charges, these motherless children, when she was helping them, her sorrows stayed at bay.

Stand up in your confidence, came to her. What did she have to lose? She stretched taller and banged her fist above her head. "Help! Someone, please help! I want out!" Her raised voice was unusual to hear. But since there was no one around, she yelled over and over. "Tallie! Come back! I'm locked in the cellar!" At least it helped keep her blood from freezing solid.

"Anyone. Help! Will!" her voice crackled. "Will, please find me." She banged on the wood door until her hand ached. Will, so strong and serious. His dark eyes and perfectly etched, manly face. His scraggly locks made him look wild and determined, yet his words came from a tender heart. Yes, her new husband had a tender heart. "Will. William!" She tried again. "Please, please find me!"

The wood rattled only inches above her head, and she stepped back down the last steps. The left cellar door flung wide, and after holding her hand against the glare, she could make out his face. "Oh, Will, thank God." She held her hand out and climbed the stairs until she felt his grip pull her into his arms. "Thank God, it was you." She clung to him and his warmth. The bright sun made her eyes water.

"You're freezing." He squeezed her tight and rubbed his hand up and down her back.

Anna could feel their chests rising and falling, his warm breath in her hair and quickly pulled back.

"What happened?" He still clutched her forearms, looking her over.

"I don't know. I went down to get the meat, but there wasn't any, and then the door slammed, and I couldn't get out."

"Someone had barred the door." Worry deepened the shadows of his eyes. "Why, Anna. Why didn't you wake me?" He shook her arms once.

"I thought—I was sure—I would be back before…" She could tell there were no words to appease the lines creasing his face. She twisted away from his strong grip. "I didn't know someone would lock me in the cellar," she murmured to the ground.

Will stepped back and took in two or three deep breaths. "So this is it. This is where you used to live?"

"Yes." She brushed the damp dirt off her dress. "How did you find me?"

"This is the only house around the pond that had my horse tied next to it." He shook his head, watching her. "Did you see who barred the door?"

"No." She looked around. "It was dark."

"Anna." He shifted his stance. "I don't understand you. Now that your husband is gone, do you *want* to come back here? Do you want to live here again?" The tension in his face deepened. "You can be honest. This is a fine home. You've been cooped up in a dog house compared to this." He looked up and down the side of the two-story, brown house.

Anna watched him, a deep warmth and belonging stirred her heart. The man had come for her. "A month ago, I thought I did, for five minutes." Her breathing finally calmed. "I thought Tallie and I could keep it up and running. And I once thought I would be content. Anything without Mr. Plugg would make me content. But I love helping you and the children." She huffed, looking down at the empty cellar. "I'd hoped the meat we cured was still in there. I wanted to bring it back for the family."

Will looked at the ground, shaking his head.

"And my sewing box. If I could find my sewing box," she glanced at the brown house.

"No." Will grabbed her hand and pulled her around the house to the waiting horse. He folded his hands together, making a step for her to use. "Get on, Anna."

She carefully swung her leg over and arranged her skirts. Will gripped the girth of the horse and jumped, landing behind her with the agility of a true Indian brave. He grabbed the reins from her hands, his arms squeezing her tight in front of him.

"It could've even been Vernon," he said. Giving the horse a kick, he led them out to the side of the pond. "He knows when you turn your back to hang laundry."

She tried to follow his words but couldn't deny the encompassing strength of his protective arms surrounding her. Was it just the warmth or did being rescued have more to do with it? Her body began to relax, like the first moments in a hot bath. Allowing herself to settle lightly against his chest, the peace and security she was feeling was unfamiliar and overwhelming at the same time.

"Thank you for finding me, Will," she whispered. "I often thought I would die in that house, but I didn't think I would die in the cellar."

"What? I'm not sure it was Vernon, I don't think he would kill anyone. It could've even been a neighbor that saw it open and closed it to keep trespassers out." Turning the horse between two trees, she could feel his body move with hers. "I'd a hunch where you went. But you should have told me, Anna." He pulled the tan horse to a stop and pulled her shoulder back to see her face. "Don't do this again. Please." He tugged on her arm, and she couldn't help but stare at his sharp eyes, waiting for her compliance.

"I—I don't know how *not* to look after myself." Her shoulders slumped.

"I know you don't want to be married." He raked his dark hair from his face. "But now I rely on you, as do the children." He leaned back behind her and gave the horse a nudge forward.

It was true she didn't want to be married. Something in her being relaxed at his acknowledgment, but she felt alive and important caring for this family. "I'm sorry. You, Will, are the head of this family, and I will try not to run with my impulses." That apology sounded strange, but it was much stranger never to fear an onslaught of pain when someone reprimanded you.

17

A T DUSK THAT night, she'd asked Milo and Maribelle to put away their paper and signed to Della to wash up for supper. She hated that all they had was a scoop of porridge and a flapjack each. Trying to remind herself to be thankful they were all well and safe in the cabin, she stirred the hot mush. Certainly, this was the usual fare they ate before she came. But something about picturing chunks of ham and beans filling those bowls dismissed her of her gratitude.

Will and Nathan's entrance filled up the little cabin more than usual. Robbed of the delight in serving them something hearty, she squeezed her eyes shut. Will's rescue at the pond house and the lack of food waxed hard in the back of her throat. She wanted to look at him and offer a smile, but some strange embarrassment was plaguing her. Rare for her, tears were starting to form. Nathan came close and washed his hands, jerking the towel from Della's grip.

Della moaned out. "Auupp."

Anna turned and motioned her hand across her palm. "Stop" was a common sign used at Lennhurst; *if* she could get her attention. Della jerked back on the towel and Nathan pulled back, bumping Anna into the hot stove.

"Both of you stop!" Every face froze and stared at her, except Della who began to laugh. She gritted her teeth and pushed away from Nathan and Della. It was only four steps to her room, and she glared at the sagging, shredded blanket. Why didn't they at least have a proper blanket to hang? Feeling unavoidable emotion rising, she didn't want any of them to hear her, so she reached for the cabin door and quickly let herself out.

Only a few steps past the hot water pot, she knew the footsteps behind her belonged to Will. "Please." She swiped her face, looking out at the last thin glow of the day. "I'm fine. Just go on and serve everyone." She pulled her white apron up to cover her wet cheeks. Anger rose quickly inside the dark mood she was feeling. She'd learned the hard way that tears just made Mr. Plugg madder. She stomped out toward the distant tobacco barn.

"*He* could be mad about everything, but not me. I had to hide everything." She growled, untying her apron and throwing it hard to the ground. "Shut up, Anna. You're a lunatic from an insane asylum," she mimicked his cruelty.

"No, you shut up! You are old and fat and mean!" she cried out to the dim landscape. "You hurt me and Tallie, and you never cared!" Picking up a rock, she leaned back and gave it a heave. "We did everything for you, and you never did anything kind for us." Her steps quickened until she was running. "I hate you!" She panted, running faster. "From the first night… in…" she sucked in a sob, "your bed… I was young and you… you were a heaving pig. You were cruel," she wheezed. "All I wanted was to be away from you." Tears streaked across her face, and she wobbled as her legs beat against the layers of her skirt. "I hate you. I'm glad you're off this earth. You deserve to rot in the hottest hell—"

She ran faster with lungs burning. Making out the open door to the barn, she could only hope the darkness inside waited to envelop her. At the last second, she turned from the outstretched darkness and slammed her swinging fists into the barn siding. The impact knocked her to her backside, and she crawled forward, gripping clumps of dirt. Smearing the clods of dirt into the wood, they crumbled between her fingers. Next, she pounded her fists up and down the rough wood until her arms shook.

"I ha-hate you." She collapsed in the dirt, her clenched fist unable able to rise to pound the wood. "Never. Never will you trap me, hit me, hold me down. Never again." The dizziness was suffocating. Unable to find her breath, everything went black.

⟜

"CAN I BRING you another wet rag?" Nathan asked from the end of the bed.

"No, I think this one is still good," Will said, dabbing it on the purple lumps on Anna's head and cheek.

"So she just ran straight into the side of the barn? Was it that dark? Did something spook her so that she couldn't find the door?"

Will was sure from her screaming and running that it was intentional. But it was too hard to explain to Nathan. "It's late, go ahead and go to bed." He sighed.

"You'll tell her I'm sorry for the horseplay in the kitchen. I didn't mean to—"

"No, Nathan, trust me, it wasn't from that." He watched Anna move her head from side to side. "It was other things."

"Goodnight then." Nathan turned and left.

Will pulled off his boots and lowered his suspenders. He propped his pillow against the log wall and lowered himself to sit. He would try his best to stay awake. Pulling the blanket over her shoulder, he heard her murmur something.

"Anna," he whispered. "Can I get you some water or food?"

She put a hand to her head. "I have a terrible headache." She pulled her hair back. "Ooh." Her eyes peeled open. "The cellar, did I fall down the steps of the cellar?"

"No." Will chewed on his bottom lip. He'd never seen or heard any human run and carry on as she did. By the time he caught up with her, she was out cold. "You ran into the big tobacco barn."

"Ohh," she moaned, her eyes shifted to him. "I thought you'd gone back inside."

"No, I saw everything." He gritted his teeth, seeing the two purple bruises in the dim lantern light. He flashed her a crooked grin. "And didn't you tell me just this morning you would work on those impulses you get?" He lifted her hand and held it on his. "I'm just glad you're okay." He waited, fingering her fingers. "*Are* you okay?" The silence lingered as she stared at their lightly touching fingers.

"This morning," she whispered, "when I was trapped in the cellar." She blinked slowly, "I think I heard God. I'm not sure. Do you think God talks to people? Especially people like me?"

Will shifted lower in his spot and crossed his ankles, still holding her hand. "My mother would say, yes. She loved the Bible stories of how Jesus loved the sinner." He turned toward her. "I'm not saying you are a sinner, but I'm going to say, yes, the Lord talks to people today."

"How do you know?"

"My mother would read to us after Della or the little ones fell asleep. That's how Nathan and I learned to read. One night, I think I was ten or eleven, she was in the last book of the Bible—I don't remember what it was really about—but I'll never forget it. It said something to the like that in the end, Heaven will be filled with every nation, every tribe, and people." He lowered her hand to her chest and pulled his pillow down next to hers. "When Mr. Ford ran the tobacco fields, the slaves would come in to work at harvest time. They would sing deep and rich songs about God, and heaven, and glory." He stretched his shoulders from side to side and yawned. "I liked that God. I liked to think that his Heaven had a welcome mat for the blacks and the tribes, or half Indians." He lifted the corner of his mouth into a smile. "The sinners and the saints." Sucking in a quick breath, he let it out. "My white ma and my Indian father, too. Something settled down in my soul. I felt like the truth of God's love for all people was real."

"Mmm." Anna closed her weighty eyes. "I think, as a child, I shared that, too, but then life became so harsh and forbidding. I supposed God's love couldn't apply to me. I had so much hatred in my heart." She turned yawning and gripped his arm like she had the night before. "But in the dark cellar, I heard, *'Do not fear, I am with you.'*"

Will tried to fight the drowsy dropping of his eyes, wanting to enjoy her warmth close to his side. "That's good," he mumbled, knowing she'd likely fallen asleep. "God doesn't give us fear."

His thoughts floated in between sleep and awake. "I prayed for you, or maybe for me." Quiet peace filled his being. "That first night you came." Reaching to turn the lantern down, he carefully scooted down closer to her, thankful she seemed to have recovered from her spell.

He truly hoped she had.

18

THE NEXT MORNING, Anna walked slowly while Della and the little ones ran down to the creek. The air was crisp, but the sun brought a bearable touch of warmth to her stiff bones.

"I usually can't bring Bellie fishing." Milo walked ahead of the girls; pole slung over his shoulder. "She talks too much and scares all the fish away."

"I do not." Maribelle skipped around in a circle and grabbed Anna's hand. Another's warm touch gripping her cold skin tugged at Anna's emotions. This family, these little ones unearthed desires so long buried. At first light, Will had told her to sleep, and he would feed the children. Of course, she couldn't sleep. Lying in bed only brought more confusion and shame for her ridiculous outburst. She joined the simple breakfast only to have everyone stare at her. Will gave them some story about walking into the barn at dark isn't a good idea; always take a lantern. Maybe the tender abrasions were the reason she couldn't find any vigor. The bruises felt too familiar.

"Can I make mud pies?" Maribelle jerked on her hand, bringing her back to the moment. Milo had already found a spot a few feet away. He pulled a worm from his pocket. Della was twisting branches into a wreath for her hair.

"Yes," Anna whispered.

Maribelle had already sat, scooping and patting the mud into little circles.

Anna looked around. It should feel good to get out of the small cabin. Usually, she enjoyed teaching the children their letters and numbers. Milo was already reading. But today she could barely find any favor for any of it.

How could she be so disheartened in this day? Mr. Plugg was indeed dead and gone. What did she have to fear? Will had only been kind and patient. She shook her head and watched Milo fling his line into the water. If she turned to Will Gibbs any more nights and held his arm, it wasn't going to be long before he wanted his due from her. Hadn't she just said she would never cross to his side of the bed?

She sighed, rolling her stiff neck backward and then side-to-side. It was a hideous act only worth enduring to make children. She walked in a circle and pulled her shawl tightly against her chest. Mr. Plugg already had sons, so it was obvious something was broken in her. So there really was no reason for it. She'd told Will from their first meeting she was barren.

"Bellie!"

Anna looked up, Maribelle was standing next to red-faced, temperamental Milo.

"Maribelle, come back over here and show me what you've made," Anna called. Maribelle skipped up from the creek bank and back to her creations. Anna knelt down to hear all about the different flavored mud pies. "I would love a bite. Thank you." Anna pretended to enjoy the invisible bite.

"Does your owie hurt?" Maribelle lightly touched Anna's bruised cheek.

"No, not really."

The little girl searched her face; so unusually serious. Maribelle lowered her little mud circle to the ground and threw her arms around Anna's neck, almost knocking them over.

"Oh, my." Anna put her arm back to steady them.

Maribelle pulled her face from Anna's neck and pressed a long kiss to her other cheek. Hugging her tighter, she nestled back in the crook of her neck. "I love you, Anna."

The melancholy reappeared without fair warning, and Anna couldn't get her voice to work. She blinked hard, but the tears came anyway. What was wrong with her? Two days of this in a row?

"Don't cry." Maribelle leaned back and swiped her muddy little finger across Anna's wet cheek and kissed it again.

She touched the little girl's cheek. "I love you, too, sweet girl." Anna turned and kissed the little soft cheek. Elias, her little brother from Lennhurst, came to mind—the only other person in her life she'd ever said I love you to. Why, oh why were her insides getting shredded left and right, up and down of late?

Twisting quickly to the sound of a branch snapping, Anna stood up, grabbing Maribelle by the hand.

Vernon Lack stood on the opposite bank.

Milo watched Anna with dropped chin, and Della, with her back turned to the creek, was unaware.

"What now, Mr. Lack." Anna sized him up again, feeling confident she could use her fists on his slight frame if she needed.

"I just wondered if you'd talked to Will, about the family and me coming home. Did you explain what he saw wasn't anything bad?" Vernon looked at his boots.

"I did as you asked." Anna moved closer to Della, not sure if the girl would run into the water to him. "But I have a question of my own." Swiping the dampness from her face, a rod of iron seemed to rise up her back. "Why do you feel you must take Della when no one is watching? You must know it sends the family into a panic. She cannot be out alone, and it seizes them all with fear. Why do you find *that* necessary?"

He leaned against a tree and scratched his forehead. "It's just when I can round up extra grub. First I feed her, cause she's always hungry, and then I try to get her to take the food back to the cabin, but she won't do it. She don't like touchin' anythin' dead or anythin' that's got blood on it."

Anna glared long at him. "And in your same attempts to sneak around to get her, you couldn't just leave the food?"

"She always wants to...I..." the man fumbled for words and looked everywhere but at Anna.

They all turned to Della as she rose and placed her new crown of branches on her head, giggling and making a funny face at Anna.

"Auugg." Della clapped her hands together and started toward him. Anna grabbed her sleeve, but Della growled and pulled free.

"Milo, please join me." Anna dragged Maribelle along and reached out for Della again. By the grace of God, Della allowed Anna to lead her back away from the water.

"And another thing, Mr. Lack, from now on, there is no reason for you to follow women and children and expect us to do your bidding." Without taking an eye from him, she moved her group backward. "You can speak to William Gibbs yourself. Only a coward preys on women and children." Regretfully, she wished she could catch those last accusatory words back. Something was clearly a bur in her brain today.

"I don't *prey*," he barked back, "on my own children, Miss."

"Very well." She clenched her teeth together. "Then you-you will speak to him, not to me, from now on."

"And I will see my children whenever I want!" he hollered after them as they moved away.

Anna could not get her heart to slow down. Had Mr. Lack followed her and shut her in the cellar yesterday? Would he do her harm? With her living at the cabin, it had made it more difficult for the man to come and go as he wished. Now it was obvious she sided with Will's wishes, and he had no ally in her. She approached the cabin still dragging Della and Maribelle by the hand and froze. A dead chicken lay on the stoop.

"Is that one of ours?" Anna's nostrils flared, dropping the girl's hands.

Milo looked over to the coop and counted with his finger. "Nope, ours is all in the coop."

"Ours are in the coop," Anna corrected automatically. She huffed and whisked it up by the rubbery feet. Surveying around the yard and trees, she dropped a hand on her hip and let the dead bird dangle next to her skirt. Debating on how she could hurl this bird and clock Mr. Lack upside the head, she almost snickered.

Realizing her dark mood was replaced with a new resolve, she observed the children watching her. Each day she was going to have to let go of her past and pick up these days of her future, no matter how daunting. This future needed protecting, just like when Will pulled her from the cellar. It was something she'd never understood before. The encompassing of arms and strength around her were foreign. But it felt right to belong, and if you belonged, then you kept each other safe.

She smiled at the children.

And there would be fried chicken for supper!

19

THE FOLLOWING THURSDAY, Will had spoken of going to town for supplies and a stop at the bank. Anna had longed to see Mrs. Hart from the Mercantile. Though she had no supplies for sewing the baby gowns and tatting lace for them, at least she freely could walk in the front door without repercussions.

"Will's got the wagon ready." Nathan came inside Thursday morning, dropping his jacket, and warming his hands by the cook stove. He peeked at her twice, and she covered the little strands of twisted hair she'd pulled back into her plain low bun. Feeling stupid for doing her hair different, she contemplated taking it all apart.

"Maribelle, get your jacket," Anna said, looking into Milo's long face. She reached over and tussled his growing short brown hair. "This time you help Nathan, and I will bring you something from town."

"What?" He scowled at her.

"A surprise," Anna smiled.

"I want a surprise," Maribelle whined.

"Now you've started it, Anna." Nathan shook his head, smiling.

"We will go," Anna eyed Nathan and then Della like a protective hen. "And you *will* watch for Mr. Lack?" She caught herself practically scolding Nathan. Now she sounded like the overprotective sole caregiver.

"Yes, ma'am," he nodded.

AFTER LOADING MARIBELLE into the middle of the bench seat, Anna took Will's outstretched hand and sat. It seemed like a lifetime ago they'd ridden on this same seat together. She straightened her skirt layers. What a strange beginning, and what a warm, excited feeling she possessed now as they pulled away from the cabin. Maribelle's wriggling little body matched her insides.

"Milo gets a surprise. Can I get one, Will?" Maribelle tugged on his jacket.

"If we have time." Will glanced up at Anna. "I like your hair today." He lifted a coy smile. "You can hardly make out the old bruises."

Anna looked down at her crossed hands and felt his compliment warm in her chest. A tiny smile played across her lips. What was she thinking? She had kept to her side of the bed all week. She was certainly enjoying his approving smiles, and the nights they'd begun to read the Bible stories to the children, but there'd been no more late night talks and consolation between the two of them.

She changed the subject, "Nathan said he would watch for Mr. Lack."

Will jumped down and opened the large gate. Anna took the reins and tapped the wagon forward until he jumped back on. She couldn't help but look back, her gaze scouring the land.

"They'll be fine," Will said.

"And our daddy will just have to pray in church. Huh, Anna?" Maribelle piped up.

Will looked at her his eyes narrowing.

"I did mention he shouldn't prey on women and children. I think she didn't understand my meaning." Anna lifted a small smile.

"You were right." Will nodded at her, tapping the reins. "He has no business speaking to anyone but me."

"Do you think he only wants to help with food?" Anna asked.

Will pushed his hat back, scratching his forehead. "I don't know." He pulled it back in place. "I think if I let him in to help, it will keep me awake at night wondering if he's up to something. He was in such a stupor after my ma died. I don't think he is the same person we knew."

As the wagon dipped into a rut, Will stretched his arm across to steady them. Anna grabbed his hand, locking Maribelle between them. The road evened out, but Will still gripped her hand. Thinking she missed something, she looked at him, and he smiled a roguish grin before he slowly released her hand from his.

What to make of these smiles and extra touches? The way he'd lightly touched her back or waist when they passed in the small cabin. Surely it was impossible not to always bump into someone in the tiny confines. A tingling started in her gut as she tried to watch for the adding of houses and barns as they approached the town. She'd never known anyone like him.

He was quiet for the most part—those dark eyes keeping all his deep thoughts hidden within. But his smiles and kindnesses were pulling something peculiar from her. She cleared her throat and sat straighter. For all the obvious reasons, no man had really loved her. Now she was telling herself fables and turning into some sappy ninny she didn't even recognize. She took Maribelle's cold hands and held them between hers. Centerville, Kentucky provided a welcome distraction to them all. "Look!" Maribelle pointed. "There's the church we can pray at. Can we go, Will Yam? Can we go?"

"Not on a Thursday, Maribelle," Will said.

Or ever. Anna mouthed over her little head to Will. He lifted wide eyes and huffed. "That's settled." Will pulled the wagon to a stop.

"I will take her and do some shopping," Anna said, watching the lines around Will's face crease with concern. He jumped down and lifted Maribelle to the ground. Leaning forward she'd hoped to catch his hand, but he easily had her by the waist and lowered her in front of him. "I suppose we should have talked about this." He held her but looked down the street. "I have no account at the mercantile. I only get things after the tobacco is sold at auction."

"I understand." She moved quickly to grab Maribelle by the hand before she could dart off. "You must always stay with me." Anna got her attention and then looked back at Will. "Do you remember me saying I sold baby gowns?"

Will nodded with a stoic expression.

"If there is anything from that, I'd like to get a few things for the children."

Will looked down the wooden sidewalk and rolled his tongue inside his cheek. "I don't know. Something doesn't feel right."

"Let's go!" Maribelle yanked on Anna's hand. "We have to find a surprise for Milo and *me*," she giggled, swinging Anna's arm back and forth.

"We'll meet back here." Will held Anna's eyes, "No breaking into the pond house?"

"No. I learned my lesson." Anna felt a cold shiver run up her spine.

Will squeezed her arm and turned to walk towards the bank. He had a muscular torso and confident gate, watching him now, and feeling his touch again was mesmerizing.

"Now! Can we go now?" Maribelle whined.

Anna smiled. "Yes, hold my hand tight as we cross the street."

Nerves or some strange reaction hit Anna as they walked in the heavy door of the mercantile. The warmth, the smell of spices, and hearing the chatter of other shoppers chipped at her heart. Please Lord, forgive me for the disdain...that house of God comment, she needed strength to keep her rising emotions at bay.

"Anna! Is that you?" Mrs. Hart almost ran toward her. Anna quickly let go of Maribelle's hand to hug the beaming woman.

"Oh, my sweet dear. I have wondered how you were fairing." Mrs. Hart pulled back looking her over. "Caring for all those children. Tisk, tisk." She shook her head.

"And that one is like a little mouse." Anna had to step away to find Maribelle sitting on the floor, playing with a toy.

"She is fine." Mrs. Hart smiled. "I have to hear about *you*. I can't believe I was gone to Lexington. Oh, you poor thing, I heard the Plugg brothers locked you out of the house."

Anna watched Maribelle, and heat rushed to her face. "It's true."

"Those men should be given a few lashes for themselves." Mrs. Hart looked around quickly, lowering her voice. "The whole lot of them and their wicked ways."

"Anna, can I have this for my surprise?" Maribelle held up a wooden horse with a red saddle.

"No child, put it back." Anna looked over at the table, noticing the baby gowns missing. "Did the other ones sell?"

"Yes!" Mrs. Hart clapped her hands together with a wide smile. "I had a grandmother from Carmichael buy the last three Saturday. Let me get you your money." Mrs. Hart walked to the cash box, and Anna followed. "I'm sorry to say, my sewing box is locked in the brown house, I don't have any supplies or gowns for you to sell." Mrs. Hart dropped two dollars in her hand, and Anna frowned. "This is too much." Mrs. Hart scurried over to another counter and pulled out a bolt of muslin and roll of blue, then roll of pink string and a tatting shuttle.

"All right then, these supplies come to a dollar." Mrs. Hart bit back her smug smile.

"I see what you are up to." Anna smiled.

Mrs. Hart leaned over the counter and grabbed Anna's elbows. "You are a true craftswoman, and now we don't have to sneak around anymore." She gave her a quick shake, something endearing misted in her eyes.

Anna watched the older woman in her starched puffy blouse, and thick checkered vest. Acceptance and forbearance seemed to move with her as she loaded the supplies into a canvas bag. "And a surprise for this little one." Mrs. Hart flapped open a small paper bag and reached behind her. "A cookie with chocolate frosting for you."

"Oh, my." Maribelle's eyes widened. "Can we have another one for my brother?"

"Of course." Mrs. Hart smiled. "They seem like wonderful children."

"And often hungry." Anna smiled at Maribelle and asked for the remaining dollar to go for grain and beans, flour and sugar.

"And the oldest brother?" Mrs. Hart loaded the remaining items. "You would tell me if you were—" Another patron set a bag on the long sales counter.

"He is kind." Anna interrupted and grabbed her full bag. She dropped her head wondering if the shadows of her bruises told another story. Not wanting to explain that she had caused them herself. She suddenly was ready to get home. "I shall work on the gowns soon and be back." Flashing a smile, she turned to gather Maribelle. As soon as Maribelle gripped her hand, a rush of thankfulness flooded her, and she stopped at the large front doors. Appreciation for her new found freedom surged through her. She felt more acceptable in public today than she'd felt in her lifetime. Turning back to the kindred spirit who still watched her, she nodded. "Thank you, Mrs. Hart, for," she had to speak around the emotions knotted in her throat, "for everything."

20

MARIBELLE SKIPPED ALONGSIDE Anna holding onto the layers of her dress. Looking up, she noticed a few gray clouds had appeared. Stopping in front of the family wagon, she hoisted the canvas bag into the back. Looking around, she concluded Will must still be in the bank. Though she hadn't asked, she assumed the needs of the family were more than what last year's crop could provide. Lifting Maribelle in front of her, the child dropped into the back of the wagon. At least her small wages were going to something important.

"Can I have my cookie?" She asked, looking down at Anna.

"Yes. You may have your surprise." Anna spied a small library sign at the end of Main Street. "I wonder if the library has any books to help us with our hand signs for Della." She said to Maribelle. "Let's go look." She grabbed the little sticky hand, and Maribelle jumped off the back.

A few minutes later, a little bell tinkled from the door, and they entered the musty smelling library. Full shelves filled every nook of the small space.

"How can I help you?" A thin, gray-haired woman looked over her spectacles at them.

"We need a book for my sister." Maribelle piped up.

"The school has their own books for the children to use." The woman patted her low bun.

"My sister can't go to school. She doesn't talk or understand people." Maribelle cast a curious glance up at Anna, "Why can't Milo and I go to school?"

Anna sucked in a breath. "I believe the child is likely deaf. Do you have any books on the signs people do with their hands to speak to the disabled?"

"Heavens, no," The woman bristled. "As you can see, we are a small branch. Only the classics and religious literature." She pointed down one aisle, and then down another, "Some books on farming and maintaining proper households."

Anna felt her chin twitch—there was that familiar judgmental tone, doubting herself through another's disapproving eye.

"Thank you, ma'am." Anna nodded and grabbed Maribelle's hand.

"Probably the sister of the reverend's wife," Anna murmured, walking out. Halfway back to the wagon, a group of Negro men and women waited on a side street, begging her attention. "Tallie," she whispered. Dragging Maribelle along, she turned down the street. One woman had a familiar red and orange head wrap. Anna's step quickened. Was it Tallie? The men separated and began to form a line to load heavy seed bags in the wagon. Anna tried to see through their line of work.

"Tallie?" she calle, trying to get the other women to turn around. She walked around and out into the street to see the woman. Her heart dropped, as none of the faces looked familiar. "Do any of you know a woman named Tallie? She would have come to work in the last month or so?" Two women looked at the ground. "She is older, maybe fifty or so." Anna sucked in her frustration; of course, they didn't want to speak to her. "Please, it's very important to me to see her. What plantation do you work on?" The woman with the colored head wrap looked over at the men loading the wagon. "She isn't in any trouble. I just need to talk to her. She used to work for me." Anna strained closer, but they just looked away with large vacant eyes.

"I need the outhouse." Maribelle pulled on her hand.

"Just a minute, child, this is important." Anna dropped her yanking hand before the child pulled her off balance.

"Her son is Otis. He is practically a cripple. Do you know Otis?" She tried not to sound so anxious as they stepped away from her. "I believe they are on the Plugg plantation. Do you have any knowledge of that place?" A burly man with a tattered shirt rocked the wagon as he climbed in and sat on the bench. Quickly, the men and women jumped on the back of the full wagon as it pulled away.

"Wait! I—" Anna's shoulders slumped, watching them drive out of town. Turning in a circle, she didn't see Maribelle.

"Maribelle?" She scanned the sidewalk and street. "Maribelle!" Eyes wide with alarm, she hurried from one building to the next calling her name. Searching left to right, she ran back breathless to Main Street. Could she have come this far? Anna circled, urgently refocusing on everywhere she had looked. Winded, Anna felt panic and anger at the disobedient child mixing through her. Two blocks down Will stood by the wagon. His eyes caught hers.

"Oh, no." She turned back down the side street. "Maribelle!" She couldn't have gone far. "What did she say? Something about an outhouse?" Anna ran between openings in the buildings. "Maribelle!" She glanced down the back alley and searched the empty field behind the buildings. "Oh, dear Lord," she panted, running back to the street where she'd seen her last. A splat of rain hit her face, and Will Gibbs was marching straight for her, attuned to who was missing.

"She was right here only a minute ago," she wheezed. "She needed an outhouse."

Will's face darkened, and he spun on his heal. "Maribelle!" his baritone resonated down the street. As Anna ran back and forth on the opposite side of the dirt street, her lungs started to constrict. More rain began to fall. Where could she have gone? Did someone take her? Was Vernon Lack following them, waiting for a moment to snatch her?

She scanned the street and buildings, fighting desperation. From the back side of the gray hardware store, Maribelle came around the corner with the side of her dress tucked in her pantaloons.

"Will!" Anna called for him and pointed to Maribelle as the girl skipped toward her. Relief flooded her being, and she willed her shaking legs to move. "Maribelle, you scared me out of my skin." Anna went to reach for her, but Will stepped in front and whisked Maribelle into his arms. Before she could say a word, he'd turned away, leaving her with nothing but the swirl of his cold anger. With Maribelle tucked against his chest, they trudged back down the street, neither looking back.

Rain fell steadily, soaking her hair, making straggles of her neat, little bun. Her chest still rose and fell as she watched the protective, older brother walk away, gripping his little sister in his arms. Her breaths struggled through her constricted throat. Her head ticked, while a familiar hollowness opened wide inside her. Glancing down the road where the wagon of Negros had gone, she squeezed her chin until the pain forced the tics to surrender. She was so concerned with finding Tallie that she'd lost Maribelle. A fool in mind and deed. Her stomach rolled in pain and regret.

Why did everyone she cared about leave her? Would she ever find Tallie so they could talk and make things right again? She held her head and began pulling the little twists of hair out. Her vanity embarrassed her. The damp strands fell loosely around her cheeks. Could Will forgive her for losing Maribelle? She took a few shaky steps down the street. The cold rain soaked into her skin. Would Will leave town without her? She could hardly blame him.

Turning the corner, she stepped up on the sidewalk and blinked at the bright lights pouring from the Mercantile. Maybe it wasn't too late to ask Mrs. Hart for refuge. A few feet ahead, Will Gibbs waited with Maribelle wearing his hat. Her spot was empty, and she grabbed her skirts and climbed up, then carefully sat. Reaching behind the bench, she tucked the bag from the mercantile under the seat.

The fabric and string for more baby gowns punched her in the gut as the wagon rolled forward. The sewing was always for her future hope chest, yet after so many gowns mocking her, she'd broken down and sold them. Her own babe was never to be, just like the love she'd never received from her family.

How many years would her mistakes hound her? Now, the once kind family who took her in had no mercy for her either. She took a careful look at Will's set jaw and his black hair dripping wet. He was the older brother, but he cared for his own like an unyielding, protective father. Losing Maribelle today was an unintentional mistake, but why should anyone believe her? Just like her stepfather, who so many years ago wouldn't believe that she would never hurt the baby on purpose. Today, Will certainly regretted the day she'd climbed on this wagon and covered her head with his hat. Folding her arms over her chest, she bent forward and held her head down.

The wagon halted in front of the cabin, and Anna helped Maribelle down then seized the heavy sack. They entered the empty cabin as Will took care of the wagon. Grabbing a towel from the shelf, she helped Maribelle off with her little dress and dried her hair and skin. A note on the table said Nathan had taken Milo and Della to the barn with him. She unloaded the simple supplies and then tried to warm herself by the cook stove. Maribelle slipped on her other dress and sat in Della's spot to play with her rag doll.

Suddenly tired and feeling tears rolling out, Anna grabbed the towel and took refuge behind the blanket. Sitting on the bed, she unlaced her boots as water dripped from her hair and face. Would her soul live in darkness all her days? Surely hopefulness is better left locked away to avoid the feelings of despair it caused when it left.

She pulled the wet dress off her body and grabbed the towel. Standing in the corner, with her back to the frayed curtain, she rubbed her loose hair with a towel. An unexpected sob rose up, and she covered her face with the cool damp cloth. Leaning her head into the rough wooden corner, she let the tears fall.

A creak on the floor made her turn swiftly to see Will standing inside the curtain watching her. He quickly avoided her eyes and stepped away to pull a dry shirt from a small drawer. A chill ran up and down her spine as he began to change.

Here she was standing in their room in nothing but her thin undergarments. But really, she didn't care, she closed her eyes, holding the towel over her face. Every foul thing a man wanted had already been done to her. Will pulled on a dry shirt. If it wasn't this moment, it was bound to happen soon enough.

He sighed and dropped his head back, pushing his hair out of his face. "Anna, I know you feel bad. I don't think for a minute you meant to let her free." He grabbed the blanket off the bed and handed it to her. Her shaking hand rose to take it, and it slipped to the floor. He stepped closer to retrieve it, and she pressed back into the corner and suddenly dropped down into a ball.

"Anna," he pleaded, crouching in front of her. He touched her knee.

She ducked her head and yanked the blanket from his hand and pulled it over her head.

"What is this about? I'm not going to hurt you." He waited. "Maribelle said you were looking for Tallie. I know she meant a lot to you."

"I need her," she whimpered from under the blanket. "I need a mother." The pain cracked through her broken words, "And a father and a friend," she groaned out. "And a baby." She could feel his hand rest lightly on her head and carefully slide down over her ear.

"Please come out so I can see you." Will pulled the blanket carefully off her head. She kept her face buried in her knees.

"I know we are no replacement for those things." He lightly brushed his fingers across her forehead, pulling her damp hair back. "But you have us. We love you and want you in the family."

Anna knew those words were supposed to mean something pleasant, heartwarming, but no warmth rose.

Peeking up, she rested her chin on her knee. "But what am I to do?" she whispered, wiping her wet face. He was only inches away, and she looked long and steady into his piercing eyes. "I know who I am. I'm keenly aware of my days on this earth, and I don't deserve to have any of you."

21

WILL SCRATCHED HIS head and watched Maribelle sitting on Della's pallet. "I will take Maribelle with me," he spoke to the blanket between them. "We can all work in the barn for a while. You'd probably enjoy some time alone."

Anna appeared around the blanket, buttoning the top button to her red blouse. Maribelle stared up at Will with a pale expression.

"Don't you trust me to care for her?" she said to the ground, patting her hair flat.

"Yes, I do." He tipped his head and sighed. "It's up to you." He reached out and touched her arm, and she moved away.

Pursing his lips, he shook his head. Why did it feel so natural to comfort her and yet so familiar for her to move away?

"I'd like her to stay." Anna pulled the fabric from the burlap bag and unfolded it on the table. "We could get some cutting done before the family needs the table."

"All right." Will reached for his coat and hat. "You can bang a pan with a spoon if you need us." He hesitated, looking around the cabin with his hand on the door latch. Finally, he walked out.

THE GRAY RAIN was steady as he jogged across the field. Looking to the left, something under a large tree caught his attention. His grandfather had returned. He stood stoic and proud, watching Will come under the barren branches.

"Come to the barn." Will gestured to his grandfather. "We can talk there."

His grandfather shook his head. "The others are in there."

Will let out a huff. "Would you come to the cabin? It's only Anna and the little one, Maribelle, in there."

His grandfather shook his head, rain dripping from the brim of his leather hat. "I offer you your birthright and yet you choose to stay here. I offer a healing woman for your mother, and you still break your legacy by marrying a white woman."

Will tried to coax the frustration out of his voice. "I want you to know, I am thankful for your invitations."

"It's in the smoke," his grandfather's forehead creased between his lowered brows. "The way it rises over the river." He made a sweep of his hand, and his deep wrinkles creased thicker. "There is a dark spirit over this land you protect. I have seen it three times. It comes with the white woman you have taken in. There is no brilliance in her star. It is dark, foul, and troubled. Now you will live in darkness. Your foot will break under the weight of it."

Will stepped back. His grandfather often talked in the folklore of his people, but he didn't feel like entertaining his grandfather's words on this cold, rainy day. "She is a child of God. There is no evil in her." Will heard his declaration and tried to swallow it himself. "She's not here to do us harm. She has come to help us." The strength in his tone was unusual for him, especially used toward his grandfather. "I must get to work in the barn." He turned and walked away, wondering if he'd just broken the last small thread holding him to his grandfather's legacy.

ENTERING THE LARGE barn, Will nodded to Nathan and pulled off his hat. Della and Milo were making mounds of dirt in the long planters, then Nathan helped them to plant the seed.

Someone had told their mother Della had a demon, but look at her now. She tapped Milo's shoulder and made a muffled grunt at him. Milo understood her correction and nodded back at her.

"How did it go at the bank?" Nathan asked, moving the dirt filled wheelbarrow near Will.

"I told them you were to be eighteen on Sunday. The Fords should now release the land into your name." He blew out a breath. "I suppose I can't tell them what to do, but paying half of all our profits to be working this land is robbery. It should be yours. If it weren't for Ma's death, we both would have found ourselves on the list to fight for the Union." Will shook his head.

"Humph." Nathan picked up the shovel. "I appreciate you trying," his expression sincere. "Each day you put in all the sweat and strength you have and then fight for this to all be mine. You know I'll always see it as belonging to both of us."

Nathan looked out the barn doors. "I saw your grandfather waiting all morning for you. He is stubborn, and I know he wants you to help what's left of the tribe." Nathan squeezed the top of the shovel handle so hard his knuckles turned white. "You being married now, I haven't said it, but thank you for that, too. I know you did it for us." Nathan waited for Will to look him in the eye. "Anna has made an old dirty cabin into a home. It's been a few years of adversity, but each of us is doing better." Nathan waited while Will took in two deep breaths. "What's wrong?"

"Anna lost Maribelle in town today." Will threw his head back and shut his eyes, sucking in another long breath.

"What? What happened?"

"I think it was a simple mistake. Maribelle had to find an outhouse, and at the same time, Anna was trying to find the Negro woman who used to live with her at the pond house. Apparently, they saw a group of Negroes. I—" Will shook his head, "don't know what to think sometimes. Then my grandfather had some vision of Anna bringing darkness to this land."

Nathan rubbed his moppy hair and looked back at Milo and Della working in the dirt. "Tell me, Will, what do *you* think about her? Do you trust her? Do you care for her?" He waited for Will to respond. "Have you two, well you know—" Nathan left his question hanging and raised his eyebrows.

"No." Will shook his head and grabbed the wheelbarrow pushing it forward. He dropped it quickly and turned back to

Nathan. "I swear to you, Nathan, I don't know how it should work. She looks at me like I'm a disease, and if she gets too close to me she might catch something fatal. But then the next minute she feels like the closest friend I've ever had. I know there are certain things I have carried inside me that only she would understand." He slapped his forehea, wondering why all these things were pouring out of his mouth. "And because she rarely mixes her words, when I listen to her, I feel as if I can understand her and why she feels different from everyone. How did this simple plan of wedded bliss grow more confusing?" His voice groaned, rolling his eyes, "I don't know if something is wrong with me," he groaned. "I think she is beautiful and interesting. I feel lucky to have her." He shook his head, blowing out a long breath, "but I don't *have* her."

Nathan frowned and stared out the barn door again. "Ouch. That's grim."

"You know when you have a bad bruise?" Will asked him, "kinda like the ones she had on her face?"

"Yeah," Nathan's eyes narrowed.

"At first everything hurts to the touch." Will scratched his chin, wondering if this even made sense to him. "Then it turns purple and doesn't hurt as much."

"Uh huh," Nathan tried to follow.

"I think she's had a lot of bruises before she came to us. Not just the outside kind. Even the inside kind that tell you how worthless, how undeserving you are. I don't know, but it takes a while for them to turn yellow and then go away. You know?"

Nathan nodded slowly. "If they ever do."

22

THE FOLLOWING WEEK Will had planned to speak to the banker again about Nathan turning eighteen. Even though the last frost had passed and the planting was going well, they had no money to last until the next harvest. Most mornings and evenings, Anna had been quiet but content to care for the children, cabin, and work on her little baby gowns. She'd asked to accompany him on his next trip, but he didn't want her few earnings to be their only supply. Vernon Lack's hadn't been present of late. Will didn't like his meager offerings left at the doorstep, but with all the children helping with planting, it was dark before he or Nathan could do any hunting. Feeling the agitation in his gut, he pulled the wagon out front for Maribelle and Anna to climb on.

"Can we see the lady with the cookies today?" Maribelle asked, leaning against Anna's arm. Will noticed the paper bag with the folded baby gowns sitting in her lap.

"Yes, we will see her, but I don't think we will get cookies. We need other things more."

Will flicked the reins a little harder than usual. "What does the store pay for those little smocks?" The wagon bounced off a rut. He really didn't want to know. Pinching his lips together, he felt something festering. He should be giving his wife money to buy their supplies.

"Thirty-five cents."

"Ohh, that's a lot of money, Anna." Maribelle swooned. "Enough for a cookie and a candy stick." Her bright smile latched onto Anna's face.

"We'll see, child. Your brother Nathan had a birthday, and he didn't get any candy or cookies."

"But he's big like Will," she whined. "You don't get anything when you are big. Huh, Will?"

Will rubbed the tension lines between his eyebrows. Nope, you work like an ox and scrape to find something to ease the void in your stomach. You try to be kind and cordial to the woman you sleep next to, but you don't get anything. Will shook his head and looked around at the green grass and buds trying to break out of bare-branched trees. Truthfully, she *had* given back to him, just like he asked. To take care of the children—then why was he feeling so cantankerous?

"Anna," Maribelle broke the silence, "Do the rhyme about the old mother and the empty cupboard."

"No," Will piped up. He needed a clear head to approach Mr. Frost at the bank. The man had always seemed helpful, but today, he needed a favor. Maybe he should have brought Nathan.

"What's heavy on your mind, Will?" Anna asked softly.

Will glanced over at her soft, green eyes. Dare he tell her, that one gentle touch from her could sooth all his frayed edges?

"Just the meeting at the bank."

"I can always ask Mrs. Hart for credit. She knows I will—"

"No." His jaw tightened. "Don't do that."

"But I've eaten the family supplies and increased your burden." She gripped the bench as Will jerked the wagon to a stop.

He jumped down and secured the horse and came back and lifted Maribelle to the ground. Reaching for her, he met her eyes for a moment then grabbed her waist. "And you work and care for your keep." Lowering her, he released her waist. As she moved away, he thought he saw her frown. Quickening a step forward, he grabbed her arm that cradled the baby items. His grip slackened, and he tried to govern his voice. "Don't hear that wrong, Anna. I don't see you as someone who works for us, for me." He gently drew her next to him, to a thin breath away. She smelled good, and his eyes narrowed. "I see you as family. My wife."

She gazed down the street, likely embarrassed by his actions. Maribelle stood looking up at them. He leaned forward and brushed a kiss onto Anna's temple before he turned her loose. She rolled her lips tight, suppressing a smile or maybe a frown. Drawing in a needed, clear breath, he headed toward the bank.

ANNA WAS THANKFUL Mrs. Hart wasn't too busy. She needed the distraction from the handsome man, Will Gibbs, and the serious attraction in his eyes and body. She tried to find her bearing's as Mrs. Hart complimented her over and over for the tatting on each baby collar and the little touches around the sleeves. After she was able to get a few supplies, Mrs. Hart brought out a catalog with various items to order. While Mrs. Hart helped another customer, Anna knelt down and let Maribelle look through the pages with her. Each item that had a picture caused the little girl to ask more questions. She finally understood the only thing they were looking for was a book to buy for Della.

"Look, there are books to order," Anna flipped the pages past the medical books for rashes and growths, fevers and colic.

"This is it! I knew it was a real thing. She'd seen some of the nurses at Lennhurst use hand signs with the patients. "The National Society of the Deaf Handbook for hand signs. Oh, it's thirty-five cents." Anna chewed on her bottom lip. "That's a lot."

Mrs. Hart came back around the large oak counter. "What have we found to order?" She smiled.

"I'd like to order this book." Anna turned the catalog to show her. "How long does it take to arrive?"

"Coming from Chicago, I'd guess about a month or so." Mrs. Hart wrote the name on an order form.

"May I possibly pay when I pick it up? Anna asked.

"Of course, dear," Mrs. Hart's gaze shot up. Anna followed it and saw Will standing behind her. He handed Mrs. Hart a dollar.

"For the book, Ma'am." He lifted a kind smile at Anna and handed her two-dollar bills. "Can you get whatever else we need? And fabric for shirts and dresses if you don't mind."

She looked at the money and looked at him. Dare she ask where this money came from? Had he sold the horse?

"Maribelle, pick a new slate and paper." Will turned her to the table with the school items.

"I've seen you teaching them to read and write. Is there anything else?" He asked.

"No." Anna turned to face him. "Did something happen at the bank?" she asked carefully.

"Were you praying for me?" His eyes held her with rogue familiarity.

Slowly, she shook her head. "No." Watching him, she couldn't help smile; his countenance had changed entirely from an hour ago.

"Nathan is now seventy-five percent owner of the tobacco farm." He announced. "On his twenty-first birthday, it is all his. All the land, a shabby cabin, the cow, and our four old chickens, all the plants, all the profit. We just got a twenty-five percent inheritance. Well, really, he did. But it's all for the family. So, tell me, Anna Gibbs, what is something you need?" He looked around the large store. "Something pretty," he fingered a roll of purple velvet ribbon sitting on the table.

Anna slowly pulled his hand away and held it in hers. *Anna Gibbs.* Use of his name with hers in this very moment almost felt oddly right and real as the earlier touch of his lips. "Sir," she offered a sweet smile, holding his hand with the good news filling her mind, "I have all I need."

23

"YOU'RE NEXT," ANNA whispered into Milo's ear, interrupting his reading of the new sign language book. For some reason, her sewing the last weeks had started in order with making Will's shirt and then Nathan a new shirt. Della a new dress and now it was his turn. He watched her arrange his old shirt on top of the new red checkered fabric."

"We have to cut way out here to make it bigger." She drew her finger along the fabric. "Do you want to try the scissors?"

"Yes." He grabbed them.

"Always cut from the closest corner. Then we can have extra fabric for other things." Anna tried not to correct his every snip. She would have to stitch over his jagged cuts.

Will stepped into the cabin. It was too early for the end of the workday. Anna looked concerned as Maribelle went to hug his leg.

"Look, Will, I'm a sewer girl," Milo said, snickering and holding up the scissors.

"Seamstress." Anna corrected. "What brings you in?" Anna stood from the table.

"I've chewed on it for weeks," Will gave her a sly expression. "You said you wanted nothing from the store."

"Ouch." Milo dropped the scissors and shook his hand. "I cut my finger."

Will grabbed the scissors and placed them on the shelf. "Milo and Maribelle, we are taking Anna for a walk."

"Why?" Milo sucked the tip of his finger.

"Because it's a beautiful day, and I found a gift for Anna." Will pulled the door wide open.

"Will," she tipped her head, "I told you, I'm fine. Really there is nothing—"

"Everybody out," he cut her off, then he closed the door after they'd all filed out. He stepped toward the small barn, and everyone followed.

"A new chicken that lays eggs?" Anna said, noticing Della and Nathan had come in from the fields. Without a clue, she couldn't see anything or figure what he'd got for her. "A pad for that wagon bench?" she guessed letting out a short laugh. "My backside would thank you." Why was the family all gathered? It was impossible to guess. She shook her head at everyone staring at her.

Will turned and gently held her arms. "Close your eyes."

"Will, things are all good. We've all been eating more than— "

"Close your eyes," he said, putting his fingers lightly over her face.

Anna pulled in a deep breath and complied. He turned her back in a circle toward the clothesline. With his hands gripping her shoulders, he whispered in her ear. "A gift for you, from me." He let go and told her to open her eyes.

Anna blinked against the bright light. Maribelle was jumping up and down. Her eyes rose to some movement behind the sheets flapping in the sunshine.

"Is this how I taught you to keep them sheets white?" Tallie's thick shoulders peeked from around the white fabric. Her wide grin and white teeth shone against her dark molasses skin. Bright, loving eyes were outlined by her orange and red head wrap.

Anna's heart leaped from her chest. "Tallie!" she screamed. Tears instantly flooded her eyes as she ran for the kindred woman. Tallie ran towards her, and they collided in the front yard, a rocking mass of arms and hugs, smiles and yelps.

"Na, look at you." Tallie breathed, pulling back from their embrace. "All grins and watery faced. Ain't nobody supposed to be this happy to see me." Tallie laughed. Her voice and cackle were like the first bite of a sugar plum pie.

"I have missed you and *pined* to see you again." Anna squeezed the callused worn hands. "Have you been well? I've wanted to say I'm sorry for—"

Tallie dropped her head and wagged it back and forth. "Whose all these youngin's lookin' at us carrin' on." She pulled Anna back around to face the cabin.

"This is Will, and then Nathan and Della, and these two are Milo and Maribelle." Anna wiped the tears from her wet cheeks.

"Are you Anna's Mammy?" Maribelle stepped forward.

"No, child." Anna shook her head and then looked at Tallie. "Well, maybe so." She laughed. "Everything I know about biscuits and gravy, dumplings, and johnny cakes…really all my cooking and baking I learned from this woman."

"Then we would all like to be the first ones to thank you," Nathan stepped forward and shook Tallie's hand. "To greet you, and welcome you to our humble home."

Tallie looked at Anna wide-eyed. "You done found a strange place to live."

Anna laughed, and Maribelle grabbed Tallies' hand. "You should come on in. Anna has some turnovers from this morning."

"And this little one can take over when I'm gone," Anna pinched Maribelle's ear.

"Ohh, weee." Tallie walked in and pulled her shoulders back. "There anit' much room for each of ya to have your own breath." She moved around the table for all the siblings to enter. Anna swept the sewing off the table and offered Tallie some coffee.

Della signed to Anna she would get the cups.

"Whata ya got doing that with your hand's fur?" Tallie pointed at their hands.

"Oh, I believe Della is deaf. We use our hands for words." Anna poured her a cup. "Remember when I talked about helping at the asylum?"

"Yes, um" Tallie's thic, calloused hand took the cup and sipped.

"I learned a few hand words there." Anna pointed for Tallie to sit.

"Then we got this book just yesterday." Milo put it in front of Tallie and opened to the alphabet page. "See this is your name," he used his fingers to make the T A L L I E.

"Oh, Lordy," she shook her head, "how's a body to remember all that."

Della made a grunt and signed something to Anna. "She says, welcome to our home." Della set down a plate of turnovers.

"All yous looking at me with those light eyes and bright faces, I reckon' Jesus is gonna walk in next."

They all laughed, and Anna eyed Will. He met her eyes, and they shared a small smile. Something she'd never felt before dipped in her stomach.

"Everyone," Will said. "Let's go out and give them time to catch up." He opened the door, shuffling everyone out. How could this humble man be so thoughtful, so good? Was it just his nature, all the time? He turned to tell Anna. "I have to meet her son on the bend of Prairie Road in about an hour. He'll take her back to the plantation."

Anna stepped closer and touched his arm. Words of deep appreciation wouldn't seem to form. She hadn't felt this depth of happiness since she'd left Lennhurst. Blast it, it started as a pinch in her nose and quickly made her eyes fill with tears. Tallie had never seen her cry more than two or three times, and now she seemed to be crying on a weekly basis over things like fresh bread and full bowls of butter beans.

Will bit back his smile, "It's okay." He lightly brushed a strand of hair behind her ear, "We can have her back as soon you need her."

Anna swallowed, nodding her goodbye to Will, and wiped her face again. Taking a deep breath, she turned back to sit with Tallie. "I want to hear how you are doing."

"Mmm hum," Tallie dropped her chin and gave her a crooked grin. "Not doin' as good as you. That big, dark-haired boy is done in love wit you. I think he'd pull the clouds over to shade your face. Mmm humm."

"No, Tallie, it's not what you think. Did he tell you we had to marry? He was desperate for someone to help around here." Tallie of all people would understand her loathing of being anyone's wife again. "I was desperate for a place to live. The reverend and his wife had limited forbearance for me and practically pushed me into this tiny cabin. At first, I wanted to abide by the plan until I could leave, but his brothers and sisters, they've rescued me," her words stopped her. The revelation felt true up and down her tingling skin. "Silly as it sounds, they make me feel as if I have rescued *them*."

Tallie's thick ebony face stilled and her chin started to quiver. Reaching across the table, she wrapped Anna's small thin fingers inside her own and squeezed them tight. "Good people gots a good woman. So I'z reckonin'."

24

THAT EVENING, ANNA added a few small logs to the cook stove. The few dishes were all dried and stacked neatly on the shelf. She turned to enjoy the warmth on her back and noticed the feet of the sleeping children in the loft. What a glorious day, she sighed, walking around the table. Seeing Della asleep, she carefully bent to remove the hardbound sign language book from her arms. She set the book on the table and looked up.

Poor Nathan, she frowned. He was curled in a ball in the small loft without an inch to spare. They all seemed to have gained weight, and she wondered how long Nathan could occupy such a small space. Was he still growing? She sat at the table and pulled the low lit lantern closer. It was Will's night to stay up until she was asleep, and since he took the time to bring Tallie and take her back, he'd wanted to work longer in the barn. After such a wonderful day, she'd wanted to tell him again how much the kindness had meant to her and that he could go to sleep first.

The door opened quietly. Will dropped his jacket and hat on the peg. Looking around, he nodded and smiled. "Still up, I see."

"Yes, I thought I'd work on Milo's shirt for a bit."

Will walked to the kitchen counter and poured some water. As he sat down at the table, his shoulders relaxed, and he looked into his cup.

"You can retire first if you want," she said as she licked her finger to knot off the thread. "I don't think I can find any words to tell you how much your kindness meant to me today. Tallie was my only friend, my only rock to lean on." She pulled the needle in and out of the soft, checkered fabric.

"In the wagon, she told me a bit about that, just as you have." Will looked up, his face drawn. "I think she was making sure I was nothing like your late husband."

"Not one hair, or breath, or drop of blood do you have like Mr. Plugg," Anna glanced up from her sewing. "Tallie is living with Otis on the Plugg plantation. I suppose you knew that. She said they don't seem to notice her much. She helps her son with his chores, and the two of them talk and sing and read the Bible at night. She said Otis has been preaching on Sundays to the other workers, but he doesn't know how to read."

Anna lifted the corner of her mouth and then stilled. "She said Mr. Plugg… he used her," her chin ticked downward, "if she didn't give him what he wanted, he'd have Otis sold." Anna froze, and her needle trembled over the fabric. "She said, tolerating his advances was what she had to do to keep Otis safe. She is relieved, now they can be together." Her nostrils flared, and she swallowed hard. "I still hate that man." She stared at her hand, but couldn't seem to resume her sewing.

Slowly she put the thread and needle in a little tin box and folded the fabric. "I got to tell her I was sorry I took her honey and things from the house." Anna's chin ticked again. "She hadn't seen my mother's spoons or sewing box. I'm sure the Plugg brothers have them." She finally met Will's patient eyes. "I would never go to the plantation. I promise."

"I know." His hand rested on her sleeve, then gently stroked down her arm to hold her hand. "Your hands are cold." He held them in his. "When we were walking in with her today, you said something about when you leave, Maribelle can take over."

Anna straightened up. "I-I was jesting. Maribelle plays the pretend hostess so well."

"Yes, I've seen her." He pressed his lips. "She never played or did make-believe before you came." His eyes narrowed. "But *are* you planning to leave? Did you and Tallie talk about it?"

"No, Will. I—" She pulled her hands free. "No."

"I saw your eyes when Tallie discovered how small this cabin is." He sat back in his chair.

"I had forgotten about that till she said something." Anna ran her hand across the rough table. "I'm so used to it now."

Will locked his fingers behind his dark loose hair. "When do you think you will be used to me?" he asked reservedly. His face flushed, watching her, "I think we get along well, and I have a true affection for you and—"

Anna rose quickly and set her sewing things on the rock mantel. "I'm tired. But thank you for everything today." She moved past the table and behind the frayed curtain. As soon as she sat to slip off her boots, she knew he'd followed.

"But you find nothing in your heart for me? Is that what your silence means?" he asked.

Covering her face with her hands, she couldn't look up and see the disappointment in his earnest face. There was an old, familiar dizziness coming over her as she took in short breaths.

She could go back to Lennhurst in her mind. The Pennsylvania springs made the front garden lovely. Many a day, sweet little Patience would sit next to her as they read a book together. She loved teaching her English. She was such a bright girl who loved fairies and butterflies.

Anna stood and began to unbutton her dress. As long as she kept her eyes closed, she could see the bushes and ivy growing along the wall. She pulled her dress down and stepped out. At least he wasn't demanding. She pulled the ribbon loose from her chemise and let it fall off. Just stay in the garden, and it will go away soon, she thought. He had brought Tallie today. Of course, she owed him something.

"What are you doing?" Will's short tone made her eyes snap open.

"I'm getting undressed to get into, uh, the bed with you. You have done me a great favor." She swallowed hard, her chin twitching down "I know what you want back. You just spoke of affection. I need to repay the kindness."

Will huffed, eyes narrowing. "No, you don't. You've slept next to me for months fully dressed, and now you—" He raked his hand through his hair and squeezed his head. "I don't want you in my arms because you *have to*." He grabbed the blanket off the bed and covered her bare shoulders. "Oh, Anna." He wrapped his arms around her and held her. "What am I to do with you?"

She pulled back and squinted at him. "As a young man, do you know what to do with a wife?" Her chin jerked again as she nodded at the bed.

"Yes, I know enough." He sighed softly, and a reserved smile curled his lips as he kissed her hairline. "That's not what I meant. You said I was nothing like your dead husband, but suddenly you treat me like him? You owe me a service in that bed? Yes, men are men, and husbands want their wives. But I want you to want *me*. Not because of a nice gesture here and there. But because you trust me, love me, and desire me without reservation."

Anna rested her cheek on his shoulder. "You've been patient with me, but I know with every small touch and smile that your heart and body are closer to me than I am to you. I don't want to hurt you." She carefully lifted her head, but couldn't look him in the eye.

"It would hurt me more to have you in my bed without your heart." He tightened the blanket around her. "Go to bed. I'll wait at the table until you are asleep."

Before he moved away, she gripped her fingers into his shirt. "I have heard what you've said. I do feel things changing. I think my hate has suffocated me from the inside." She risked a glanced at his stoic face. She dropped her hands, and her shoulders slumped. "I know that makes no sense. But my time here… the needs of the children, their bright eyes, their laughter, has…has…. I don't have the words. Do you remember the story we read the other night with the children, about Nicodemus? He asked Jesus how he could be born again without entering back into his mother's womb."

Will nodded.

"It feels a bit like that—that I have been given another chance to be who God created me to be—something greater than my hatred is being born in my heart. I would have thought it was too late, but I suppose anyone can change. Is that something you think God does for people? Even if they have been angry and bitter inside?"

Will pulled his fingers through her hair and nodded. "I think it is the very purpose of God for his people."

After Will stepped around the blanket, Anna stood for a long while. Will had pointed out the obvious; it'd been months that she still slept in her dress. She opened the small wardrobe and fingered her nightgown. With a strange impulse, she jerked it over her head and dropped her stiff corset to the ground. Her back and chest felt like an animal trap had been opened. Her skin tingled with freedom. Laying down and pulling the nightgown around her legs, she cuddled up with her blanket and pillow. Remembering Tallie's laugh today, a new caress of comfort saturated her being, inside and out.

WILL ROLLED OVER on his back in the middle of the night, bumping her arm. Usually, it woke Anna up with a start, but in the past few weeks, she realized she could take it in stride and fall back asleep. Tonight a sliver of moonlight fell perfectly through their window and across their bed. Rising on her elbow, she took a long look at him sleeping.

The cabin was plenty warm, so as usual, he slept in his sleeveless cotton undershirt and canvas pants without a blanket. There was truly nothing wrong with his appearance. From the moment she looked at him in the church, she found him agreeable. His arms were long with lean muscular curves. Even in the shadows, there was barely any hair seen on them. Tonight, those arms had wrapped her in care and safety. His grip was different than the moment he pulled her from the cellar at the pond house. Those arms were tense and urgent. Tonight his arms were gentle and warm as they wrapped the blanket around her shoulders.

How much patience could a man hold? He could've been upset, but she was coming to believe he truly cared about her and wanted her as a wife. The soft moonlight revealed a bit of copper mixed in with his dark black tresses. Her stomach did another unfamiliar flutter as she thought about dragging her fingers through his hair. If he awoke, could she say to him, she loved him?

Right now as long as he was asleep and unmoving, she could. She rolled her eyes. As long as he was asleep, she desired him? That was strange, indeed.

25

THOUGH JUST A tease, spring tried to make an appearance on the fragrant Kentucky farmland. With the door left open, Milo ran inside in a fury, making Anna jump from kneading the dough.

"Anna." He panted. "There is a black man with a funny leg. He says he's here to see your man."

Anna wiped her sticky hands on her apron and peeked out the window.

"Who is your man?" Milo blocked her from getting to the door. "Can I be your man?"

"He means Will, child." She turned him around, "Go run now to the field and bid Will to come quickly." She spied Maribelle still napping on her bed.

"Oh, heaven's sake." She blew out a sigh as her brows dropped in concern. Walking into the sunlight, she wondered if something had happened to Tallie. "Lord of mercy, please." She nodded to the young man standing in the yard fidgeting his hat. It had to be Otis. He and Tallie shared the same broad face and stocky build.

"Hello." She bowed slightly, trying not to stare at his bowed leg.

"You the Missus Anna?"

"Yes. And you must be Otis."

"Yes, ma'am." He looked at the ground. His clothes tattered and patched. It was strange to be looking into the face she'd pictured from all of Tallie's stories.

Anna glanced up to see Milo still running to tell Will. He hadn't even made it halfway out to the field. "May I offer you some water or coffee?"

"No, ma'am."

"It might be a few minutes." She squeezed her hands together. "I'd be obliged if you told me how your mother is faring?"

"Ahh, she doin' good."

Anna felt her insides relax.

"She been helpin' in the big house, sum time in de kitchen, sum time I seen her hangn' laundry." He looked out where Milo had run. "I supposed I should have just took my wagon on out yonder." His eyes only reached hers for a split second. "I'd almost get me in trouble if I ain't stopped and give you dis." He reached under the wagon seat and handed her a basket. "Momma said dey yous favorite."

"Thank you." Anna nodded taking the basket. She lifted the cloth to see pumpkin muffins. "These are my delight. Would you tell her so?"

"Yessum, I do dat." Otis rocked down on his damaged leg. "I'll just amble my way out to yoh fields." He climbed up on the wagon and tapped the reins.

"If you would be so kind," Anna jogged along the wagon. If she has a day off soon, to ask her to come again."

Otis tipped his hat. "Yessum, I tell her."

Anna stopped and hefted the basket up and down. Walking back to the cabin, she thought she heard something. A strange sound was coming from the basket. She set it on the table and lifted the muffins out and set them on a plate in the middle of the table. Lifting the cloth to shake out the crumbs, she noticed another cloth underneath. Pulling the hidden weight out, she pulled the fabric apart — twelve silver spoons. Her throat tightened as she carefully placed each one by size along the rough wood table. Her mother's spoons. Four for soup, four for the meal, and four for tea. She fingered the smallest one. The engraving was from her grandmother's set. They seemed so out of place without their fine red velvet case for display.

A sleepy Maribelle came from behind the blanket and reached for Anna. Though the child was heavy, Anna swung her up onto her hip as Maribelle wrapped her arms around Anna's neck and buried her face on her shoulder. "Oh, that Tallie." Anna rubbed Maribelle's back. She wondered if Tallie had taken some of the Plugg silver and replaced them in the pretty case. No one to be the wiser, she thought amused.

"NOW, WHAT SMELLS good?" Nathan entered the cabin at dusk. His smile and appreciation always brightened Anna's heart, but today she'd spent the whole afternoon worrying about why Otis needed to talk to Will. Funny thing about living with fear each day as Mrs. Plugg, dread was the house guest she'd grown accustomed to. She couldn't recall the exact day that fear had moved on. As Mrs. Gibbs, maybe she was so distracted with the care and needs of the children, she hadn't noticed. But the familiar foe, like a belly ache, had come for a visit today.

"It's cinnamon cookies." She watched Nathan snatch one off the plate. "Where is Will?"

"He was heading to the creek." He poured a glass of milk. "Milo, run a towel out to him."

Anna reached for the towel but stopped before handing it to Milo. "He'll need clean clothes, too."

"Yes," Milo nodded with a smirk, "you've taught us. It's no good to put the dirty clothes back on."

Anna stepped behind the blanket and reached for a stack of Will's clean clothes. She hesitated before she handed them over to Milo.

"I know." She didn't want to wait any longer. "I'll take them out."

Milo moved back to the table. "Can I have another cookie?"

Anna shot Nathan a frown. "Yes. Just one." She pointed a finger at both brothers. "And I *will* count."

The brisk walk to the creek was something she should have done earlier. All afternoon she'd been pacing the cabin, fretting about whether Floyd or Bernard Plugg had threatened Otis and Tallie. Will should have planned Tallie's first visit after dark. Had someone seen Tallie meet him? Was it the missing spoons? Those brothers were as mean and cruel as their dead father, probably trying to— Anna stopped suddenly at the edge of the creek.

Will had his back to her, and he was bathing. She blinked in shock, looked one more second, and then spun around quickly on her heel. Frozen by what she'd just seen. Her pulse raced inside her body.

"Anna," water splashed behind her, "I wasn't expecting you." His voice came up the bank, and she jerked the towel from the pile and held it out behind her with a stiff arm. Looking at the powdery dirt, she wondered how to drop his clothes and move away before he came too close. Too late, he took the towel and brushed her hand with his. Her stomach fluttered in that strange way it did when he touched her of late.

"This is a nice surprise," he said, coming around to her side. The towel was wrapped snug around his waist, and he reached for his clothes.

Anna stood frozen, trying to remember where she'd left her common sense—to come here and interrupt a man bathing. "I," she cleared her throat, "I'll see you back at the cabin." Her feet finally moved.

"Wait," he spoke a few feet behind her, "I'm almost dressed. We can walk together."

Anna pressed her fingers hard into her skull. What was going on? Seeing him washing in the shallow water, of course, it should be no surprise he was strong, lean, and muscular. But why did those things rattle her head to toe? Goodness, this was the strangest thing. An unfamiliar longing jumbled around in her body and soul. Chills competed with heat all over her skin. She must be getting sick. The evening had turned cool, then why was she now overheated? Likely from fretting all day. How could just seeing him and hearing his voice make her tremble all over? This had never happened before.

"How are you?" He came next to her, rubbing the water from his hair.

She glanced up into those dark soothing eyes, a light, bashful expression on his face. It was happening all over again, possibly worse. "I was talking to myself, and I didn't think when I walked up."

"I noticed your face was red." He tucked his dirty clothes and towel under his arm. "Are you breathing, Anna?" He lightly touched her chin.

"Yes." She smiled, holding her hand to her cheek. "I suppose I'm embarrassed, that's all. Can you forgive me?" Now she could almost see the humor in it all.

"Umm, maybe I could." He smiled and moved closer.

Her heart spiked, and a quiver ran up her spine. She turned to find the path leading away, but his hand touched her back and came up her neck, gently pulling her face to his.

Oh Lord, her eyes darted side to side.

"I want to tell you why I love your interesting expressions. Like the one you have right now," he whispered, drawing his thumb under her bottom lip. "These very lips give away your words, your thoughts, and your breath. These all bring life to me. Like your soft eyes, they draw me to you like nothing I've ever known. Every moment I'm away from you, your voice, your smile—I miss everything about you. I know it sounds crazy." He waited, only a breath away. "But since we are alone, can you kiss me, Anna?"

A little squeak came from the back of her throat. He smelled like soap and rain. Curious and craving the risk, she rose up on her toes, and with wide eyes, she brushed his lips lightly with hers.

His smiled widened, and he dropped his forehead on hers. "That was nice." His hand gently massaged her neck. "Could you do that again?"

She tried to think but couldn't remember why this was a bad idea. It felt quite the opposite. This time she clutched his shirt and kissed him slower. The split second their lips pulled away they found an urgency to kiss again. Two people wanting the same thing, and she enjoyed it. A rush of shivers ran up and down her arms and legs as if *she* had just emerged from the water. At some time, he must have dropped his things, because his arms pulled her tight against his frame. Her chest rose and fell quickly against his.

"I know you didn't want to be married." He rested his face along her temple. "I thought you would be mourning your loss. But then you said it wasn't so and I, well I started to fall in love with you." His words fell like quick breaths in her ear.

Anna tried to find her words, her breath, but the pattering of her heart was so loud. Shocked to the core by his words and her brazen conduct, she wondered how long her lips and body would tingle. His firm grip slackened from around her, and she stepped back, feeling the immediate blushing head to toe.

"I guess, I think, we should get back," she said, smiling shyly.

He nodded once staring at her like a hungry man whose only plate of food was removed before he'd taken the first bite.

26

ENTERING BACK INTO the cabin, Anna went into their bedroom and straightened her hair. An exciting warmth tried to compete with embarrassment. She'd never known such enjoyment existed with a man. Feeling her face flush anew, she wondered again if something was wrong with her. "It wasn't like the children saw us by the creek." She winced, realizing she was mumbling to herself.

She heard Nathan say, "I fed the kids... Everyone got tired of waiting."

Anna rubbed her forehead. The way he said *waiting* was a bit too exaggerated. *Oh, this cabin is small.* She took a deep breath and came out. Della was sitting at the table with Milo and Maribelle. Her sign language book was wide open as the three of them tried to talk using their hands. Nathan had a funny grin, and she looked away and made a plate of food for Will.

"I," good Lord, why did her chin just tic? "wanted to ask about Otis." She kept her eyes on the plate as she set it before Will. Nathan was likely still having fun at her expense. "What did Otis want today?" she asked.

"We'll talk later." Will squeezed her hand. "This looks good." He took a bite. "Thank you, Lord, and thank *you*, Anna" he nodded chewing.

AFTER EVERYONE WAS asleep, Anna pulled the silver spoons off the shelf to show Will. "I never knew my grandmother, and I barely knew my own mother." She stood, tracing her fingers over the engraving. "If we need to sell them for the farm. I will."

"No," Will groaned, settling his hand on her waist. "I think we are doing fine. By the end of the week with everyone's help, we should have all the plants in the ground." He brought his hand around and dragged it back and forth over the rough table. As his silence prolonged, Anna felt her stomach clench.

"It's probably nothing. But with Tallie working some in the big house, rumors get spread. She heard some kitchen help talking. Supposedly the Plugg brothers are still talking about having you put away for murder."

Anna stepped back. Then slowly came to sit at the table.

"I don't want you to worry about it," his gaze deepened, "You told me what happened. No one can charge you with a crime when it was really an accident, or like you said, he might have had a heart seizure of some kind."

"But you don't know them." Her countenance sunk. "I had a feeling all day, like I've been living a dream." She shook her head. "But good things never last."

"Nothing is going to happen to you, Anna, we're married. I will protect you."

She closed her eyes and shook her head. "I know you want to. But I couldn't get the law, the sheriff, to help me. They're all together in their hooded masks, a night raider group of the same mind and creed. They chase and threaten the freed slaves bent on all kinds of hateful mischief. The Pluggs have their hand in everyone's pocket."

"Don't worry." He squeezed her arm. "You've left the pond house, and there's little to gain from you going to jail." He rubbed his jaw.

"Except revenge for their father's death, and more desire for hatred fulfilled." She whispered.

They sat in the silence for a few minutes. Della turned in her sleep only a few feet away.

"I know this is strange," Anna sighed. "But as a young person, I cherished my time at Lennhurst. I didn't realize how important the work was until it was all taken from me. I left there easily because I'd convinced myself it was time to leave, to belong to the *real world*." She huffed, trying to keep her eyes on the strength in his face. "But this time, here with this family, it has enthused my soul like nothing else. I have found more than love. I have found peace with God. Possibly mercy for my sins, and in peeks and glimpses, I can see my future. And then like a puffy cloud taken by the wind, it expands out to nothing but air." She pulled the pins from her bun, and her soft hair fell around her shoulders. Crossing her arms on the table, she laid her cheek down. "I don't think I can sleep. You go to bed."

He tenderly pulled her arm towards him. "Come with me." He pulled her to standing.

She gripped the corner of the table, resisting his pull. "I don't know, Will. I feel as shredded as that blanket. I don't want to get close. It will only hurt you or the children. What if the brothers find a way to have me jailed? Murder. My Lord. I would never see any of you again."

He let go of her arm and shook his head at the floor. "You've said more than once, you don't want to hurt me. But I can tell in your eyes, you don't believe I will protect you."

"No, it's not that." She tried to lower her voice for those sleeping all around them. "I just don't know how." Stepping behind their blanket, he followed her into their room. "I learned from a young age how to fend for myself. My own parents didn't protect me from a nanny who lied. At Lennhurst, I was rewarded for my independence. Four years with Mr. Plugg was a prison of...of…losing myself to fear and mistrust."

Will rubbed the back of his neck, his face lacking its usual ease. "I've never loved a woman before, and I don't know how to make you believe me."

"And you've never *been* a woman," she said.

He opened his mouth and then cocked his head. His lips drew into a tight, thin line. Puzzled, he blinked at her then a penetrating look came over his face. "I heard something."

WILL CROSSED TO the small bedroom window and stared into the night. Far past the barn, was there movement in the fields? Some animals or—he pushed past the blanket and pulled the door of the cabin open.

"Anna, stay here and put the beam across the door." He pinned her with his eyes before he jerked the rifle from its rack. He heard the plank fall in place as he ran from the front yard. A strange figure came around the side of the large tobacco barn. Even in the shadows, it looked like his grandfather. He pulled his sprint to a stop.

"Grandfather! What are you doing?" he panted, searching the area with eye quickly growing used to the dark. "I thought I heard something in the fields." Will slung the rifle behind his back.

"There were three men on horseback, and they wore strange cloaks over their faces." His grandfather spoke as Will went into the tobacco barn and lit a lantern. Everything in the barn looked the same as he'd left it.

"They dragged large tree branches behind their horses," his grandfather said, impassive.

Will turned to face him with a start, "The new plants." He marched out the back door of the barn. He didn't need daylight to see the young rows of plants on the left had all been trampled. He stomped through the dirt to where the large thick branches had been cut loose. Many of the tender plants he'd grown all laid uprooted around the limbs. He exhaled a long breath. "Did you see any markings on the horses?"

"No, but I nicked one of them in the arm."

Will noticed the bow the Indian always carried and shook his head. "Did they see you?"

"No, Red Wing," his grandfather laid a heavy hand on his shoulder.

The use of his Indian name was to make a point. The man still knew what he was doing. He had survived this long, where many had not. Wasn't it just moments ago, he was angry with Anna for not believing in him? His ability to protect her? He walked along the trampled rows. "If you hadn't been here, it would have been much worse. How were you to be here at this time?" Will bent and pulled a trampled plant upright.

"I told you of my dream. The spirits quickened me tonight."

Will gazed up at the man and brushed the dirt off his hands. "And you told me I should follow the Indian way and plant the tobacco among the stumps and dead trees." He stood up. "If I had, these plants wouldn't have been destroyed tonight."

"So twice you do not listen to my words." His grandfather's eyes narrowed. Will stepped away from the damaged rows turning toward the barn. Breathing through frustration and anger, he looked over his shoulder. His grandfather was gone.

27

IN THE MORNING sunlight, Anna studied the last of the sweet baby gowns she'd made. Every seam was tight, and thread snipped. Folding them in a small stack, she thought about the visit with Mrs. Hart. The friendly owners heard a lot of news at the Mercantile. Maybe she would ask her about last week's raid on the fields. Will said they couldn't prove it was the Plugg brothers, but the fact they were wearing hoods along with Otis's warning pointed to the only possible culprits.

All six of them had helped with the replanting this week. Ten thousand hills was daunting. Even so, Will seemed to think their small farm was no threat to the other plantations near them.

Since the violation of his crops, he'd been distracted of late and spent long hours in the barn. Nathan offered many a night to relieve him, but Will refused.

There'd been no more late night talks with Will. She wondered if there could have been any worse moment to try to help him understand her than that night last week. However he took her words, a wedge had slipped into their growing closeness. Maybe it was better this way, she sighed, drawing her hand across her face. She'd asked Will about talking to a lawyer, but he brushed it off as unnecessary. Turning, she added a few pieces of wood to the cook stove.

Anna leaned over the counter, looking out the kitchen window. Della marched with her body swinging side to side across the long field. Her face was cross, and fingers moved rapidly in the air. Anna had to smile. Maybe all women talk to themselves from time to time.

"Maribelle, let's get to work on that garden dirt." She brushed the child's soft brown curls off her face and into her hands. "I told you your pretty hair would all grow back." She tied a string around the bundle of thick hair. They headed to the cow barn as Della let the outhouse door slam behind her.

A few minutes later, another slam as Della exited the outhouse. "I'm tired of this." Della signed to Anna. "What, the long walk?" Anna set the garden hoe aside and signed back.

"Yes, and my back hurts," Della signed and rubbed her back.

Anna wondered if something was wrong. The teen had walked funny just a moment ago. Della hadn't worn the new dress she'd made her in weeks. Celia's loose dress hung on her, but Anna noticed something strange. She stepped closer and met Della's tense eyes. "Is your tummy well?" Anna signed and carefully placed her hand on her belly. It was round and firm, and Anna froze.

"Maribelle, take the hoe over to the garden dirt and get started," Anna said, gripping Della's hand. She pulled the teen inside the small barn with the cow and chickens.

"Drop your dress." Anna signed to Della.

Della grunted and turned away from Anna. Anna quickly stepped in front of her.

"Something is wrong," Anna spoke and signed at the same time. "Do it."

Della looked around with a scowl and began to undo the buttons. As soon as the dress hit the hay-covered ground, Anna stumbled back and covered her mouth.

"What!" Della's hands flew around in front of her. "What's wrong?"

Anna rubbed her brows back and forth and looked again. It couldn't be. But it seemed like, oh Lord, this poor child was pregnant. Anna grabbed Della's dress and shook out the hay and dropped it over Della's head.

Della's face was flaming red as she redid her buttons. "What is wrong with me?" She groaned and signed to Anna.

Anna rubbed her temples. She had to tell her the truth. But how? Who did this? Vernon Lack? Of course. Will had been right. He was *not* to be trusted around her. Anna felt her stomach curl with nausea. Della jerked on her arms, bringing her back.

"You...you." She pointed to Della's chest. "You have a baby." Anna cradled her hands together and swayed her arms back and forth. "Inside."

Della shook her head rapidly. Her hands were adamantly working in front of her, "Too much food," Della signed, "now fat."

"No," Anna said, wide-eyed, "Baby." She'd seen women in the back H at Lennhurst pregnant. It was the same round, out front belly. It happened too often to the disabled. Her adopted brother, Elias, was born from someone's wrongdoing at Lennhurst. How would she tell Will? He would surely go after Mr. Lack and... what? Kill him? This baby was a sibling to Milo and Maribelle.

She turned and signed to Della's stunned face. "We keep this to us. Yes?"

Della hung her head despairingly. "Just fat." Her fingers barely moved.

Della walked back to the fields. Anna tried not to stare as she joined Maribelle in the garden area. Della did walk differently. How many weeks did she have to keep their secret? A month possibly? Anna dug the spade into the dark soil. Will would be fit to be tied. First the Plugg brothers' threats and now this. Was she sure Della was pregnant? She looked up and saw her far in the distance. Had she just jumped to that conclusion? She'd never shown any signs of sickness in the morning, but she did sleep longer than anyone. Maybe when she went to town to take the baby items, Della could go and they could find a midwife.

Vernon Lack was a sick man. Candy and treats to do his bidding.

Anna slammed the spade hard into the ground. No wonder he was nowhere to be found. He knew from Celia what a pregnant woman felt like, and now he was long gone. Evil and a coward, Anna ground her teeth. Della had come so far in being able to communicate, but nearing seventeen, she was still such a child herself. Anna stood up from pounding the dirt and leaned on the handle. She would help Della learn to be a mother, she thought, trying to find her breath. Glancing up at the cabin, she exhaled a long sigh. Six bodies and one about to appear, seven bodies, how would they fit?

ONE OF THE first nights that week, Will sat at the table with the family. Anna tried to concentrate on his prayer over the food.

"Thank you, Lord, for provision and safety. For the sunshine and strength each day to plant. Make us grateful for this food and all your gifts. In Christ's name, Amen." He looked up, and everyone began to eat.

With his absence and her falling asleep before he came in, she wondered if she could hold the news any longer. "Are you staying in tonight?" Her voice came out more demanding than she meant.

"I can." He chewed, glancing at her.

Anna watched Della stab a slice of potato. Now her stomach seized up again. Della had had such a good week. No complaints of back pain; maybe she shouldn't say anything.

"Wonderful." She forged a smile. "Maybe we can pick up again in the Bible tonight."

"Can we read about Noah and the whale?" Milo sat up.

Will shook his head. 'No, we can't." He rubbed Milos's wavy brown hair. "But we can read about Noah and the Ark or Jonah and the whale."

Maribelle giggled and pointed a finger at Milo. Milo elbowed her, and her smile dropped into a frown, "Ouch." Tears sprung to her eyes, and her face turned bright red. "That hurt, Milo." she whimpered, fighting the tears.

"Milo." Anna had a sudden urge to shake his arm. "You are never to hit a girl, ever. Do you understand me? You will become a gentleman, like Nathan and Will."

So rarely scolded, Milo looked wide-eyed back and forth between Will and Nathan.

"She's partly right, Milo." Will wiped his bread across his plate. "But Maribelle, no gentlemen wants a woman pointing out his faults. To be a proper lady, you shouldn't have laughed at him." Will handed her his napkin, and she swiped her wet face.

"Women are much weaker," Nathan added. "So if you and I elbow and horseplay, we like it. Women don't." Nathan smiled at Milo.

"That is also only partly true." Anna corrected Nathan. "Women like to laugh and have fun, and they aren't *much weaker*. In fact, in many ways, women have superior strength to men."

Will and Nathan both leaned back. "How is that so?" Nathan lifted a corner smile.

"Umm." Anna looked around the cabin. "I count the fact many a Negro woman works side by side in the fields with men. I count that many women oversee the woodpile, the water, the garden, and the meals and…and the safety of the children, often at the same time." She knew there was more but wondered if her point was being lost on the three males staring at her. "At Lennhurst, the women in the back H played a game, kicking a canvas ball back and forth in the yard." She nodded, "Really. They enjoyed the running and competition."

Will and Nathan didn't seem convinced.

"I have the canvas ball you made me!" Milo jumped up from the table. "Show us that game, Anna." He picked it up from the corner and stood between Will and Nathan.

She looked into the curious faces of these three family members that she'd called gentlemen.

"Boys against girls," she smirked, narrowing her eyebrows at them.

28

THE LAST REMNANTS of light were fading fast as Anna watched Nathan draw a stick across the dirt and weeds in the front yard.

"This will be our line for the win. And *if* the ladies," he swung a long arm out toward the three females," can get the canvas ball past this line," he ran to the other side of the yard, dragging another line, "you gain a point. What number shall we play to?"

"Twenty," Milo yelled, jumping up and down.

"Five," Will said, shaking his head.

Anna suggested two. It was almost dark, what was she thinking? Della and Maribelle? She said a small prayer as she turned to the girls. "Here's the plan," she said and signed to Della. Maribelle giggled, and they spread out to face their masculine opponents.

Will stood an arm's length in front of her and squinted at her. 'I will win.' He mouthed at her. She bit her lip and tried to make a mean face—which only turned into a jolt of laughter.

"Just feet, no hands." Nathan held the ball up in the air. "I will throw it up, and as soon as it drops, we begin." He tossed the ball upward, and Maribelle squealed and ran to Will and attached herself to his leg. Just like their planned trick, Della went up to Nathan and began to tickle his armpits. As he was turning to get away from her, Anna moved swiftly around Milo's confusion and kicked the ball over the line for the win. The girls jumped and cheered as the boys looked stunned and not too happy.

"If that's how you want to play," Will gave her a pirate sneer, pulling Maribelle off his leg. Scorned, the boys huddled together.

"Okay, girls, they're on to us." Anna felt her heart pounding. "So this time, Maribelle you take Nathan and you, Della, kick the ball while I take Milo." Della nodded her understanding with a big smile. They all turned to face the boys' resolute faces. Nathan tossed the ball, and Maribelle did her same squeal as she headed for his leg. Right before she could fasten, he swept her up in his arms and kicked the ball. Anna ran after it, blocking its roll to their line. Before she could turn toward her goal, Will and Milo surrounded her, and a mad flurry of feet stirring up the dirt followed. By some miracle, Anna got her foot on the ball, and it rolled out of the pile. As she went for another kick, someone's hands locked around her waist, pulling her back. Will easily pulled her off her feet and up against him stopping her kick.

"I like this game," he nuzzled her ear before he set her down. Anna watched as Nathan, still holding Maribelle, did a dance around Della and kicked the ball back over the boys' line.

"And I called you a gentleman!" Anna swiped at Will's arm. Milo and Nathan celebrated as Maribelle ran after the ball.

"We will win this battle. Would you like to claim defeat now or later?" Will pulled her against him and kissed her cheek.

"None of that with the enemy," Nathan boomed, holding the ball above his head. Game three begins!" He tossed the ball, and this time Anna squealed. She'd no time to plan their defense. She ran in circles with the others, trying to find the ball in a flurry of darkness and dirt. This time Milo came from nowhere and tapped the ball over the boys' line. "Two to one!" he bellowed, dancing in a circle.

Anna tried to find her female teammates, but Della and Maribelle were already teasing and provoking their brothers. Their behavior needed no prompting from her. Girls did indeed enjoy a bit of horseplay.

"I will start the ball this time," Anna announced, grabbing it from Nathan's hand.

She stood in the middle of their playing field. "Ready." She held the ball over her head as Milo and Nathan came closer. "Step back, young man. There will be no cheating!" She made wide-eyes at Della standing near their line. "Ready? Begin!" She tossed the ball over to Della's feet. And Della easily kicked it over their line.

The girls did a jig, swinging each other around, while the boys called out their rebuttal. "Who said no cheating?" Will stalked closer, glaring at her. Laughing and moving backward, her heart jumped. Just as Will was about to reach her, she pulled to the right and took off running. Drawing her skirts up, she ran left and then right out to the big field trying to avoid his capture. "I have a bad aim!" Her lungs were starting to constrict, wondering if she could make it to the tobacco barn. Something strong seized her arm and yanked her skirt layers from her grip. The folds of fabric tripped up her running, and she fell onto the grass. Will's weight was attached to her as he fell on top. Their chests heaved for air and Anna surrender to her exhaustion.

"You. *Are.* Half. Indian," she panted, looking up at him, "I should have known better than to have run."

He laughed and jumped up. Grabbing her hand, he pulled her up and led her toward the tobacco barn. Anna looked back toward the cabin. The others played, and laughter still drifted out front of the cabin. Pulling her around the corner, she smelled the old wood and hay. She felt a light, refreshing breeze between the open doors. Will stopped and smoothed back the loose hair falling around her face. The minute she looked into his eyes, she knew what was going to happen. He winked with a roguish expression before his lips found hers as passionately as before.

Strange shimmers began in her stomach and coursed up and down her limbs. Each kiss left her wanting more as he pressed their bodies together. Was it right for her to feel the same hunger as he? If her skin couldn't touch his, she couldn't satisfy her craving. She pulled her fingers through his black locks, and his kisses fell to her neck and cheek. "I'm sorry for neglecting you. I shouldn't have worried over the crop," he said in a husky voice.

Before her mind could register a response, he turned and went back to the large barn door. "The others have gone in." He pushed the tall door partially closed. "Could we spend time alone?" He stepped close. The irresistible wanting in his eyes overwhelmed her. "I will try to be a gentleman." A sly smile arose as his hand climbed up her back.

The stirring from her insides came over her again. She couldn't suppress her smile. "I think I would like that."

He pulled his fingers over his lips, pushing back a wide grin. Carefully he reached behind her and pulled the pins from her hair. "I think you're beautiful." He traced his fingers around her face and let them drop to the buttons below her chin. He undid each one, watching his hands and then lifting his eyes to check her expression.

What should she be doing? This slow undressing mixed with anticipation was nothing she'd ever known before. How many times had she told herself there was no enjoyment in this marriage act? Could she have been wrong? A wave of strange heat flooded her skin as her blouse slipped from her shoulders. He stepped back and undid his buttons and pulled his shirt free. She recognized those thick-muscled arms—her first nights with him, she'd clung to their comfort.

She took his elbow in her hand and lifted it. Placing small kisses on his bicep, she could taste the salt on his skin from playing their game. Slowly, she kissed her way to his collarbone and neck—they shared a sweet smile before their lips found home. She belonged to this family. He undid the buttons of her skirt, and it fell to the ground. She belonged to him, and he belonged to her.

"I know just the place." His hand was warm as he pulled her back into the corner of the barn. Six large hay bales lay together on their side. A single, sliver of moonlight came through the slats in the wood siding. Grabbing a tarp hanging on a peg, he threw it over the hay bales. He glanced at her smiling shyly, and then at the homemade bed, then glanced back at her. She couldn't help but smile again; he was trying his best to be patient.

"You are fast, but so worth the chase." He brought his hands around her neck and let them run down her shoulders. He kissed her mouth again, deep and without a trace of reservation. His arms were around her body, and he pushed her back to their hay bed. She laid back and reached for him as he came close. She looked forward to their lovemaking. This is how God must have intended. If only she could have their own little...

"Wait." Anna pushed him back. "I have to tell you something. I can't do this and then tell you." Sitting up, she opened her mouth to say more but chided herself for being so lost in the moment. She'd clearly confused him. She blew out a long sigh. It felt like she'd been deceiving him. "I've known about something for a week and haven't had the time to tell you. You've been out here many nights."

Will sat back on the hay bail and ran his hand down his face. He sighed and said, "You can tell me anything."

Anna squeezed her hands together and took a needed breath. "I think Della is pregnant." Quickly she stood up and stepped back from him.

He tilted his head to the side and glared at her with dark, piercing eyes. "What are you saying?"

"I could be wrong, but I saw her for myself. I think I'm right." Anna cupped her hands around her twitching chin.

Will stood and walked back to his shirt and yanked it over his arms. "It was Vernon. I knew what I saw." He picked up Anna's things and handed them to her. The fabric felt cold as she refastened it against her.

"That man is going to pay," he growled. "She could give no consent."

"I will help her, Will. She has come so far. Can you imagine being trapped in a world where you never heard a word? You never understood what was happening minute by minute. Then losing your mother, I think if she could have communicated—"

"It's a bit late now!" He walked in a circle, raking his fingers through his hair. "The night we married; was but what? Four months ago? I saw what I saw about three months before that— when I kicked him out. I did not misunderstand." He shook his head, looking at the ground. "To think, I'd questioned my haste to get rid of him. I"d felt as if I'd torn Milo and Maribelle's father from their life." He rubbed his forehead. "Do you suppose this is why we've not seen an inch of him or his offerings? Of course, it is," he answered himself. "He said once he'd kin in Alabama." His face turned red." I tell you, Anna, if I see him, I will…" He dragged his fingers across his chin as his eyes bore into hers. "I should be thanking you. I don't know what I would do if he'd taken her and Milo and Maribelle away with him." The silence lingered. Anna looked up as a bird fluttered up in the high rafters of the barn.

"Come." He took in a deep breath and held his hand out.

Anna walked into his arms, and they held each other. "Your game antics were lively." He pressed his cheek against her hair. "I haven't seen my brothers and sisters laugh and be children in so long. Likely, you gave us the medicine we needed before the next storm comes upon the land."

29

A FTER A COUPLE of days of spring rain, the land was soft and moist. Will dropped off Anna and Maribelle in front of the mercantile. Anna entered the tall glass door and returned a wave from Mrs. Hart as the businesswoman helped a few older ladies. Maribelle went to look at the table of toys as Anna set the baby gowns on the store counter. Would she have to explain to Mrs. Hart her need for yards of flannel for blankets and diapers?

She fingered the yellow and green cloth. Would it be a boy or a girl? Which gender would be easiest for Della to handle? Her heart constricted painfully. As Mrs. Plugg, how long had she held to her hope for a baby? Having her own little one was the best dream to dream. She had hoped to have a girl first, and from there it didn't matter. She laid the flannel on the counter for cutting. She would rise to the challenge and help Della with her new life of motherhood. And she would *not* begrudge the Almighty. He'd been good to give her a peaceable man and a family to care for.

"Now what are we making with this?' Mrs. Hart came back around the counter and unfolded the fabric. "Something for me to sell?" She smiled.

"Well," Anna felt like a coward as she turned from her simple question. "Let me make sure Maribelle isn't into mischief." She bent down to peek through the stacked canned goods and said, "Could I have three yards of the green and three yards of the yellow?" Anna walked away to see Maribelle sitting on the floor with the same wooden horse she loved to touch.

"Please be gentle with the toy, child." Anna took a few minutes to watch Maribelle reenact a horse's gallop while Mrs. Hart cut the flannel. How would they explain Will's sister was in the family way? She looked around at the other shoppers. It would be the talk of the town. She could picture the reverend's wife's judgmental scowl and hear her critical voice question Anna's ability to care for the children.

"Oh, Anna. These are lovely," Mrs. Hart said, looking over the baby gowns.

Anna smiled and went back to the counter. "Can you take the flannel, a bag of coffee and a pack of carrot seeds from my wages?" Anna looked at a bowl of yellow fruit on the sales counter. "Are those lemons? They look as pretty as a picture."

"Yes, dear," Mrs. Hart turned and brought out another small bag. Smiling, she dropped a lemon into the bottom of the bag. "For a pitcher of lemonade and two licorice sticks for the little ones."

Maribelle jumped up and joined the ladies. "For me?" Her eyes shone brightly.

"And Milo," Anna handed her the small bag. "Thank you, Mrs. Hart, I imagine Will is waiting for us." She gathered her items.

"Oh, did you tell me, Anna? What that flannel is for?" Mrs. Hart asked.

"No, ma'am, I," she shrugged. "Just for around the house." Anna took Maribelle's hand and led them out the door. *House,* she chided herself. *It was a cracker tin of a cabin.*

Chewing on her thumbnail, they waited out on the same sidewalk where she'd first met Milo and an overburdened Will Gibbs. When the wagon rolled in front, she noticed Will had purchased more fencing. He reached for them and pulled them up to the bench seat. She started to open her mouth but knew better. There would never be enough spools of wire to keep the evil out and the good in. She could tell with his sober temperament of late, and long nights in the barn, he carried the burden of a family always stretched to its limits.

"I've got a few things for the new arrival." She glanced at Maribelle, her lips and mouth covered in black candy.

Will nodded, keeping his eyes on the road.

"Have you told Nathan?" she questioned carefully.

He squeezed his hand over his nose and mouth. "Yes. He wants the same revenge I do." His scowl deepened. "But what are we to do now? There is nothing we can do. It's too late. Our sister..." Will pursed his lips and looked away.

Anna looked out at the familiar farms and landscape they passed each time. "I can tell you for a fact, it does no good to hold the anger so tight. It will poison you from the inside, and then the person who deserves to suffer is free to go about their business while your burden is still there. Week after week, month after month, year after year. You'll lose your faith. You'll lose your joyfulness, and your reason for living," she whispered and watched the tan horse bob his head seemingly in total agreement with her as he pulled their load. "I don't know if I can say before God and Jesus that I have forgiven Alfred Plugg. I can't rightly say what God was doing during my suffering, but I know He brought me out of Egypt and into a promised land."

Will turned to her, squinting, "We are your *promised land*?"

"Yes." She smiled at him. "And you tried to scare me off. 'There is no blessing,'" she imitated his low voice.

"I didn't know you. It was a fair warning." He straightened his back. "Truth is, that night I was desperate. I didn't expect the reverend to join us in marriage on such a miserable night. I was only trying to find Della. "I," he tapped the reins. "I was ready to send Della away to keep her safe and thought maybe Milo and Maribelle might be better off in someone else's family. I thought maybe the reverend would help me there."

"Huh?" Maribelle licked her sticky fingers.

"But God had a better plan." Anna pulled a sticky strand of hair from her cheek. "Help came to you." She smiled at Maribelle. Glancing at Will's strong profile, she wished she could have relieved him of the responsibility that had befallen him after losing his mother, and then the corruption Mr. Lack inflicted upon their desperate state. He didn't seem convinced she would be able help teach Della how to care for her baby. No one could stop what'd already happened. But they could make amends for the future.

"And another funny story, Maribelle. When I met your brother..." She smiled at Will, and he glanced at her. "I agreed to help with Della, and Milo, and Maribelle. I would do chores, cook, and teach. I was coming to do a bunch of jobs." She smiled at the bright upturned face. "When I was younger, I had a job at a place with a lot of different types of people, but the children were my favorite." She could see Elias and his trusting eyes on her. Patience, the little, timid, glass-doll sort of child. She'd found love and gave it freely to those unwanted ones.

The wagon bench rocked as Will jumped down to open their gate.

"You all helped me remember why I love children. It's never been work because I love helping. I'd almost forgotten until I married your brother."

"But Nathan and Will Yam ain't children," Maribelle said in her petit southern drawl. The wagon bench rocked as Will led the horses forward.

"Do ya love them, too?" Maribelle asked.

The wagon came to a stop as she waited for Will to jump back up after closing the gate. Instead, he looked over the horse's rump at her. He held the reins steady as he lowered his chin. His sharp eyes creased, expecting an answer.

Anna bit back her smile. "Yes, I love them, too."

Will's jaw rocked to the side, still waiting he swatted a fly and scratched a knuckle under his nose.

"I love Nathan like I love you, and Milo, and Della." She couldn't seem to take her eyes off his dark, penetrating gaze. She knew what he waited for. This man could communicate many things with those deep, silent eyes. Her midsection fluttered. "And because Will is my husband, I have a special love for him." She sucked in a breath, holding back her embarrassment. Would that satisfy both of them, for the moment?

Maribelle giggled. Will drug his fingers across the rim of his hat and with a slow nod of approval, he leaped into the wagon seat and tapped the horses forward.

30

THAT NIGHT, ANNA pouted looking at Will's untouched dinner plate and glass of lemonade. He'd worked past supper again. The children had gotten such a delight out of the lemonade, he of all people needed a diversion from his worries. Picking up the plate and cup, she set them on the small kitchen counter and stared out the cabin window. Looking down at the lemonade, she sighed. Like a cup of sugar and lemon water was going to lift his spirits. She had never wanted to carry any burdens with Mr. Plugg. Funny how many times a day she wondered what she could do for Will Gibbs. After watching out the window a few more minutes, she grabbed a cloth, flung it over the plate, and reached for the cup.

"Nathan, could you open the door for me and at the end of the hour, help the little ones to bed?"

"Yes, ma'am." He set his book aside and opened the door.

WILL FLIPPED A fence board over on the saw horses a little harder than usual. The light flickered dimly, adding to his pent-up frustration. He could never fence off all the acres of fields or ask his sullen grandfather to be the night watchman. He let the hammer fall from his hand and slam onto the wood. Someone had purposely torn into his crop, gotten his deaf sister pregnant, and all the while he was trying to convince Anna he could protect her.

He'd let the truth out of the bag today. Before she came, he was ready to break up his family. His own flesh and blood had been barely surviving under his watch. Hearing his own words today, somehow soured his stomach. He grabbed the stack of posts and wire and carried them over to the pallets and let them drop with a thundering slam. Wiping his forehead with his shirt sleeve, he turned to see Anna standing in the large doorway, a plate and cup in her hand.

"I'm sorry," he blew out a breath. "I missed supper again."

"The night air and walk were good for me." She came to where he worked and held out the items. "I made lemonade."

He took the cup from her, feeling almost shy from her personal attention.

"Your siblings were circling the table," she smiled, "waiting till my back was turned to have the last cup." Kind eyes and simple womanly understanding covered her face. So many things were heavy on him, how did her sweet expressions, her walk, her words touch him, pushing him to a lighter place.

"Thank you." He brought the cup to his lips and raised his eyes over the rim to see her. From the first taste of the sweet drink, he tilted his head back and drank it all without stopping. It was good. He swiped some from his chin, smiling. She smiled back. The flickering lantern danced the light around her and the dark barn. Every instinct and desire he'd ever had for her burned to life.

Wasn't it just a few weeks ago, after their kickball game, he'd wanted her touch, and she seemed to want his? He glanced over to the corner where the hay bales still waited. Another grin couldn't be held back. Did a husband ask? Or just see if… He reached out and took her hand. "Do you expect anyone to follow you out here tonight?" He pulled her close and began to remove the pins from her hair.

She cleared her throat, "No." She closed her eyes as her sandy, blonde hair fell around her shoulders. He drew his roving fingers under and through it. The delicate turn of her neck beckoned him as he lowered his mouth to taste her soft skin.

"Maybe we won't be interrupted," he breathed into her ear. Without waiting for her to respond, he pulled her over to the corner where they'd been before. This time she wore her gray dress. The small buttons pulled tight across her chest, making a line down the center. His fingers tremored as he tried to release the tiny clasps. For weeks he'd tried to take his eyes from her curves. In a small cabin, he'd forced himself to appreciate her laugh and her ease with the children, but being a man, he was drawn to her ever-enticing form.

He watched her swallow hard and slowly close her eyes. Was she surrendering passively to him or as overwhelmed by the attraction as he was? He knew one way to find out. Holding his aggressive need back, he kissed her slowly, tenderly until she pulled her arms free from her dress. Passionately, without reserve, she kissed him back. Her fingers were in his hair, over his back, and gripping him tighter. Her body answered his question, pressing into his until he lifted her off her feet and lowered her onto the hay. His things dropped quickly to the side as he came nearer, feeling the astonishing warmth of her soft skin pressing against his.

NIGHTS LATER, ANNA rolled next to Will's body. His shoulder and chest became her pillow, and her arm rested upon his bare skin. Trying to fall back asleep, somewhere into the late night hours, was proving difficult of late.

Running her fingers lightly over his torso, she wondered about her recurring dream. Could it be from the new way her body and heart found such appreciation in the marriage act? The dream was always lovers outside, a warm quilt beneath them and the shade of a large tree over them. Most nights, her dream was interrupted by her husband's feet running up her calves or the way he pulled her closer and whispered sweet words in her ear. Every time she assured herself she could keep a distance and fall back asleep, the desire for his caress won out.

Would they enjoy these new liberties every night? Last night he referred to what potion had she put in that first night's lemonade. The snickers had started low and erupted with each ridiculous guess. They covered each other's mouths so as not to wake the others until that became a tumbled wrestle of arms and legs.

Tonight, blurry with bliss, she yawned. The familiar rise and fall of his chest meant he'd fallen asleep. Love and desire was a commanding sensation. The simple gifts, like the way his smile made her feel approved, like being someone he truly enjoyed and valued. From their first weeks together, his gentle countenance and small touches made her feel cherished and wanted for the first time in her life. The delight, the euphoria, changed the way she did the laundry and cleaned the cabin. She'd surged with more energy for the children's nursery rhymes and lessons.

Even today, after finishing all the new baby items, she tried to teach Della how they could dress and care for one of Maribelle's dolls. *Just like your new baby*, she had signed to her.

Anna released a slow breath. The teen had swung at Anna's arms as she made the cradle motion to sign "baby." She hadn't seen her aggressive like that in weeks. Whispering a quick prayer, she needed inspiration for how to reach the girl.

The afternoons they all helped in the fields, only fueled her desire to have him alone. Often he would watch her, and she would watch him. Lover's glances with an intimate secret only they could possess. Maybe that was where the reoccurring dream came from? She could arrange a picnic, possibly Sunday. She smiled, pleased to make plans they would both appreciate.

Will rolled to face her and pulled the blanket over their bare shoulders. Her eyes drooped closed, such comfort she'd never known. Yet a door to their tiny room would be nice.

A LARGE WEIGHT landed on Anna. Jerking her head up and her eyes open, "Child, what are you…"

Wearing the little nightgown Anna had made, Maribelle smiled while she tapped Anna's cheeks.

"Everyone's gone. How long you gonna sleep?" Maribelle scrunched up her nose and mouth.

"Mmm," Anna pushed the little girl to the side and sat up. "I must've overslept."

"You've been doin' that all week. Just tell Will Yam to wake ya."

Anna smiled to herself. Her young husband knew all too well how interrupted the wee night hours had been. Not waking her early was just another of his special gifts.

"Did everyone eat?" Anna reached for her undergarments and slid them on.

"Yep." Maribelle opened the small wardrobe.

"Did Milo and Della go out to the fields?" Anna stepped into her dress.

"I think so. Milo brought the milk in." Maribelle pulled out Anna's shoes and put them before her.

"Thank you, Bellie, child. What shall we do first? Churn some butter and sing our songs? Or get the beans on to soak?" Anna took Maribelle's hand as the little one pulled her to standing.

"Let's bake somethin' yummy!" Maribelle smiled and raced around the curtain.

LATE IN THE afternoon, after Milo had come in to do his school work, Anna peered out the little kitchen window.

"Milo, did Will take food out this morning for everyone? I haven't seen Della come back to eat." She looked long out toward the big barn. She'd never noticed Della's frequent trips to the outhouse, either.

"I don't know." He looked up from the sums on his slate. "Can I be done?"

Anna turned and looked over his shoulder. "Do the second one again. You didn't subtract right." She dropped the folded towel on her table and opened the front door of the cabin. "She was out this morning with y'all," Maribelle said.

"I never seen her." Milo redid the problem. "Is this right?" He held the slate up.

"Saw her." Anna corrected and turned from the open door. "What do you mean? Wasn't she working with Will and Nathan this morning?" Her brows creased her forehead.

"I didn't see—saw—uh her. I figured she was here with you and Bellie."

Anna's back straightened, and she pinched her bottom lip. "Milo, I need you to run out to the fields." She took the slate from his hand. "If you don't see Della anywhere, get Will and Nathan back to the cabin." Anna pressed her hands against her cheeks. None of them could call for her. Poor thing wouldn't hear their calls. "I will search around here. Tell Will I have not seen her all day."

"Yes, Ma'am." Milo rose, and Anna followed him outside. He ran out from the small cabin, and she turned to Maribelle. "Have you seen Della today? Didn't you tell me she went with the boys?"

Maribelle lifted a shoulder and looked down.

Anna squatted close and took her hands. "Maribelle, listen to me, this is very important, and you won't be in any trouble. Was your Pa here? Did someone take Della?"

Maribelle shook her head no.

"And you saw her walk to the fields?" Anna asked.

Maribelle scratched the back of her neck. "I saw her go outside."

Anna blew out a huff and stood. Why had she overslept? She took the few steps to the front door and searched left to right. In all the routine chores today, Della was nowhere to be seen. Rubbing her forehead, she stared out to the big barn. Certainly, Milo was mistaken. She must be out there somewhere.

31

A S SOON AS Anna saw Will and Nathan running to the cabin, her heart spiked, constricting her throat. Milo lagged behind them, but Della wasn't with them.

"You haven't seen her all day?" Will panted, looking around the cabin yard. "I assumed she was with you." Closing his eyes, he tried to find air. "She never came out to the fields." He paced around the area like Anna had done a hundred times.

"I've looked and looked," her voice cracked. "I think we need to split up to look for her." She marched back into the cabin and came out with two pans and two wooden spoons.

"Milo, you stay here and bang this pot if you see her."

Will went into the cabin and came out with the rifle. "Nathan, you go along the south and shoot one shot if you see her." He handed the rifle off to him, and Nathan jogged away.

"Wait!" Anna called after him. She ran into the cabin, and then back out to meet him. She shoved a flannel blanket in his belt. "You have a knife, too?" His expression dropped as he nodded his head. "I'm fearing she might be delivering."

Nathan rolled his eyes and jogged away.

"Will, don't leave yet." Anna went back to the cabin and grabbed more flannel and her scissors. "I can take Maribelle and stay towards the north side," she said, coming out.

"I'll search the middle woods." Will pulled another flannel from the stack and pushed it inside his shirt."

"Listen for her." Anna grabbed his arm, choking on the words. Her eyes brimmed with worry and tears. "If she's birthing, you *will* be able to hear her."

Handing the other pot and spoon off to Maribelle, Anna turned. "We're going to move quickly, child. Keep up and stay close."

After a mile of searching and walking, Anna stopped and let Maribelle catch up. She pounded her fists on her hips and turned in a circle. "First, I lose you in town, and now we've lost your sister."

"Della!" Maribelle squeaked.

"Stop that now." The frustration grated in her voice. "She can't hear you, and you stop me from listening." She rubbed the palm of her hand back and forth on her forehead.

"Lord, please help us," she whispered as they marched on through the woodsy brush.

"I think my daddy lives over there." Maribelle pointed.

Anna stopped. "Are you sure? Can you lead me?"

"Mmm, maybe." Maribelle lifted her chin and took them around a large tree. Sure enough, it looked like a bit of a worn trail through the brush. They'd only walked a few yards when Anna thought she heard something. Grabbing Maribelle's arm, she held her still, "Listen, I hear something." Anna felt her insides drop. It was Della. She'd recognize that groan anywhere.

"Della!" Anna ran forward, forgetting her own advice. Della's scream wrenched the air. Anna caught sight of Della's bent over form sitting under a tree. "Maribelle, stay right here and pound the pan."

Anna ran over to where Della leaned back against the tree, writhing in pain. She grabbed the teen's red, sweaty face and mouthed, "Let me help you."

Della rocked forward, breaking away from Anna and screamed again. The pounding of the tin pan and Della's volume was making Anna's head split. Della finally rocked back to a sitting position, and Anna grabbed the front of her skirt and pulled it up to reveal blood and water. She had to swallow down the contents of her stomach as she pulled off Della's pantaloons.

Della looked down and screamed in wide-eyed terror. The panicked teen's screech was cut off as Della started to rock up again in response to another wave of pain.

"Push!" Anna yelled and signed, even though the young woman's eyes were tightly closed. Della grabbed Anna's shoulders and screamed in pain. Anna had no time to think before the tiny, waxy head appeared. She took the poor girl by the chin and shook her to attention. "Push again!" she yelled. Della's head flipped back, and Anna grabbed her upper body. "One more!" She shook her until Della's eyes opened and she took a weary breath, dropped her chin to her chest and bore down.

The purple baby slipped from Della's body, landing on the inside of Della's skirt.

"Oh, my Lord. Oh, my Lord," Anna panted as Della leaned back against the tree. Her body and breathing froze at what lay before her. A tiny waxy arm jerked forward. In wide-eyed shock, she stared at the movement then the air jumped back into her lungs.

"Oh, blessed be," Anna sputtered and reached for the flannel and scissors tucked in her pocket. "It's a girl, Della," Her voice held a mixture of awe and delight. "You have a baby girl." Anna cut the cord before she wiped the baby's face and wrapped the flannel around the little jerking limbs. She pulled her to her chest as Della's legs began to shake.

"It's over, brave one." She whispered, even though Della's eyes were closed. Tucking the little bundle in the crook of her arm, she tried to smooth the wet hair from Della's forehead. Della let out a raspy groan and turned away from her touch.

Anna looked down, and her eyes fixated on the little tiny cracks of dark eyes that looked at her. Her throat tightened, and she rubbed Della's arm. "Please, Della. You have to see this. She's trying to open her eyes. She is perfect. You are a mama." Hot tears poured down Anna's face. Something in the woods became silent and holy, and Anna looked up to see Will holding Maribelle and Nathan squeezing Milo's shoulder.

"Whose baby is that?" Milo broke the sacred moment.

Anna felt the familiar hole in her gut and took one last gaze of admiration at the very creation of God. "This is Della's baby girl."

ANNA THOUGHT SHE couldn't have any more esteem for her husband, but she found a bit more as he cradled the newly bathed baby girl in her clean diaper and towel. In the difficult hours after getting back to the cabin, Anna realized she couldn't get Della's attention, try to talk with her hands, and hold a newborn all at the same time.

"She'll only take a sip of water," Anna said, standing in the blanket door. "I've tried, you've tried," Anna blew out a long breath. "She won't even hold her or look at her."

Will adjusted the towel tighter around the baby. "Maybe it's just the pain. My ma said a woman forgets about the pain sometime after the baby is born."

Anna chewed on her lip. "I've helped her walk and bathe. I know she saw me when I spoke to her. But when we bring the baby near, she turns away."

The baby let out a squeaky cry, and Will lightly bounced her in the crook of his arm. "I would do this for Maribelle when she was this small." He looked at Anna and touched her arm. "Don't worry; she'll take to her."

The baby let out another squeal.

"And she needs to nurse her." Anna frowned. "I tried to show her. I told her it would help her, too."

She looked down at Milo and Maribelle yawning at the table. "You two, off to bed." Exhausted, Anna pulled out a chair and sat. "Maybe Nathan should go after the doctor, maybe he would know of a wet nurse in the area."

"Anna, no need to fret, look how good I am at this. This baby is already asleep," Will announced with a crooked grin. "Let's give it till tomorrow. I'm sure you can reach her." He glanced up at Nathan. "Remember Maribelle's baby bed?"

Nathan went behind the curtain and came out with the bottom drawer to the wardrobe. Setting it on the table before Anna, the two brothers smiled as Will carefully lowered the little bundle in the space between the clothes Nathan parted.

Anna wilted, staring at the little bundle, not knowing whether to smile or cry. "She looks healthy." Anna stood and swept a gentle touch over the infant's two little wisps of dark hair. She lifted a sad smile to Will.

Wrapping his arms around her waist, he kissed her temple. "God has kept us this far. You go sleep with Della." He whispered, kissing her cheek. "I'll take Della's spot."

"Is it safe to leave the baby on the table?" Anna glanced down, her confidence from her years at Lennhurst crumbling away in the whimper of her voice. This felt a hundred times different, the shock, the reality of weeks of suspicions now asleep in a drawer on the families' supper table.

"She's not going anywhere," Nathan said before he turned to go up the loft.

"Maybe I should just tuck her in with me? How will we know when she needs us? She might not stay warm enough."

Will looked down into the makeshift baby bed and smiled patiently at Anna. "Go to sleep. She'll be fine."

32

ANNA TRIED AGAIN to close her eyes but felt like she'd had too many late night cups of coffee. All the events of the day kept swirling through her mind. Della seemed to sleep soundly without discomfort. Anna looked back and pulled the blanket around the exhausted teen. Poor child, why did she leave the cabin? Did she think she would find Vernon Lack today? All this time, she assumed Mr. Lack had lured her away from the cabin. Maybe Della went out on her own accord? It didn't really matter. Della had been truly pregnant, and now she was a mother. Similar things had happened to girls at the asylum. Some of the babies stayed, some were whisked away— Anna had always hoped by caring family members. This baby was a tiny peanut. She yawned.

She'd never seen a baby born before, only heard the nurses tell the details. It was shocking and miraculous all at the same time. Anna took a long breath and prayed a prayer for Della to awaken from her shock.

Sleep finally came, yet a little squeak woke Anna with a start. The baby. Did it just squeak once and go back to sleep? No, she could hear the baby getting louder. She's hungry. Anna flipped her legs off the bed. Should she wake Della? She came through the blanket door and lit the lantern. Scooping up the infant, Anna looked to see her husband sound asleep in the corner. How could he not awaken? The little squawks should've awoken everyone but

Della, the only one needed. She tucked the blanket around the baby and gave her a little jiggle. The little head turned to the side and opened her mouth. "Oh precious, I have nothing for you," she whispered. The baby closed her eyes and then let out another squeak. Now what, should she awaken Will? What could he do?

Anna walked around the table five or six times, stepping over Will's legs. The jiggling seemed to hold the cries back for a moment, and then they would start again. Feeling her nerves rattle, she knew there was only one way to solve this. Anna stepped into the bedroom and pulled back Della's blanket. Tapping her shoulder, she grabbed her wrist to pull her up to sitting. Della rubbed her eyes and finally focused on what was lying in Anna's arm. Della grimaced and rolled back to the bed. Anna pulled on her elbow. Della jerked it from her grasp and tucked it under her pillow. Anna tapped on her shoulder, and Della rolled away from her. The baby swung its little head to the side again—squeaking with a searching open mouth.

Anna felt her own growl rising from her throat and took Della's upper arm and pulled. Della jerked to the other side of the bed and Anna came around to the other side to meet her. Pushing her way to sitting, Anna tried to bring the baby closer to Della. Della moaned a loud cry and rolled quickly to the other side. Anna stood up and came back to the other side. Frustration was building as the baby squawked and Anna had only one arm to control Della with. Della screeched at Anna and rolled up in a ball. Anna felt her heart pounding as she circled the small space, trying to settle the little hungry babe. Movement from the shadowy curtain revealed Will watching through the opening.

"This baby needs her," Anna heard the desperation in her voice. "Can you talk to her, make her see?" They both looked to where Della still had her limbs tucked under her in a ball. Will motioned for her to come out to the table. He reached for the bundle, and Anna felt her arms go limp. "Why won't she even look at her? She must have some kind of maternal instincts."

Will rocked and shushed the fussy infant. "Get the pitcher of milk." He nodded to the small kitchen counter.

Anna brought it over to the table. Will stuck his pinky in the milk and held it to the infant's mouth. The baby quieted for a moment and then squalled louder than before. "She *is* hungry." Will repeated the same method. A drop of milk made the baby open her mouth and quiet; needing more, she began to fuss again. "This isn't fast enough." He looked around. "Dip the corner of the towel in milk and see if she will suck on it."

Anna lowered the tip of the towel in, and Will held the baby near as she tried to drop the milk onto the babies' tongue. The little head jerked for attachment, and the milk dripped down her cheek and neck. "Try again," Will said, as he held the infant closer.

Anna felt her hand shake as she carefully tried to drip the milk on the infant's tongue. One, two, three drops seemed to get in until the baby stilled, choked and sputtered.

"She's choking, Will!" Anna stepped back as Will flipped the infant onto his other hand and patted its back.

"It's okay, Anna." He flipped the baby back over like a bag of beans. "They will do that. See, she's breathing."

Anna flinched, and she felt exhausted tears rising. Will went back to dipping the milk onto his pinky and setting it on her lips. At least the poor babe wasn't screaming.

"What are we going to do? Maybe Tallie knows of a wet nurse we can get from the plantation?" Anna urged.

"No." Will shook his head. "I don't want any of us going near that place."

"Then at first light, you'll go to town and ask." She drew a ragged breath.

"And what am I to say?" His eyes brows narrowed. "Whose baby is the milk for?" The baby seemed to settle down and doze, and he set it back in the drawer. "For my deaf sister's baby? Born out of wedlock? Presumably raped by her own step-father?" He chewed his bottom lip. "I don't think so." He tossed the towel back on the counter.

Disconcerted, Anna drew back. A strange air of calm and civility washed over her. "Will Gibbs, you know this little one won't survive on just drops here and there."

"It happens. My mother lost two after Maribelle. If Della doesn't take to her, she won't survive." He shot her a stern look.

"And I know what you are thinking, but I don't want you naming her or any of that."

They both turned to the table. Another squeak came from the drawer, and a little fist jerked loose and knocked into its face. Anna leaned over and tucked the arm back in the blanket. The baby looked up with blurry eyes as if begging for a chance at life.

"I cannot abide by your thinking," Anna said, without looking at him. Anytime she'd crossed Mr. Plugg, she'd paid a painful price. Her head twitched down in rapid secession. "You hold her and care for her yourself, and I can't…" *Blast it.* She took a calming breath. "…See you *not* wanting her to live." Her chest ached with the thought that this baby had dropped into her hands only hours ago, and she couldn't, she wouldn't let her suffer and die.

"Will." She met his eyes. "Listen…to…me." She touched his cheek. "She *has* to live." Her eyes pooled. "This baby has to live." She choked. "I can't have my hands near another infant's death."

IT TOOK WILL a moment to understand Anna was referring to what happened to her own baby brother. He'd seen this determination in her eyes before. The first days of coming to this family he thought she would crumble under all the needs, but she daily pressed into every burden with a gentle fortitude. In so many ways, she was the greatest answer from God, and he almost didn't have the faith to believe it. And now as her husband, lover, and yes, friend he wanted to please her; make her happy.

"I just don't want to see you hurt," He searched her eyes. "You've been through a lot, Anna." Pulling her hand from his face, he kissed her palm.

"Just as you have," she said wistfully.

"But I've barely ever thought of being a father, having a child. You said this was your only dream." He stilled as loose tears rolled down her cheeks. He moved closer and cupped her face and wiped the tears aside with his thumbs. "Let's make a compromise." He waited until she nodded. "We'll think of something to help her eat, but I don't want you to name her yet." His arms encircled her body. She returned his warm embrace with her face resting against his shoulder.

It still amazed him to relish her touch, her warmth. Did she know the encompassing power she had over him now? She'd become his beautiful companion, his comfort in this torrid life. More trust and hope had taken root, more than he could even dream of. He did not doubt her ability to care for an infant, maybe he just wasn't ready for the truth in living, kicking, squalling form. He hadn't been able to protect his sister. Would this baby be a constant reminder of that?

33

THE NEXT MORNING Anna scooped another helping of oatmeal for Milo as Will tried again to cradle the unhappy infant while dropping drips of milk on her tongue.

"I'm done." Maribelle pushed her bowl forward. "Can I hold the baby now?"

"Not yet." Will bounced his arm up and down. "She's unhappy or just hungry." Will wearily looked toward Anna. Neither had gotten more than a few hours of sleep.

Nathan appeared from the blanket opening with an empty bowl. "Della finished all this." He set the bowl on the table and glanced at the baby. "But when I asked her about the baby, she said, give it away." He frowned. "Is this the sign for away?" He held his finger near his chin and pushed it from his face.

"Yes," Milo and Maribelle said simultaneously.

"All right," he nodded. "I thought that's what she said."

Will shook his head and handed the baby to Anna. "I need to get out to the fields."

"Will," Anna pleaded, "she can't go another day without nursing." They all looked at each other. The baby piped in with a short squeak.

"Why can't you use those?" Milo pointed to Anna's chest. Nathan and Will looked away, shaking their heads. "What?" Milo croaked. "That's what you told me they were for," Milo squinted at Nathan.

"I...I..." Nathan shook his head, holding his hands up, then backed away. "He asked one day. I...I..."

If she wasn't so tired, Anna might have smiled at the confusion. "Only the woman who births the baby can feed the baby." Anna touched the soft velvet ears of the darling peanut. "And Della doesn't want to."

"Maybe you could just try to Anna." Maribelle's round eyes pleaded. "That's what you always tell Milo and me—just try."

Anna shook her head and stilled, chewing on a thought. What if she showed Della how painless and easy it could be? "Nathan, could you take Milo with you this morning?" She turned to Milo. "We'll do your lessons this afternoon."

Nathan opened the door, and Milo followed him out.

"I wondered if Della could see how easy it is." She looked curious at Will. "Would you help me get her attention?"

He nodded and followed her through the curtain. She handed him the baby as she sat on the bed. His eyes looked to the side and then back to her as she unbuttoned the front of her dress and pulled her corset and chemise loose. "You're in here to get Della to watch." She smiled at his flushed face as she reached for the baby. Not sure if the baby would even latch on, Anna pulled the infant in close to her skin. "Tell Della to..." Anna swallowed hard. The baby found what she'd wanted all along. "To...to...see how easy...." Will shook his head and tried to sign to Della to watch. Even Maribelle came in to get Della's attention. Determined to help, Maribelle tapped on Della's arm as she held her rag doll to her chest for her own example.

"Can you get...?" Anna looked wide-eyed down at the nursing infant, the baby's hunger magnifying the sensitivity in her empty breast. "Get...her to turn towards me? This baby is going to get furious at any moment." Anna's impromptu plan fell apart as Della turned from everyone's attempt.

Will walked from the room and brought in the pitcher of milk and the towel. Sitting next to Anna, he dripped the corner in the milk and set it on her breast. Anna pushed the corner of the baby's mouth away from her nipple as the milk rolled in. Anna glanced back to where Della was rolled into a ball. "We need her to do this, not me." She blew out an astonished breath. Knowing she was barren, never in a hundred years did she think this kind of maternal moment could actually happen to her.

"I said we would find a way to feed her." Will dipped the towel in the milk and held it again. "Though as much as I am enjoying this, I can't be the nursemaid assistant all day." He nodded to Maribelle. "We want Della to do this. But today if she won't, will you help Anna dip the milk on the towel?" Maribelle came close. "See how I do it?" He showed her.

She nodded to Will. "I can do that."

"Thank you, Maribelle, you are a good helper." Will handed her the pitcher of milk. "Sit here next to Anna." He stood with a certain glimmer in his eyes that made Anna's stomach feel like something was wrong and very right at the same time. He bent forward with a twitch in his smile. His first kiss and the second one were fuller than his usual peck goodbye. The knowing smile he had when he turned away made her flush from head to toe.

ON THE THIRD day of her stand-in feeding of the baby without any response from Della, Will agreed to take Anna to town. She'd told him it was safe to confide in Mrs. Hart. Even though the baby seemed attached to their makeshift feeding system, she didn't know if nursing her every hour was really necessary or if the poor thing was calmed from the small improvised suckling.

ANNA STEPPED DOWN from the wagon as Will called Maribelle to go with him to the lumber yard. Her feet moved forward, but her body broke out in a cold sweat. Anna held her hand on the doorknob of the mercantile and debated calling them both back. A fear, close to panic, suddenly overcame her. Urgently she wanted to be home with the baby in her arms. What were they thinking, leaving a hungry infant with Nathan?

Two ladies with feathery spring hats bumped Anna back a step as they tried to leave the store. She took a deep breath and walked in, wandering among the baby section, like she'd done many times in the past—but today it held importance like never before.

"Anna," Mrs. Hart came near, "did you bring me some of your lovely baby gowns today?"

"Not today." Anna looked around the store to see if they would be interrupted.

"You look a little pale, dear." Mrs. Hart laid a comforting hand on Anna's elbow. Have you been feeling all right?"

"Do you have a moment? I need to confide in you, and I don't want to interrupt your work." Anna looked around again, feeling another cold sweat coming on. "It concerns Mr. Gibbs sister, the one who is deaf?"

Mrs. Hart nodded. "Yes, yes."

"Someone had...little to our knowledge...someone..." Anna looked around and blew out a breath. "She delivered a baby girl four days ago."

"Oh, gracious," Mrs. Hart covered her open mouth.

"I found her in the woods and helped deliver the infant. Because she can't talk, she's being difficult and...just...*so* difficult. Miraculously, the babe seems healthy. It's the sweetest thing you ever saw." Anna lifted a quick smile.

"The flannel from a few weeks ago?" Mrs. Hart dipped her chin. "How disconcerting for all of you."

"I don't know what to do." Anna sighed. "I've tried everything to get Della to notice the baby or take a little interest." Anna stopped as a woman with her son came close to finger the baby blankets. Anna and Mrs. Hart took a step away. "But she won't. We've been giving the poor thing drops of cow's milk and—"

"Oh, that won't do." Mrs. Hart turned. "You're going to need a pap boat."

Anna felt her nerves quiet for the first time in days. Mrs. Hart turned and handed her a little silver bowl with a tiny spout. "You need to mix up some bread and flour. And enough water and a little sugar if you want. But," Mrs. Hart shook her head, "I can tell from your voice you're already attached to that poor infant."

"Yes, ma'am." Anna looked at the floor.

"Anna," Mrs. Hart said, hushed, "most babies whose mothers don't feed them, don't live. Please, I hate to see you trying so hard. Maybe the babe isn't meant to be here." She rubbed her arm. "What if she has all those problems your Della has—what a desperate life."

"I already love her and want her." The words slipped out unbridled. "I know about desperate lives. I have one, and I'm overcoming one. I know if I can do it, anyone can."

Mrs. Hart pressed her lips together as she studied the young woman for a moment then puckered them to the side, causing a dimple to appear in her cheek. "All right, what else?"

"I will try the pap boat and limit the cow's milk," Anna said. "Do you know of any wet nurses close to us?"

Mrs. Hart shook her head, "No, I don't, but," She walked back to where she had her spices and flipped open a small bag. "take this fenugreek seed and hide it in with tea leaves. Every new mother I know says four or five cups later it makes the milk flow like a fountain in a city square." Mrs. Hart chuckled. "Della won't be able *not* to nurse."

Anna took the small bag and the pap boat. She opened her reticule to find her money.

"No, no." Mrs. Hart put her hand over her efforts. "Your hand-tatted baby gowns are loved here. I know you have your hands full, but in between feedings I would love to have some more."

Anna thanked her and stepped from the store. Waiting out front for Will and Maribelle, she looked long at the two items. *In between feedings*, Mrs. Hart had said. She hadn't told her she was the one getting along with the wet nursing or at least pacifying. She lifted the little brown bag, one to help milk flow and give a baby a chance at life. The pap boat a hopeful attempt. But without some change in Della... She sighed, chewing her bottom lip. Why not try the tea for herself? This little girl was close to needing a name.

34

A WEEK LATER, Will came into their room at bedtime. Della had returned to sleep on her pallet by the rock fireplace.

"You're okay with Della helping in the fields today?" Will asked, as he sat on the bed and pulled off his boots. "I had her walk and pull hornworms off the leaves. Nathan hauled the bucket when it got heavy."

Anna laid on her side in the bed with the babe nestled against her breast. "I am." She feathered her fingers across the baby's neck and face. "She's begun to speak to me again." The babies arm swung up, and Anna met it with her finger as the little fingers entwined around Anna's. "But whenever I would offer for her to hold the baby, she would growl and turn away or go outside." Anna sighed. "Milo and Maribelle take turns holding her, and I see Della watching them. I'm still at my wit's end, but at least she's speaking to me."

"That reminds me." Will stood pulling down his suspenders and yanking his shirt up and over his head. "My grandfather came by today."

"How did it go?" Anna asked, watching the baby's eyelids open and droop close.

"I left it back in the barn, but he brought you a cradleboard for the baby, for a papoose."

"Really?" She looked up at him.

"I thanked him. It was a peace offering of sorts. He still thinks you're trouble." Will smiled and put his knee on the bed. Reaching for the light, he hesitated.

"But this is where trouble really is." He crossed his arms over his chest and looked down at the baby nestled against her. "Can a man be jealous of a baby? No, that's not it, maybe envious?" His eyes held hers, and he reached out for the infant. "I do like that you can pacify the little squealer. But I don't want to share my bed every night."

ANNA FROWNED AND wrapped the blanket around her bundle then lifted her up. Will took her in his hands."

Anna rose on one elbow as Will put the baby in her drawer-bed for the night. "Her name is Charity." She waited to read Will's expression. He didn't appear angry, only lost in thought perhaps.

"I figured by now you might have named her." He blew out the light and laid beside her. Pulling her onto his chest, he tucked her hair behind her ears. "And dare I ask what her last name is?"

"Gibbs," Anna whispered. "Like ours." Softly she brushed her lips against his.

His eyes closed and he kissed her fully without a trace of reservation. "Mmm." He began to nuzzle her cheek and neck. "I see how this works."

"I don't want to disrupt your delicate…" She stopped. Oh, she loved the way he massaged her back. "Sensibilities. Not that any of us have much of that." She smiled and pulled back. She caressed his handsome face with feathery fingers as his ardent expression and dark eyes wooed her.

"Charity can be ours. Many a family member has adopted another as their own." Anna's stomach flipped. He was too attractive for convincing tonight.

He nodded with understanding and a faint smile before he closed the distance to her waiting lips.

A FEW WEEKS later, Anna walked the garden next to the cabin with Della and Maribelle. Charity slept in the cradleboard, strapped like a little butterfly safe in a cocoon on her back. She looked back and forth at the abundance of vegetables on their way. Maybe it was just the spring air, but each day brought more vitality to her body and soul. Della had returned to the family in sign communication and help. The only thing she didn't want to do was care for the baby.

Anna wondered about a mother who could never hear her child's cries—it must limit them to want to offer care. The only reason she questioned Della's missing maternal instincts was that something bizarre was happening to her. After weeks of brewing the tea for herself and allowing Charity to nurse at her breast, the baby's squalls could only be soothed with her nursing. Once she'd settled, Anna could get a few drinks into her mouth with the pap boat. The sweet little thing was gaining weight. Weekly a new roll of fat found home against those sticks she had for limbs. And when Charity cried, she could feel it rattle in her own body. Like an urgency only satisfied at her bosom.

A week ago, Otis had brought Tallie for Sunday supper. The children were so excited to have company that Anna had little chance to talk freely with her. She did ask about any women who were nursing around the shanties. Tallie had thought of two or three women she knew of, but Anna didn't ask more. She knew Will would never agree to take any help from the Plugg plantation. The one mystery she might have asked Tallie about but hadn't been able to find a quiet moment to talk was that she rarely used the pap boat anymore. Anna stopped and bent over, packing some dirt around a sagging carrot shoot. Had God done a miracle within her body? Could a woman who was barren, sustain an infant from a once-empty breast?

Anna shook her head and watched Maribelle and Della from the end of the row. They signed back and forth about something to bake today. Anna carefully touched the hard thickness around her ample chest. How could it be? A breeze blew the sandy strains of her hair across her face. God had done so many miracles in her life. Delivered her from desperation, given her a good husband and family who'd taught her how to give and receive love. Her eyes misted with tears as she stood. And now this little gift of Charity. Anna peeked over her shoulder. She didn't know if she could contain another ounce of joy.

After they'd told the family the baby's name, Will had read from the Bible, "Charity suffers long, and charity doesn't envy or boast." Remembering God's word, Anna smiled walking toward the girls with Charity strapped to her back. She thought, *We all should live with God's hope and faith, but the greatest thing from God and for us to give to others is God's charity.* Wiping her hands on her apron, she stopped. Maybe with these changes in her body, she needed to work on holding greater faith.

LATE THAT EVENING, Will walked around the bed and spied the two tucked in the blanket. Anna laid on her side with Charity snuggled up against her. "Sorry I missed supper. My grandfather comes with a few rabbits now and then. I think he just wants somebody to sit around the spit and talk old tales with." He began to undress.

"I understand. Nathan told me he saw him under the trees." Anna took a deep breath, looking down at the sleeping Charity. She wanted to tell Will about the milk supply for the baby. Her stomach twisted, maybe she should have tried to get Della to take the tea? He blew out the light and laid down. Laying on his side and reaching for her hand, he recited his nightly thanks to God for the crop, weather, his grandfather, and siblings. He thanked God for her, and all she brought to his life. She swallowed hard, another quiver of emotion tried to squeeze her throat. He continued and thanked God for Charity. He prayed health and thanksgiving over the child, not yet called his daughter. Squeezing her hand, she knew he was done and would listen while she prayed for the wisdom to raise their family. Safety and protection over all the children. She waited. His deep breathing signaled he'd already fallen asleep.

Sometime in the middle of the night, Charity let out a squall, and Will shot up. Often, Anna had to hold back a snicker. He woke like someone was chasing him.

"It's all right." Anna reached for his arm. "I've got her right here."

He fumbled for the matches and held the flame to the lantern. "What do you need? Do you want cow's milk or the pap boat?" He sat on the corner of the bed, rubbing his face.

"Neither," Anna said, as she slipped her nightgown down off her shoulder. Charity rooted and began suckling.

Will looked back at them, squinting. "But that substitute won't last long." He yawned.

"Will, I've wanted to tell you something." She reached over Charity and touched his arm. "But I don't know how to say it."

"I knew it." Sighing, he twisted toward her and leaned his elbow on his leg. Raking his fingers through his long dark hair, he looked at the bed, shaking his head.

"What?" Anna pulled on his arm. "What do you know?"

"You're pregnant." He muffled still looking down. "I could tell you've gained…" He finally looked up at her and twirled his finger toward her chest."

"I told you I was barren," she whispered. "I don't think I could ever…" She stopped. Is early pregnancy what made this milk come in? "Oh, now you have me confused. I thought nursing stopped a woman from being fertile."

"What do you mean nursing? The milk from the pap boat?" He squinted at her.

"Will, take a close look at Charity. I'm not just pacifying her. I'm feeding her."

"Are you sure?" He scratched his head. "Can that happen?"

"I haven't used the pap boat in days. She's getting milk from me." Anna stilled, watching his face freeze expressionless.

"Is it because you are with child?" His voice was sympathetic.

"I never thought that I…" Her mouth hung open. "I…don't think so." She blinked, confused. "Would you be upset if I wasn't?" She slipped her gown back over her shoulder and turned Charity over on her tummy. Patting the sleeping baby's back, Charity released a small burp.

"No, never." He brushed his fingers across her chin. "I'm not upset, I got sidetracked thinking of all mouths to feed, and how many drawers can we fit on the floor of this cabin."

He lifted a small smile, and his eyes relaxed. "And now you are feeding her, that's one less to feed, I guess." He took the quiet baby from their bed. "She's getting big." He leaned over and tucked her in her drawer.

After he blew out the light, he laid down next to her and held her. "You have been her mother from birth. Maybe the milk is just God's way of confirming the bond you have with her."

Anna pulled back to face him. "But you know, never in a thousand years did I want to take this away from Della."

"We all know that." He held her close and kissed her forehead. "And you fought for her to live. You are in the right place as her mother."

Mother. The word seemed so foreign in light of her unorthodox life. Baby Charity's *mother.* Anna let it touch her again. Maybe she hadn't allowed her heart to hold such a lost dream. But when Will said it, the dream blossomed in her breast, finding its home back in her being.

35

THE WARM, SUNNY afternoon felt as good as butter on warm bread when Nathan dropped her off in front of the mercantile the following week. Anna struggled to balance Charity, the bag of new baby things for Mrs. Hart and open the door. "I should have brought your cradleboard," she smiled to the sweet, wide-eyes looking up at her from the crook of her arm.

The rich smells of new merchandise for sale wafted around Anna as Mrs. Hart looked up from a thick ledger and smiled. "There you are!" She came around the long wooden counter. "And look who you've brought." She touched the blanket around Charity. "She looks healthy. You must be doing something right."

"Thank you for all your help." Anna handed her the bag. "I have a surprise in there." She smiled and followed Mrs. Hart to the counter.

Mrs. Hart pulled the new baby items from the bag. "What are these?" she beamed. "Bonnets! With the matching tatting around the brim, same as the gowns." She looked to Anna wide-eyed, "They are lovely. Just lovely." She fingered the satin ribbon Anna had used for under the chin.

"I don't know why I hadn't thought to make them before." Anna chuckled. "Well, actually, I do. Will's grandfather gave us a cradleboard for this little papoose. She loves traveling around on my back, but as the sun is getting hotter, I wanted something to keep her head shaded. Charity was my practice. I think with the length of ribbon, they will fit up to a year."

Mrs. Hart held them up. "I think we should sell them as a set." She smiled at the baby. "You've named her Charity? Or has Della?"

Anna took a deep breath, searched the store, and felt her stomach drop. The reverend's wife was being helped by Mr. Hart. "Will and I are going to raise her as ours." She lowered her voice. "I tried over and over to get Della to warm up to her."

Mrs. Hart nodded and flipped the pages of her ledger. "The way you've taken on the care of the other children, this one will fit right in. They are so lucky to have you."

Anna looked again catching Mrs. Horworth staring at her. She turned and pulled Charity closer. The back of her skin crawled as she knew without looking, the harsh woman approached.

"Well, unless God is making babies in less than six months. Who does this little one belong to?" The short square-faced woman frowned looking at Charity.

Anna crinkled a smiled back to Mrs. Hart and pulled out her list for purchases. "These things, too." Anna's throat constricted, couldn't the busybody see she was with Mrs. Hart.

"Will and I have taken on the care for a family member. She is unable to…" Anna sputtered. Mrs. Horworth knew of Della's disabilities. Would she deem Charity demon-possessed too? "Well, she needed some extra help."

"Quite the helper you are." Mrs. Horworth's tone held little sincerity.

Anna forged a smile. "Really I should have come by sooner to thank you. Before you were to throw me out into the cold dark rain *in the dead of winter*—you pushed two gullible people into a marriage. And little did I know," Anna watched Mrs. Horworth's slow sneer, "that it was truly the providence of God. Will is a strong and caring husband. The children have come to fill my heart and hands with an abundance of love I never knew possible. Even this little doll is a gift to my life that I would never have had if it weren't for you." She grinned at Charity and touched her soft cheek.

Mrs. Horworth's chin pushed down, making the rolls on her neck protrude. Quickly she tilted her chin up and cleared her throat. "Beyond your young years, I do understand the ways of God. I'm glad you now see my interference as a blessing." Mrs. Horworth lifted a patronizing smile.

Anna nodded back. She felt the truth of her own words and wanted to hold no malice against the woman. She knew God's forgiveness and grace had changed her. As grace had been freely given to her, she would give it in return.

Mrs. Hart slid a large wrapped package toward Anna. "I believe I got everything on your list."

Anna nodded to both women and took the heavy bag of supplies in one arm and balanced Charity in the other. She stepped from the store, feeling thankful for the clear spring air and that Mrs. Hart hadn't said anything about her request for more fenugreek seeds.

A couple of blocks down the street, the sun dappled the back of their tan horse who waited patiently with their wagon. Anna decided to tuck the packages in the wagon then look up and down the sidewalk for the medical dispensary. Even though everything about lovemaking had changed with Will for a husband, she didn't understand how her womb could work. With such irregular lady's days, she didn't feel pregnant. It was so difficult to communicate with her own husband about the fenugreek, and breast milk, and possible pregnancy, how would she explain her unusual changes to anyone else?

Carefully balancing Charity, Anna lifted on her toes and slid her shopping in the back of their wagon. A sudden shadow blocked the light of the day.

"Looky here, Floyd."

The sneering words from behind her made her knees buckle. She turned quickly to walk around the wagon. Bernard Plugg's massive girth blocked her path.

"Excuse me. Get out of my way," her tone firm with a slight tremor. Wrapping both arms around the baby, she huddled Charity against her body.

Floyd Plugg now boxed her in from behind. "It's our dear, old step-mother. The murdering sow," he said.

"She can't be a sow. She never produced anything of use. Never even had enough meat on her bones for a good snack." Bernard ran his finger down her face. Anna flinched away and tried to find an opening from their smelly round bodies. Charity began to squirm under her tight hold.

"She must be a gilt then," Floyd pulled on the blanket and Anna twisted away.

"Touch her, and you'll be seeing your father in hell," Anna growled, shocking herself at the words flying from her lips.

"Oh, oh, oh." Bernard held his hands up. "Is that so?" He bent low in her ear. "We know where you live. We been hungry for a lynchin',and we know just the right slave woman and her son. Maybe if we can't get you to swing for murder, then you can come out one fine morning and find them hangin' from a tree." Floyd said, his fat belly pinning her and Charity against the wagon. Just as desperation told her to scream for help...

"Anna!"

She heard her name as the Plugg brothers backed off and crossed the street.

Nathan ran to her side as soon as she began to wilt. He grabbed her elbows as Charity let out a cry.

"Are you all right? Did they hurt the baby?" he huffed.

"Can you hold her for a moment?" Anna passed her over to him. "I'm shaking so bad that I don't trust myself." Anna's fingers gripped the wagon as she laid her forehead against the wood. Such fear hadn't invaded her being in months. How could the sound of their voices take her blood and bones back to the pit of darkness she had lived in?

"Let me help you," Nathan supported her arm as she climbed into the wagon. He handed Charity up to her, and Anna tried to comfort the squalling baby. Charity continued wailing as Nathan jumped up on the wagon.

"No, they didn't hurt us," Anna tried to jiggle the baby. "I think she must be feeling the same terror I am." She glanced over at Nathan. "Threats and intimidation," Anna said and shook her head as Nathan *snicked* to the horse and the wagon headed out. "I *didn't* kill their father."

WILL PACED AROUND the black pot in the front of the cabin. She knew as soon as Nathan retold what he saw in town, Will would stop everything and want to hear from her what had happened.

"They said they'd have a lynching? You think they meant Tallie and Otis?" Will stomped by red-faced.

Before Anna could answer, the cabin door opened and Milo stepped out.

"Leave us be Milo!"

Milo stepped back in and closed the door. Regret lined Will's face. She knew the regret came from his raising his voice at the boy. She'd never heard him raise his voice to any of his brothers or sisters.

"I'd forgotten what it was like to live with someone making their aim to bully." She shook her head. "I was just in the wrong place at the wrong time, and I was foolish."

"What, what did you do?" Will stopped pacing and eyed her.

"Floyd pulled on Charity's blanket." Anna rubbed the side of her face. "I told him if he touched her, he'd be in hell with his father."

Will dropped his chin and looked at her through the top of his eyes. "You did?"

"A woman should never provoke a man's anger." She rubbed her forehead. "It just flew from my mouth. I…I … She's tiny and helpless, Will." Her voice cracked, and her eyes pooled.

"If they ever hurt you or Charity or any of mine, I'll shoot them in the head and never look back." He started to pace again. "If you want, I will try to get to Otis and have him watch his back."

"That's all Tallie and Otis have ever known. A master coming for them, taking from them, abusing them. Watching their back is normal life for them." Anna swiped her face, gritting her teeth. "I thought I'd let my hate go. I felt a chunk of it leave today when I saw Mrs. Horworth." She shook her head and rolled her eyes. "God knows I've tried to let the Pluggs go."

Will came to her and wrapped her in her arms. "They'll cool off, but until then, I'll get another rifle from my grandfather, then we'll have one for the barn and one for the house. We will protect our own."

Anna exhaled into his shirt. Mothers protected their brood. What would God say if she shot first and asked later?

36

ANNA DROPPED THE hoe in the garden's soft, dark soil. The cabin had gotten too quiet after Maribelle asked if she could go with Della out to the fields this afternoon. The rifle lay across her hamper of dry clothes, and Charity slept tight and safe on her back. She'd a few minutes to weed, and then a loaf of bread would be ready to come from the oven. Its fresh warm scent beckoned her to check on it. She set the hoe against the fence. The small stove could be temperamental, she reasoned.

Entering the cabin, she took a rag and opened the heavy stove door. The top was dark, and she was smart to pull it from the heat. Popping it from the pan to cool on a rack, she tapped the hard top as her mouth watered. Debating about a thick slice with butter for herself, she grabbed the knife and stilled. Did she hear something? Charity hadn't made a peep from sleeping strapped on her back. Was it a wagon from the road to the south?

She went to the door and looked around, her heartbeat spiking. Sounds of horse hooves came closer, and she gripped the knife. "Good Lord," she clenched her other hand into a fist. The rifle was outside with the laundry basket. Still clutching the knife, she came to the stoop and looked out. One of the riders she recognized as the short, balding man from the sheriff's office. She put the knife back on the counter. As long as she didn't see any Plugg brothers, she could steady her breathing.

Covering the glare of the sun with her hand to her forehead, she nodded to the two men as they came to a stop in front of the cabin. The lawman from the night she'd nowhere to go, pushed his wide-brimmed hat back.

"Mrs. Plugg" He leaned his forearms on the saddle horn. "You remember Sheriff Pruett."

"Mrs. *Gibbs*," Anna corrected him, nodding at the sheriff.

"Yes, Mrs. Gibbs. Is your husband about?" The sheriff glanced down to the rifle leaning against the basket of laundry.

"He's just out there, past the large barn. Would you like me to get him?"

"No, Ma'am. I don't think we have to bother him. Just a few simple questions." The sheriff pulled his hat forward and scratched his eyebrows. "Ma'am is that baby strapped to your back your's and Alfred Pluggs?"

"No." Anna tried to hide the raucous disgust the question brought to her tone.

The sheriff's wrinkled eyes drooped. "Ma'am, whose baby is that?"

Anna stilled. Were they going to take Della away? Could they? Was it Mrs. Horworth, the evil nosey—

"Mine." She spouted.

"Ahh, Laud, woman." The older sheriff swung off the horse and looked around. "Can you leave the baby with someone and come into town? We'll just be an hour or so. Maybe two, but it will save you a chicken coop of time."

Anna shook her head. Was this a trap set by the Plugg brothers? These men didn't seem dangerous. "No, sir. She must come with me. Only I can feed her. What is it that you can't just ask me right here?"

"You're telling me, that baby is yours, and only you can feed it?" The sheriff put his weight on one hip and lifted his thick brows, staring her down.

"That's what I said." Anna felt her patience thinning. "That hasn't been a crime that I know of."

The sheriff walked closer and pulled his handcuffs from his belt. "It is if you are being accused of murder." He snapped one over her wrist and pulled her other wrist out front and snapped it on.

"Anna Pl...I mean Mrs. Gibbs, you are under arrest for the murder of Alfred Plugg."

He pulled her forward to his horse.

"Sir, please stop!" She strained to see someone out by the big barn. Jerking aside, she tried to turn from his leading.

"Ma'am. I can hog tie you if you want. The Plugg brothers say they have someone who saw you push Mr. Plugg into the ice and hold him under."

"They're lying! I tried to pull him out! He was too heavy for me." Tears rising, she pleaded with the older sheriff. "Those indecent liars saw me in town yesterday. They pinned the baby and me against the wagon." Her words came out in short bursts as she tried to find the right words through her growing panic. "I...I...was upset, and I provoked them." Both men listened without response or sympathy. "Please, sir, let me get my husband."

The sheriff grabbed her at the waist and tossed her belly first onto the saddle. "He can come see you in jail." Twisting left to right, she tried to sit up and search for just one of the children, what would they think? "Can you please tell them where I am?" She pulled herself forward with the saddle horn and pleaded with the other short man. "There is a slate on the table. Please," she cried. The sheriff had already jumped up behind her and Charity. He nodded to the other man, "Go ahead, Donny." He kicked the horse forward.

Anna tried to look back. "How can you put a mother and baby in jail?" she sobbed. "What kind of lawman would do that?" Her chin twitched down.

"The law is fair for all. I wasn't gonna take you in. I told them boys you didn't have no reason to kill your husband. Pluggs' one of the richest men in the land, slaves and stock aplenty in this county. No reason for a woman to want to be widowed. I told them they had no cause."

Anna stopping looked back and tried to listen to his words. "Why am I going to jail? Why can't you listen to my side? To the truth." She felt Charity stirring against her back.

The sheriff let out a long sigh. "I'm sorry, miss, with all that family money." He cleared his throat and straightened up on the horse. "They got a fancy lawyer from Lexington. I'm probably not supposed to tell you this, but I heard them talkin'. Something about needin' a motive. So I was supposed to come ask you about this here baby."

The back of her throat constricted painfully. "What? What about this baby? How can it matter?"

"Looks like your motive was to kill Mr. Plugg so you could have your lover's baby."

"What? No! That is ridiculous. This is a family member's baby. I've never given birth. I'm barren."

Charity picked the wrong time to begin to fuss. The sheriff told her she'd better not change her story around with him. He wasn't the judge, but he wasn't stupid either.

As they entered the town, Anna hung her head. Charity was in full bawl, and as usual, Anna's breasts reacted to her demanding cries. The sheriff jumped off the back and tied the horse. What could she do? Her wrists were cuffed together. She glanced at the mercantile on the next block. Could she get word to Mrs. Hart? The sheriff pulled on her arms as she and Charity slid from his saddle. Maybe if she asked for a pap boat? The sheriff pulled her inside as she looked over her shoulder. Her forearm brushed her full breasts, and her chin tics began relentlessly. The tears formed again, only distracted by Charity's hungry cries. The sheriff's keys rattled as he opened a cell and undid her cuffs.

"Just have a seat. Maybe you can get her out of that Ingin thing and quiet her down." He locked the door and turned away.

Anna swallowed her sobs and unlaced Charity from the pack. A rancid smell caught her attention. An old tin bucket, sitting in the corner was the chamber pot. Glancing up from the baby, she could see the urine stains all over the cinder block wall. Turning back to Charity, she tried to swing her in her arms and smile at her. Maybe it was her red tear-soaked face, but the baby would have none of it.

"Please baby girl. Please." Anna crooned through her hiccups. "Momma can't feed you right now. There are too many people watching." Another cry got trapped in her throat. She held Charity against her shoulder and walked in a small circle, patting her back. The baby swung her head back, and Anna had to catch it in her hand. "I know, love. I know, love." Charity howled louder, and Anna turned her to face away, bouncing her.

"Can't ya just feed her?" The deputy named Donny came to the bars.

Anna felt her sorrow turn into rage. "Is that my fresh baked bread under your arm?"

He looked at the floor and whirled away.

"Sheriff this can't be right," she pleaded. "This baby cannot be...in ...such a filthy place. This jail is what is upsetting her."

He looked up from his writing on his desk. "If I come in there, you won't like where I put her. She's evidence now."

"Evidence?" Anna felt every muscle weaken. "Good Lord in heaven, she's just a baby."

"And a loud one," he smirked and turned around. The deputy leaned over and said something in the sheriff's ear before he walked out. Charity arched her back, screaming and butted her head to Anna's chest.

Nostrils flaring, back stiff, and sucking in short whimpers for air, Anna began to slowly unbutton the front of her dress. As long as his back was turned, though she already knew he was no gentlemen, she could hide Charity's feeding. Trying to force the searing tears back, she sat on the dirty cot and turned away from the man at his desk. Pulling her dress off her shoulder and her chemise back, the room instantly quieted as Charity began to nurse. The very thing she thought was a gift from God would be her undoing. If she didn't birth her, then how could she be feeding her right now? He was probably watching her this minute. Writing on his paper— *...the woman who denied giving birth was seen putting the babe to the breast. Baby quit screaming as soon as it* *was satisfied with the mother's milk* — sufficient proof for the Plugg's fancy lawyer from Lexington.

"Oh, Charity," she whispered, wiping her tears off the baby's cheek. "I'm so sorry. I don't know what else to do." She gulped, her lungs squeezed for air. "When we are separated, I will always love you, my little one. Always." Anna curled over the hungry baby and wept with deep grief from her long incomprehensible life of loss and misfortune.

37

RIDING HARD TO town, Will chastised himself for not paying more attention. Why hadn't he pressed her about the details of Alfred Plugg's death? He tried to pray and listen for direction, but his mind circled into bargaining with God. He would give up the land, the crop, everything he'd worked for to see her free. They could take the family and start over somewhere else. Pulling to a stop, he jumped from the back of his unsaddled horse. She'd asked about getting a lawyer, and he shrugged it off. Heaven above, this was a ludicrous mistake. He yanked open the door of the sheriff's office.

"I demand," he caught the agitated eye of the sheriff and tried to steady his harsh tone, "that you release my wife and baby at once." His chest swelled, reminding himself not to grab the lawman by the collar. Before the man could answer, Anna made a squeak in the jail cell closest to the entrance.

She stood inches from the iron bars. Her eyes were red and watery. Using her hands, she signed to him. "This can't be your baby." She held her lips tight, but her eyes demanded he understand.

He raised his palms up and shook them back and forth. Then tapped his middle knuckles against his chin. "What? What's wrong?"

"She can't be your baby." Anna signed back.

He brushed his hand along his temple and made a fist in front of his chin. Was it the right sign for 'why not?' He gritted his teeth, wishing he'd paid more attention to the others as they learned the simple words.

"Hey. None of that secret Injin language, you two got." The sheriff stood from his desk. "You can talk to her," he sneered at Will. "You have to use words."

Will took in a deep breath and bore into the sheriff. "Why is my wife in jail?"

"I'd already done told her this." The sheriff nodded to Anna, and her chin tics bounced up and down. "The Plugg brothers got some fancy lawyer, and they're going to press charges for the murder of their father. They have a witness that saw her push him in the ice water and hold him under."

Will gripped his head and rolled his eyes. "And I have a witness that said he fell and knocked himself out."

"Well," the sheriff shrugged, "maybe so. But since you two gone an had a baby, and Mr. Plugg has only been dead six months, they figure you two had a reason to see him dead."

Will stalked two steps toward Anna, hesitated, and then spun back to the sheriff. "Who can prove she wasn't pregnant with Mr. Plugg's child when we married?"

"I already asked her." The sheriff glanced at Anna. "She said it wasn't his baby."

Will felt the air leave his lungs. "No, it's not Plugg's child," he said emphatically and stepped closer to look at the baby. Charity slept in the cradleboard laying on the cot. "And it's not my child, either." He reached in and found Anna's shaking cold hands, and tried to rub some warmth into them. He turned back to the sheriff. "The child belongs to my sister. She gave birth under a tree on our property about seven weeks ago. My sister is deaf. We try to talk to her with hand signals. We have an idea who the father is, but the child is a bastard, and so Anna and I call her our own."

"Uh huh." The sheriff rolled his tongue inside his cheek. "I ain't no midwife, but my wife birthed all five of our youngin's at home. No sister of hers could walk in and feed them. Only the woman who birthed them has the means to feed 'em."

Will stared long at Anna's pale, drawn face and shook his head. A rock fell hard into his gut. He was beginning to understand the implications. "Come here." He whispered, pulling her close with the cold metal between them. "We'll work this out." He cupped her jerking chin as the tears fell over his fingers. She closed her eyes and entwined her fingers with his.

"Listen to me," he said, as she opened her eyes. "We can fight this and we will. It's just one person's word against another's."

"You have an idea." Anna wearily breathed out, "But those brothers are as mean and horrible as their father. Like a bulldog in a fight, they never let go." Her watery green eyes looked to the side. "The sheriff doesn't believe us. I had to feed her an hour ago. She was screaming and I—I—tried but," Anna bit back a sob.

"Of course, you did." He wiped her tears with his thumbs. "We could have Della tell the sheriff or the judge."

"And who would interpret for her signs? One of us? Nathan, her own brother? Even though they could, not the children. Milo and Maribelle are too innocent to be embroiled in this." She frowned, rubbing her eyes. "I've thought of everything that could possibly prove what we say and dismissed it all at the same time." Her shoulders dropped.

She looked at Charity, and this time her chin was still. Barely above a whisper, she said, "All I know is I love you and the children. Every moment with your family has been the best moments of my life. Thank you for that."

"*Our* family." He tipped her chin until she looked at him. "You are the reason Maribelle sings little songs all day and Milo can read and add. Della has gone from curled up in a corner chewing on her hair, an angry spitfire, to a helpful young woman. I never understood what was wrong with her. You had her communicating with us in a week, and really talking in a few more weeks. This is just the beginning of who you will be, Anna Gibbs."

He felt the truth like he knew his name. His eyes widened. "The *beginning*. We have to put our faith in God and believe for the future. We are going to have a future. We've yet to see the sunrise turn to noonday, but we will." Wrapping his hand around the back of her neck, he tried to support her weary head. "I know you can't see any light at this moment. And I want to say I'm sorry a thousand times for not protecting you."

"Will," her tone and expression held deep despair, "you have."

"But I will rely on God for my failures and my future. Will you?" he pleaded. "Don't thank me like it's over. Please, Anna, stay strong. Don't give up."

She nodded slowly and kissed the tips of her fingers and brought them through the bars until they touched his lips. "You are the best life I've ever had," she whispered.

Eyes shifting around the cell, his anger spiked. "I'm going to ride back home and get you food and a blanket. Do you want me to take Charity? I can use the pap boat tonight."

Anna rubbed her forehead. "They won't allow it. The sheriff said she is evidence."

Will stilled, the blood rushing to his face like a man facing a battle without a weapon. He remembered his grandfather's visions and warnings. Would his own faith prevail over his grandfather's prophesy? Was this affliction brought on by his careless desperation to marry Anna? He'd lacked the ability to protect his own sister. If Charity hadn't survived, this wouldn't be happening.

Will fought the growl rising in the back of his throat. Hadn't he just asked Anna to stay strong? He blew out a long breath. *The battle is the Lord's*, he thought he heard inside his head. His agonizing stilled. A strange, powerful calm subdued his churning insides.

"The battle is the Lord's. He will go before us," he spoke firmly as he regained his composure. "I'll be back with some necessities for you and Charity."

ANNA WATCHED HIM go and turned to pick up Charity off the dirty cot. Sitting, she gently laid the cradleboard across her legs and stared at the content, sleeping little cherub. "Your daddy has great faith," she whispered, brushing her fingers across the back of the tiny hand resting on her narrow chest.

In her mind's eye, she could see Will back at their cabin. The children would all bustle around him to ask question after question. He would try his best, but his words and the gathering of her things would cause more ruckus. She released a heavy sigh. Since Charity had been born, someone else had had to read Maribelle a bedtime story. Remorse washed over her; she hadn't been as attentive to the others as she once was. Many of the chores they used to do together, Anna had found it faster to do herself. No wonder Maribelle had wanted to go out to the fields today. This little one took so much of her energy.

Anna yawned, fatigue making her body droop. How did Celia do it? She hadn't thought of the children's late mother in weeks. If she were alive, would she see Will's new wife as a blessing or a curse? This little one would've been her first grandchild, now locked behind bars. Barbaric. Anna's eyelids drooped.

Her childhood nanny was pointing a finger at her. Screams from her mother's mouth rang in her ears. The baby covered in white powder. Blue lips and nose, turning purple. Breathe, baby brother, breathe! *She felt the impact of the floor where the nanny pushed her. Swept up by his ankles, his lifeless body swayed, head dangling above her, as the nanny pounded on his back.* Baby, cry. Cry now! *Wake up and take my mother's pain away!*

"Wake up." Anna startled at her own voice, as her body flinched to attention. Charity blinked sleepy dark eyes at her. Maybe she was mistaken in her fatigue, but Charity appeared to lift a quick smile.

"Did you just smile?" Anna asked, pulling her from the cradleboard. "Either way, thank you." She kissed the baby's nose and held her close. Will would be back soon.

38

THE MORNING SUN had entered the open office window, penetrating the gloomy jail cells. Anna dozed from a restless night with Charity, tucked under their blanket. Her throat was dry as she tried to open her eyes. Will had stayed with her long after dark until the sheriff forced him out. What she hadn't expected was the sheriff would lock the front doors, leaving her and Charity in the building alone. It had been wonderful for her to tend to Charity throughout the night without anyone around, but now she feared another day of people coming and going while she sat in a dirty jail cell with a baby.

Hearing the jangle of the keys in the door, she sat up quickly. The sheriff nodded at her as he hung his hat on a wall peg.

"Sir, now could I be released to my home? If I have to await a trial, I cannot," She wrapped the blanket over Charity and stood. She felt ruffled body and soul, "tend to my needs and the baby in this cell."

He scratched behind his head. "The charges are too great to release you until trial." He took out the guns from his holster and ignored her by cleaning them.

Anna sat next to Charity and looked to his back. "May I have some water?"

He stopped what he was doing and dipped a smaller bucket into a larger one from the floor. "I planned on you being less trouble than the drunken reprobates I usually have to listen to." He unlocked the door and passed the bucket in. For a moment, she thought of pushing him aside and running out the door, but she reached for the water tin. Leave Charity or risk getting shot in the back? Her mind was still jumbled. Maybe she should try for another hour of sleep.

After she took the damp cloth to her face and neck, she brushed her hair and pinned it back in a low bun. The water was too cloudy to drink, but she could use it as a rinse for Charity.

The door opened, and the sunlight hurt her eyes. A large woman with a thick, dirty apron sat down a tray where the sheriff had the pieces of his gun taken apart.

"Just one today, you say," the large woman stopped and gaped wide-eyed at Anna. "What the devil?" She dropped her fists on her wide hips. "And looky there, an outlaw with a baby. You've got a woman *and* a baby behind bars!" she snorted. "Sheriff, work don't get any tougher for you." She slapped the sheriff on the back. "Maybe you can let her out so she can pour your coffee and sugar your oats," she snickered.

"Enough, Sal." He nodded at the door.

Smirking at Anna, she shrugged and let herself out. For a moment, the smell of coffee and buttered biscuits covered the other rancid odors. The sheriff poured his coffee and brought a second cup of coffee to Anna. He tossed a spoonful of oats in a mug and grabbed a napkin with a biscuit. Anna thanked him as he handed the items through the bars.

Half an hour later, Charity still slept, and Anna could fret no more. "Sir, I need to use the outhouse if you don't mind."

Frowning, he unlocked the cell and let her out.

"Can you watch for the baby while—"

"No," He snapped, cutting her off. "This ain't no ladies hotel." He grabbed her upper arm and led her back past the other two cells and out the back door.

Anna used the small wood-sided water closet as fast as she could. Stepping out, the sheriff grabbed her arm and led her back inside.

They both stopped short as two large men faced them. Anna's heart dropped. The Plugg brothers.

"Oh no," Anna whimpered, looking for where she had left Charity. Thank God, she was still in the blanket, asleep.

"Boys." The sheriff continued forward, and Anna stepped back in the cell.

"Just comin' to make sure y'all still had her." Floyd tipped his hat at the sheriff. "We got some of our slaves buildin' gallows outside town."

The sheriff shook his head. "We won't need any gallows built, and you know it."

"Got plenty of good trees to do the trick." Bernard nodded at Floyd.

"That's sore true enough," Floyd's vulgar smiled matched his voice. "Done hung an old theivin' blackie and her son just the other night."

Anna gasped before her hand could cover her mouth. Tallie? Otis? Those stupid spoons. Her heart fell from her chest, and she had to grab the bar to steady herself. The Plugg brothers turned to her, laughing.

"Now yous about to cry? You done no cryin' over our pa." Bernard glared at her. "Yous just sitting in that nice house sippin' your tea. Inviting yous lover back to your bed like nothin' happened." His lips tightened into a thin white line. "How you like this box?"

"We already gotta pine one, you might like better," the evil crackled in Floyd's snicker.

"Do you hear this?" Anna moved to the side of the cell, trying to get the sheriff's attention. "They hung an innocent woman and her son," she whimpered. "Please."

The Plugg brothers laughed and turned to the sheriff. "She's proven crazy head to toe, you know. Have you seen the way her head flinches? Crazy wretch from an insane asylum." Bernard turned to face her, "Why would we hang our property? They are worth somethin'. Wheres you ain't worth nothin'," he sneered. "You and that bastard baby can share the same noose."

"All right, all right. That's enough, boys." The sheriff opened the front door. "I'm sure you got something better to do than this."

"Yeah, we do," Floyd smirked, "but this is more fun."

Anna staggered back, her body covered in a cold sweat. They *hadn't* hung Tallie and Otis? Is that what they said? Dizziness came on her as she tried to steady her breathing. Charity looked up with bright eyes, and Anna scooped her into her arms. Thank God, she's safe. The cell was left open, and the brothers could have snatched her and—

"Okay." She bounced the baby. "We're okay," she whispered, trying to believe it for herself.

THAT AFTERNOON WILL apologized for being gone. He'd found a lawyer to represent her and spent the morning trying to state the facts as he knew them.

"Why wouldn't he just want to speak to me?" Anna asked through the bars. "Did you tell him we'd never met before the marriage? That Reverend and Mrs. Horworth could speak to that?"

"I did." He sighed.

"Did I tell you I had run to my neighbor, Mrs. Holden, that morning when it happened? Her husband had tried to get him out of the water."

He shook his head and sighed. "No, I didn't know about that. I will see him tomorrow and ask him to talk to you personally." His dark eyes narrowed. "He said women and blacks are not allowed to speak at trials, I...I..." A shadow darkened his countenance.

"So I can't speak to what really happened?" Anna squeaked.

"That's what he is for. He said there are different degrees for murder and for a woman. The judge usually takes into account the weaker rationale that women possess."

Anna's chin ticced. "So, I'll just go to prison instead of hanging?"

Will changed the subject. "I couldn't sleep last night. But at some point, I dozed off and awoke this morning to someone cooking breakfast."

"Nathan?" Anna guessed.

Will shook his head.

"Maribelle and Milo."

Anna was confused when he shook his head again.

"Della." He scratched his temple. "Grits, gravy, eggs, and biscuits.

"Amazing," She said, fighting the homesickness. "I wish I could have been there."

"Oh, I can't forget." He pulled some paper from his pocket. "A letter from Maribelle."

Anna opened it and noted what she thought was a drawing of their garden. "Look, she has a few of the right letters for her name."

Will rolled his tongue inside his cheek, never looking at the paper. His wild eyes dimmed, aloof with the same hopelessness that was overtaking her.

"I will get you out of here," his nostrils flared with emotion, "or I will die trying."

39

THE NEXT MORNING, shortly after the cook dropped off the same breakfast, Anna was changing the baby when Mrs. Hart came flying through the office door.

"I thought it was just a vicious rumor!" She nailed the sheriff with a wicked scowl before she met Anna at the bars. "You, the sweetest young woman in this town, is being charged with murder? And the *baby* is here!"

Anna had never seen the woman so riled. She finally found her voice. "It's the Plugg brothers. They say I murdered Alfred." Her shoulders drooped. "But I didn't." She pressed her lips into a line. "They think this baby is a love child from Will and me. That's their claim, the motive I would have to kill the man."

"Humph." Mrs. Hart huffed. "I could think of some better reasons to kill him than that."

Anna whimpered, "That has to stay between you and me," she said, leaning toward the bars. "If I talk about how terrible he was, it will just fuel their account against me."

"I understand." She nodded. "How about the testimony I have seen you off and on for the last six months." She turned toward the sheriff sitting at his desk. "And I have *never* seen you with child!"

They watched the back of his head shake. "Hurry up the squawking visit, ladies," he said.

"What can I bring you, dear?" She looked past Anna and grimaced at the conditions. "Does the baby need anything? Can someone take care of her for you?"

"No," the sheriff barked before Anna could answer.

Anna rolled her hands together. "I might as well tell you this, Mrs. Hart. And if you don't believe me, it's okay." Anna swallowed hard. "Remember when you gave me the seed for the tea? For Della's milk to come in?"

Mrs. Hart nodded.

"I never gave it to Della. I drank it myself. Like four or five cups a day." She took a breath and forged on. "At first, I could pacify the baby at my breast, and then she would tolerate the pap boat. And though I felt things changing," she rubbed her hand above her breasts, "I didn't know it could happen. But now I can feed the baby myself. I have milk."

Mrs. Hart's fiery eyes opened wider, and she glanced down at Anna's bosom. "Is that so?"

"When you said many a babe doesn't survive without mother's milk, I wondered if God had seen my barrenness and given me a gift—and Charity her life."

"And maybe... *He has?*" Mrs. Hart swayed her head.

"But to a man's eye, it appears only a woman giving birth can feed the baby. So it is a furious slap against my defense."

Mrs. Hart pulled her hand down her face. "I see." The silence lingered. "But since those Plugg men have half-black children all over this county, even if it was yours, as they claim, it doesn't seem a point to hold a woman to," she growled, shaking her head. "It's a troubled time we live in—little justice for a young woman without family to protect her." Mrs. Hart reached through the bars and gripped Anna's arm. "I have to get back to the store, but I will come again tomorrow."

Later that afternoon the deputy asked Will to leave—he had to lock the door to run an errand. Anna sat nursing the baby and feeling the stuffy late afternoon heat. Maybe it was the filling beef and gravy lunch Will had brought, but she rolled to her side and laid down with Charity. Sleep came instantly. Later, she awoke to the tap of something against the metal bars. Little Charity was asleep with her mouth hung open and a dribble of milk across her face. Anna pushed back from her and quickly tightened her chemise and buttoned her dress. The reverend turned away.

"Reverend," she choked out and sat up.

He went to a corner and pulled a stool up to her cell. Swallowing, his neck revealed an Adam's apple rise and fall. He looked at his Bible. "I try to bring a word of hope to those in your situation," he said lifelessly, while he thumbed through the pages. "The word of the Lord from Psalm twenty-seven says, '*The LORD is my light and my salvation; whom shall I fear? The LORD is the strength of my life; of whom shall I be afraid? When the wicked, even mine enemies and my foes, came upon me to eat up my flesh, they stumbled and fell.*'"

Anna wished he would slow down and reread it.

"'*Though a host should encamp against me, my heart shall not fear: though war should rise against me, in this will I be confident.*'"

War? What did Will say? The battle is the Lord's, she thought.

"'*One thing have I desired of the LORD, that will I seek after; that I may dwell in the house of the LORD all the days of my life, to behold the beauty of the LORD, and to inquire in his temple. For in the time of trouble, he shall hide me in his pavilion: in the secret of his tabernacle shall he hide me; he shall set me up upon a rock.*'"

She wanted to stop him again. In times of trouble, He would hide her?

"'*And now shall mine head be lifted up above mine enemies round about me: therefore will I offer in his tabernacle sacrifices of joy; I will sing, yea, I will sing praises unto the LORD.*'" He rambled on, never looking up. "'*Hear, O LORD, when I cry with my voice: have mercy also upon me and answer me. When thou saidst, Seek ye my face; my heart said unto thee, Thy face, LORD, will I seek.*'"

Is praying the same as seeking? Anna wished she could ask questions.

"'*Hide not thy face far from me; put not thy servant away in anger: thou hast been my help; leave me not, neither forsake me, O God of my salvation. When my father and my mother forsake me, then the LORD will take me up.'*"

Anna felt her stomach clench. She didn't know those words about parents forsaking were in the Bible.

"'*Teach me thy way, O LORD, and lead me in a plain path, because of mine enemies. Deliver me not over unto the will of mine enemies: for false witnesses are risen up against me, and such as breathe out cruelty.*"

"What?" Anna finally interrupted. "Could you read that again?"

He repeated it quickly and kept reading. "'*I had fainted unless I had believed to see the goodness of the LORD in the land of the living. Wait on the LORD: Be of good courage, and he shall strengthen thine heart: wait, I say, on the LORD.'*"

Anna was glad for the break from his rumblings so she could think about those last words. It was so hard to believe she would see the goodness of the Lord. So many of her years, she wondered where God was.

"Can I ask you a question?" She chewed on her bottom lip.

He pulled out his timepiece and put it back in his vest pocket. "I have a few minutes."

"Do you believe all those words?"

He finally made eye contact. "Of course. I believe everything written in this book. It's God's holy word, and I would stake my life on it." He cleared his throat.

Anna nodded glancing at his scuffed shoes, and his socks gathered around his ankles. He smelled like boiled cabbage, but her thoughts poured out, "Can God really forgive us? Because I had thought he'd forgiven me." She wanted to pick her words carefully. "Isn't all of this life mistake after mistake?"

"I don't think I can follow you." He slightly shook his head.

"My father died when I was four," Anna said. "I don't remember him. But my mother remarried, and they had a baby boy. One day the nanny told me to get the talc powder off the shelf. She had a dirty diaper to wash."

He nodded, listening.

"I reached up over the cradle to the shelf for the powder, but somehow the tin slipped from my hand, and the powder fell into the baby's mouth. I tried to brush it away, but the baby inhaled it and stopped breathing."

The Reverend ran his hand down his long, stoic face.

"I called for the nanny, and she ran back and pushed me away. When my mother arrived in the room, her lovely baby boy was suffocating. The nanny claimed she saw me hurt the baby intentionally. My stepfather had no forbearance for me or ears for my reasoning, and one morning not long after, I hugged my grieving mother goodbye and was taken on a long carriage ride.

"I didn't understand it then. I wondered each night how long I would have to stay, but I was left in Brown Township, Pennsylvania, at a place called Lennhurst. It was an asylum for lunatics and had an area for disabled children—a school they called it."

Her head teetered. "I think it's a lovely thought, but it was the place to leave children who were mad. Most were trapped in defective minds that could barely function. Some had beautiful minds, but their bodies were spastic with crippling deformities. It was a horrific place for a child who, what did you just read? Had been forsaken by their mother and father?" Her eyes narrowed. He was watching her intently.

"But maybe the Lord did hide me there. There was a beautiful, blond little boy named Elias. He was born in Lennhurst to a derelict woman. She passed giving birth to another baby, and he had no one. I understood his tears and began to keep him with me. We would play little games. There was an old coin and wrapper we would hide for each other's birthdays. I told him he was my brother. Humm…" She tilted her head to the side. "I never thought of this, but maybe it was my way of making amends for killing my own brother."

She blinked and shrugged. "Elias became my family, and I was his. He slept in the crook of my arm until he was seven or eight." Anna smiled and noticed the reverend hadn't looked at his watch. "I came to find out he was a fast learner. We both were given a bit of schooling and then put to work. I had a natural way of calming the disruptive children. He hauled coal and other things."

Anna glanced toward the blanket and watched Charity yawn and arch her back. "I was able to name this little one Charity," Anna touched the chubby leg kicking out of the gown.

"At Lennhurst, there was another poor child who had lost her family in a fire. The burns on her back were like nothing I'd ever seen, and she only spoke Polish." A sad smile tipped her mouth. "Her doctor said I could name her, so I named her Patience because she was so patient to suffer through the burn treatments and to learn English." Anna stilled and wondered if the reverend would want her to go on. "But just as I'd come to peace with God and this strange life and the Lennhurst family I was given, I got a letter from my family. They had found a proper suiter for me. I would be leaving Lennhurst, leaving my dear Elias and Patience. I was told that he was an older, distinguished man who would not hold my past against me but provide the security and future I could be proud of, a widower from Centerville, Kentucky."

"Alfred Plugg," the reverend murmured.

"I met him on a Tuesday, and we married on Saturday." My mother cried through the entire simple ceremony. I would love to think she grieved our years of separation, but I'll never know because she spent our few moments together making excuses for her preoccupation with her other four children."

The reverend's eyebrows drew down over his eyes.

"But I think I am almost to my question." She picked up Charity and held her on her lap. "God knows from the first night I lay with Mr. Plugg, hatred entered my heart." She swallowed the large rock in her throat. "And we both know, King David's wife, Michal, was barren due to her disrespect. My only restitution from that marriage was one day I could be a mother. I sewed so many baby gowns that I had to sell them at the mercantile." She smiled, gripping Charity as she wiggled on her lap. "So I believed, as long as I carried such hate, God would have no sight of me. The barrenness continued year after year, increasing the abandonment I felt. The psalmist cried out for God, not to forsake him, as you just read. And just when I started to believe I'd been unforsaken because of my new life with Will Gibbs, because of my blossoming love for him and his family, and this little one, now, I sit here before you," her eyes held his, "forsaken again."

40

THE NEXT MORNING after the simple jailhouse breakfast, the reverend returned as he said he would. She'd told Will last night before he left that she'd told the poor man her tale of woe. Will encouraged her, saying it was good to tell someone else. But the look on the reverend's face made her wonder if she was too forthright with her desperate childhood and unlearned questions of faith and forbearance.

The thin man didn't even acknowledge the deputy on duty, pulling the stool close to her cell.

"I apologize for leaving you wondering yesterday after our visit. But I'm glad I had some time to think. It actually kept me awake last night." His small smile revealed crooked front teeth.

Anna started to thank him for returning, but he held his thick black Bible over his palm and tapped the book as he spoke, "May I be frank? May I speak my mind without my congregants looking down their noses to see if I interpret the Bible as they want me to?"

"Yes, please. I would appreciate that." She turned to see Charity still enjoying her morning nap. "Though the Bible was taught at Lennhurst every Sunday, Will and I have never been to a church."

He opened the Bible in the middle. "Then, you know this first half is the Old Testament?"

She nodded.

"Yes, of course, you knew King David's wife was barren. And the gospels start the story of Jesus and his redemption of mankind." He flipped the pages forward.

She nodded again, feeling his excitement for what he would share.

"Can a believer in Jesus be forsaken?" he said wide-eyed. "Is that the gist of your question?"

"I… Yes, I believe so."

"And this may be shocking, but my answer is no. A believer in Jesus the Christ cannot be forsaken. We know from reading the Old Testament every sin and mistake, or the breaking of the law," he watched her, making sure she was following, "had to be atoned with a sacrificial offering, a spotless lamb and so on."

She nodded once.

"Then, the long-prophesied Messiah came." He sat up a bit straighter. "The New Testament teaches, that Jesus was the fulfillment of the law: The only one and final sacrifice for all the sin of mankind. All your sin, all mine, and all the generations to come. He was the perfect lamb, and his blood flowed for us, the undeserving, at Calvary." He took in an excited breath. "Astounding, wouldn't you say?"

Anna lifted a small smile but wondered how this could help her.

"I realize I'm simplifying centuries of church theology, but I think we make it too difficult." He tapped his fingers together over his Bible. "My church only likes to hear the rules and fear of God. When I try to talk about grace and freedom in Christ, they frown and point out the Old Testament stories," the reverend sighed, scrunching his long face.

"You've had a troubled life." He looked at her. "But God has not forsaken you. In this very day, this life or death moment you are in, there is nothing you have to do. You don't have to sacrifice, promise, beg, or repent harder. Actually, believing in what Christ did for you, now gives you a place to rest, hide, and to sing, and be thankful. Just like the psalm, I read yesterday," he waited, looking for her agreement.

The uncertainty lingered on her face.

"Mrs. Gibbs, neither your childhood, your hatred, nor your barrenness and bitterness can separate you from the love of God. His son died for all our sin and mistakes." He leaned in, "The Lord has seen everything you've been through, and he holds nothing back because of it. Even though you may not feel Him, He is with you, and in the midst of your trial, He loves you. You are His."

Anna felt the same encompassing stirring she had sitting next to Will and the nightly chatter at the family table. "Thank you, sir. You've helped me see the truth more clearly. I hope I didn't sound disrespectful to you?"

"No, no," he sat back on his stool. "Your honesty was refreshing. We all have our struggles, and I believe that's why we need to talk more about the Good News. And yet so many don't like that."

"Like your wife." Anna shocked herself. "I...I...shouldn't..."

The reverend laughed and stood. "You do not mince words, young lady." He set the stool back in the corner, and Anna stood embarrassed.

"Would you say a prayer for my new family and me?" She pressed close to the cold bars. "I miss them terribly." She covered her mouth with both her hands, eyes pooling with tears.

"Of course," he said before the office door rattled open and a man with white hair and bushy mustache came in. Nodding a half smile, the reverend left. The deputy and the white-haired man spoke. A few minutes later, the sheriff entered, and they all talked and joked together.

Charity had awakened, and Anna changed her diaper. The man with the white hair wore a blue striped suit, and she wondered if he was the lawyer Will had sought out.

"I guess we'll see ya at the Black Code meetin' tonight," the deputy slapped the man with a suit on his back.

"Donny," the sheriff growled. "A bit loud, don't ya think?"

Anna felt her heart drop. Black Code. That was the group Mr. Plugg ran with at night. Her chin twitched down. How could Will know they were all in this vigilante group together? Taking a deep breath, she held Charity against her shoulder and stood to pat her back.

"Are you Mrs. Gibbs?" the older man finally turned to ask her.

Who else would be in here with a baby? She almost spit out. After one slip about the reverend's wife, she didn't want to offend this man if he could help her.

"Yes, sir."

Charity let out a yelp, and Anna bounced her.

"I've already spoken to your husband. Mr. William Gibbs, that right?" He had a thick southern drawl, and Anna got a whiff of reeking cologne from where he stood. "I'm Mr. Flanders, and I will represent you in court on Monday. The judge only comes to Centerville every other Monday, you see."

Anna nodded.

"What questions do ya need answered?"

There were so many that she didn't know where to start. Charity fussed, and Anna swung her around to face outward.

"May I tell you about the morning of Mr. Plugg's death?" She swayed from side to side with the baby.

"That's not necessary, Ma'am. Your husband already done told me."

"Umm…do you think the judge will believe me?" Her voice cracked. "The Plugg brothers say they have a witness, but I screamed for help, and no one came." Her tics notched her head up and down. He didn't look very interested in what she was saying. "If someone saw me holding him under the water, then why didn't they come forward to… to help him?"

He frowned and shrugged. "I don't rightly know, but we can ask him at trial."

"Have you spoken to my neighbor? Mrs. Holden? She was the first person to help me, and her husband came out. He saw the blood. I believe Mr. Plugg had a heart seizure before he fell."

Charity let out another squeak, and Anna knew she was getting hungry. "What about Mrs. Hart at the mercantile? She is a trustworthy businesswoman. She knows I've never been pregnant. Have you talked to her?"

"Women and blacks are *not* allowed to speak up in court. You understand now," his tone darkened. "Court is a very serious thing, and you are facing a severe verdict. If I were you, I'd spend these days tidying up your affairs, giving over your obligations."

Charity let out a cry and then another. Anna popped the babe back over her shoulder.

"Once the sentence has been read," Mr. Flanders pulled on the curve of his thick white mustache, "that baby will be removed from you. So like I said, you need to focus on arrangements for the child and—"

Missing the rest of his words, a wave of clarity hit her like the blunt impact of a certain tobacco barn in the dark night. "Am I going to hang?" Anna clenched her jaw and bounced the crying baby.

"My job is to keep that from happening. I think I can get you a lesser charge for the crime of murder. Here in Kentucky, we find it ill-mannered seein' our women folk swingin' from a rope."

The deputy snickered from his chair across the room.

Bile rose up in her throat. "You can leave now, Mr. Flanders." She knew her tone seethed and she didn't care. "All of you! Get out!" She screamed over the baby's cries. The Sheriff turned shocked, opening his mouth. "I must feed my child! So all of you leave me be! Now!"

It was only a few seconds before the Sheriff shut his mouth and walked to the door holding it open for the other two.

41

THE EVENING SHADOWS fell across the cinderblock cell, making her depressing situation even more so. Today was a long day without seeing Will. He'd ridden to the next town to see about finding a new lawyer. She didn't know how she'd communicate to Will what she was feeling. She did feel a certain peace from the reverend's words of encouragement, but after Mr. Flanders left, it was like it all blew away from her heart with a strong wind. She wanted to be strong for Will. She would do anything to see the light back in his eyes. He was carrying such a heavy load and didn't want to talk about it, but they needed to know who would care for the baby after she was gone.

These days of melancholy and idleness were taking their toll. She was used to being busy. She enjoyed the children's lessons and gardening. So many chores put a skip in her step, homemaking tasks completed lent her time for her baby gowns and bonnets. Funny how she had tasks aplenty at the pond house, but they didn't make a life. A life worth living needed tenderness and love to blossom and survive. Fear and hate had begun to suffocate what was left of her person at the pond house, but Will Gibbs showed her how to find her true self and provided a life worth living.

A letter slid under the door of the sheriff office, and he turned to pick it up. "Looks like a note for you." He put it through the bars and Anna took it.

She opened the envelope and flipped open the paper.

I have other appointments today, but I want you to know that I was praying for you. This scripture came to mind. As I wrote it out, I prayed it would bring you comfort in these next days. Reverend Horworth.

Anna sat next to Charity.

From Isaiah, chapter fifty-four verse one:

Sing, O barren, thou that didst not bear; break forth into singing, and cry aloud, thou that didst not travail with child: for more are the children of the desolate than the children of the married wife, saith the LORD.

Enlarge the place of thy tent, and let them stretch forth the curtains of thine habitations: spare not, lengthen thy cords, and strengthen thy stakes;

For thou shalt break forth on the right hand and on the left, and thy seed shall inherit the Gentiles, and make the desolate cities to be inhabited.

Fear not; for thou shalt not be ashamed: neither be thou confounded; for thou shalt not be put to shame: for thou shalt forget the shame of thy youth, and shalt not remember the reproach of thy widowhood any more.

For thy Maker is thine husband; the LORD of hosts is his name; and thy Redeemer the Holy One of Israel; The God of the whole earth shall he be called.

For the LORD hath called thee as a woman forsaken and grieved in spirit, and a wife of youth, when thou wast refused, saith thy God.

For a small moment have I forsaken thee; but with great mercies will I gather thee.

In a little wrath I hid my face from thee for a moment; but with everlasting kindness will I have mercy on thee, saith the LORD thy Redeemer.

For the mountains shall depart, and the hills be removed; but my kindness shall not depart from thee, neither shall the covenant of my peace be removed, saith the LORD that hath mercy on thee.

O thou afflicted, tossed with tempest, and not comforted, behold, I will lay thy stones with fair colors, and lay thy foundations with sapphires.

And I will make thy windows of agates, and thy gates of carbuncles, and all thy borders of pleasant stones.

And all thy children shall be taught of the LORD, and great shall be the peace of thy children.

In righteousness shalt thou be established: thou shalt be far from oppression; for thou shalt not fear: and from terror; for it shall not come near thee.

Behold, they shall surely gather together, but not by me: whosoever shall gather together against thee shall fall for thy sake.

Behold, I have created the smith that bloweth the coals in the fire, and that bringeth forth an instrument for his work; and I have created the waster to destroy.

No weapon that is formed against thee shall prosper, and every tongue that shall rise against thee in judgment thou shalt condemn. This is the heritage of the servants of the LORD, and their righteousness is of me, saith the LORD.

Anna stilled, staring at the paper. How desperately she wanted to believe. How she wanted faith and that her condemners would be silenced. She felt some small comfort. The blessing of the children: Milo, a boy who just needed a pair of socks; Maribelle, who needed hugs, clean hair and someone to sing with. The laughter and smiles were more than a barren woman could hope for. She had taught all the children, and they had taught her. How to give love and receive love, what a blessing a family could be. The pain of never seeing them again returned, starting in her eyes and constricting her throat, deliberately crushing her body and soul.

THAT AFTERNOON WHILE Charity slept, Mrs. Hart came into the sheriff's office.

"Oh, my dear one." She put her arm through the bars, and Anna squeezed her hand.

"I worry about you. Are you eating?"

Anna nodded. "My hope is fading." She swallowed the lump in her throat.

"Then, this may be helpful." Mrs. Hart pulled her arm back and grabbed some envelopes from her bag. "I was at the post office. People were talking—and who cares what they say." Mrs. Hart batted her hand in the air. "Anyway, the postmaster overheard your name and said he's had mail for you, but someone from the Plugg plantation said you'd moved away." She held the envelopes through the bars. "I can only hope there is something to cheer you up in these."

Anna forced a smile for the woman's thoughtfulness. "Denver City, Colorado and Hancock, Pennsylvania." She searched the postmarks over the scribbled word, 'unknown,' that stretched across the paper. This one is from my mother." She held up the third envelope. "It's dated after I told her of Mr. Plugg's death." She sighed and said, "I think I've already figured out, she is not coming."

"Here and take this, too." Mrs. Hart held out a little bag. "Some cinnamon cookies." Mr. Hart and I will both be there Monday. We are closing the store."

Closing the busiest store in town? For her? Anna's head shook, and the tears welled swiftly. "Thank you for everything. You have been a beautiful example of a friend to me. I will never forget your kindness."

Mrs. Hart sucked in a sob and jerked her hankie from her bag. "Until then," she choked and swished from the office.

Anna sat carefully and opened the tattered envelope from Denver City. The writing looked familiar, and she flipped the letter to the back. The signature splashed her in the face like cold water.

I still love you like a real sister,

Elias Browne

Anna sucked in a sob so quick her back hit against the thick bars. Her Elias, this was from *her Elias!* How many nights did she carry the fear of what had happened to him? She held the paper to her chest as the tears flowed freely. "Lord, what are you doing to me?" she whispered, shaking her head. She tired to find her hankie without waking Charity. Her mouth hung open, and her hand hovered over her heart, still beating wildly.

As soon as she'd wiped her face to see, she read:

Dear Anna,

I think of you often and hope you are well. I ended up in some trouble after leaving Lennhurst. As you can emagn I was a bit lost without you.

Anna puffed out a held breath. "emagn," that was *her* Elias.

"While I was in jail, I was put into the Union army and taut to set xplosives. When I left, I got cot up in that until I got shot in the side. I met a beuteful girl named Lauren who helped me recover. It's to long a story, but it's safe to say, love covers a multitude of sin. We took the wagon train from Greenlock Ohio all the way to Denver City, Colorado. That is where her mother lives. We were married in Denver City. I have a hundred sixty akers and will mostly raise horses. And any day I will be a father. That might worry you. But please smile. God has helped me to become a good man. There is nothing I want more than my family. Since you will always be my sister in my eyes. I hope I can live up to the load of love I got from you.

I can only pray this finds you well and I have included my address as I would so enjoy hearing from you.

My wife wants me to say thank you, from her.

I still love you like a real sister,

Elias Browne.

Anna fell forward and laid her head on her knees. How could this blessing hurt so deeply? A week ago, she would have written him with the glowing tales of her family, the tobacco farm, the garden, and little cabin. Retelling the blessings and trials of the Gibbs family. They would've spent years writing letters about their children and maybe grandchildren. Sitting up, she choked back the sobs and shook her head. The pain and reality of her future ached through her fingers and onto the paper. Quickly she folded the letter and put it back in the envelope.

42

WILL WANDERED UP along the creek at dusk and stopped. On this very spot, the night Anna had brought him clean clothes, was their first kiss. The fire in his belly that night had matched everything in his heart for her. It wasn't just her beauty, or gentle confidence, or the fact she'd rescued his weakening family. He was in love. He loved how her sadness had given way to her smile, how her stance of distance had faded to one who held his arm in the night. The way she had begun to trust him and love him back. The long looks they had over the dinner table, secrets and dreams only the most trusted souls shared.

He shook his head to clear the memories. He'd gone on a walk to pray. The Lord had seen his day. From Barkerville to Pine Creek, there wasn't a lawyer to be found. He'd prayed for another way, another solution, racking his brain for something he couldn't see.

"Lord, you've seen the cry of my heart. You know I've begged and promised. Please hear my prayer." He'd run out of words. There was only one idea for tomorrow, the last night before the Monday trial.

SUNDAY, AFTER COMING and going from the jail to see Anna, Will had come back to the cabin to check on the children. The cabin was empty; likely Nathan kept everyone busy in the fields. Will knew he should check on them, but his body felt pulled to the ground in weariness.

He scooped some stew from a pot into a tin with a tight lid for the ride to the jail. Grabbing a few rolls, he stuffed them in a bag. He scribbled a note to Nathan and climbed on his horse. Pulling out of the yard, he could see his grandfather in the distance. Standing under the tree where they usually met. His grandfather raised a hand, and Will could only lift one back as he turned the horse toward town.

When Will entered the office, and Anna rose. Her hair was hanging tangled around her shoulders as it'd been earlier. She was still drawn and pale, her eyes vacant of her usual life.

"Done told ya, I leave early on Sunday," the deputy named Donny put his hand out. Will didn't want to do this with Anna watching. It could upset her more. He pulled the roll of bills from his pocket and handed them to the deputy.

Donny took the supper bag and lifted the stew tin and opened it. Setting it all down he told Will to lift his arms. Anna's brow furrowed as Donny patted up and down Will's pant legs and shirt. Handing the supper items back to Will, Donny pulled a gun on Will. It didn't surprise him, but the look on Anna's face was more than he could take.

"It's all right," Will stepped up to the cell with the gun on his back. The deputy pulled the keys from his belt and unlocked her door. Anna backed up a few paces with her mouth ajar. Will stepped in, and the deputy closed the barred door and locked it. Anna stood shocked as Will heard the deputy get his things.

"I'll be back before sunrise. Before any rooster goes off. Y'all hear me?"

Will turned and nodded as Donny locked them in the office.

Anna watched him with red-rimmed eyes afraid to move for fear it was really a dream and she'd waken. "What is happening?" she asked.

"I made arrangements with him to stay with you tonight. I don't want you to be alone."

"William Gibbs," She whispered, "Is that the money you… Are you using…"

"I had it set aside to pay for harvesters. I don't need it right now."

Her face saddened, and he set the supper down.

"I've done such a poor job of helping you." He huffed. "I thought this was something I could do for you."

He never saw her step forward, but suddenly her body collided into his. Her arms squeezed his shoulders as his arms wrapped around her body. He nuzzled into her neck and cheek. "We've talked and cried and prayed. But tonight let's just be together. Let's not talk about anything. Okay?"

She nodded against his shoulder, and they stood and held each other tight. "I love you," she murmured, running her fingers through his dark hair.

"And I love you." He inched back and kissed her. "Are you hungry?"

"I have no appetite. Maybe later." She raised a small smile. "You can stay all night?"

He smiled and nodded. "I haven't been able to sleep since you and Charity left my bed. I would have snuck in her drawer, but that might have been asking a lot." He winked, running his fingers down her cheek.

Anna gripped his hand and kissed it. "Yes, true. Often I comfort myself in seeing this cell is about as big as our room." For a second, she offered him a smile, and the next, the flash of life suddenly dropped from her expression. Desperation hung in the air.

"How are the children today?" She released his hand.

"They were all out in the fields when I left." He turned and knelt by the sleeping Charity.

"On Sunday?" she asked.

"I think it helps them to keep busy." He stood as her head tilted to the floor.

"You won't be bringing them tomorrow?" she half asked, half insisted. "I would love to see them before, the, you know, before." She bit her bottom lip and squeezed her hands together.

"But I don't want them to see me like this." She turned quickly and tried to hide the fresh tears.

Will came up behind her and turned her to face him. Embracing her, he let her weep.

SOMEWHERE AFTER CHARITY'S middle of the night feeding, they sat side by side on the cot, leaning against the bars and listened to the baby.

"She's snoring." Will shook his head.

"I know, isn't it the cutest thing ever?" Anna tucked the blanket around the baby.

"All right, tell me another story about Elias." Will enjoyed listening to her. "So, you would hide the coin in the wrapper, and he had to find it?"

"Only on his or my birthday," she replied. "I wonder if the silly thing is still under the loose board of the cot in the dormitory." She pulled out the letters and held them on her lap.

"Patience has married a lawyer," she sighed.

"Really?" Will said.

"They live in Hancock, Pennsylvania, on the very land where her parents died in a fire."

"That must be difficult." The jail was dark, but he could hear the self-restraint in her voice.

"She sounds happy. She wants to make a garden for the depressed and incapacitated. She said Dr. Powell was bringing a group to her soon."

She leaned her head on his shoulder. "They have asked me to write. But I've decided against it. It will be easier for them to imagine their letters never reached me."

"And then this one from my mother," she slid her fingers back and forth across the paper, "finally hearing from her, yet it left me no time to contact them." She gripped Will's arm. "There was one consolation in her words."

"What was that?" He entwined his fingers with hers.

"She said, she knew the age difference would *not* suit me, but because he would die sooner, it would leave me with his vast holdings." She released a hoarse chuckle then said, "Should I draw a picture of my vast holdings," she swung her hand, encompassing the cell, "and send it to her?" She grabbed the letter. "You can have it." She put the letter on Will's lap. "Write her after I'm gone. But these two from Elias and Patience, I will keep with Maribelle's drawing."

Will stood, taking Charity off the cot and tucking her in the cradleboard. Setting her gently on the floor, he took the blanket and held it out. "Lay down, Anna. You need a few hours of sleep. You and I have done all we—" His own words got jammed in his throat, and unwanted tears pierced his dark eyes. He wanted to protect her like he wanted his next breath. How could life matter without her by his side? He cleared his throat and swiped his face along his shirt sleeve. "We've done all we know to do. So, you should rest."

"If you will rest with me," she patted the cot.

He slipped behind her and wrapped her in his arms. Forcing his eyes to stay open, he wanted to absorb her every scent, the faint rise and fall of her shoulder, her hair next to his face and every warm sensation of love held in his arms—possibly for the last time.

43

MONDAY, AT TWENTY to ten, Will rode to the end of town. The Grange Hall sat on the right; the street where they had lost Maribelle was to the left. Would every moment bring a memory they'd shared? Horses and carriages were tied to the few hitching posts. As people filed in, his stomach ached. This trial was all the talk of the town, and people stood outside the open windows leaning in to listen.

When he entered the building, it seemed all the chattering in the room died down. Many people looked at him and then looked away quickly. Anna sat with a straight back at a long table to the right. Her hair was back in a low bun and Charity sat on her lap. Looking from row to row, he could see the chairs in the back of the hall were all filled. To his left, was a long table with the Plugg brothers seated behind it. His teeth clenched, and he debated how he would like to make them suffer.

"Mr. Gibbs," someone said.

Will turned to the rows of people closest to Anna's table.

"Here's a seat for you." It was Reverend Horworth.

Will sidestepped the well-dressed and the country folk in the row and took the seat beside the reverend and his wife.

"Where is Mr. Flanders?" Will looked around.

"He's been back with the judge," the reverend said, "behind that door."

"Is that normal?" Will asked.

"As long as I've lived in Centerville, a woman has never been on trial." Mr. Horworth rocked in his seat. "Due to the delicate nature of her testimony, I wonder if things are better said behind closed doors."

Will felt his spine crawl. Maybe the judge was chewing the cud with another Black Code comrade.

Anna turned and caught his eye. She bit down on her lip, looking about to cry. Without thinking, he used his simple signs to ask. "Do you want me to take the baby?"

Her chin ticced down, and she closed her two fingers over her thumb, signing no.

"Enough a'that," the sheriff said from the front of the room.

A thick, brown door opened to the left, and an older balding man came out in his long black robe. The crowd hushed as he took his seat behind his long desk. Anna's lawyer came to sit beside her.

What was only minutes, but felt like hours, the judge read through the papers in front of him. Sometimes reading and then looking at Anna.

"Welcome everyone. Today we have Mrs. William Gibbs on trial for the murder of her first husband," he squinted at the papers, "ahh, Mr. Alfred Plugg of Centerville, Kentucky." Will's mouth went dry. The man had to look at his paper. How could he not know of Mr. Plugg? Maybe that was good?

"I've chosen to read over Mr. Flanders' detailed testimony for Mrs. Gibbs. Due to the delicate circumstances involved, he felt this better implemented as a verbal testimony. So we will begin with Mr. Grubber and your testimony."

Will leaned into the reverend, "Is that right? How do we know what he put on paper?"

The reverend sighed and slightly shrugged.

"Thank you, your Honor, and may I welcome you to Centerville. Please send our deepest condolences to Judge Monroe for his mother's passing."

The judge nodded.

"I'd like to open my remarks with an article from the Chicago Institute for the relief of persons deprived of the use of their reason." He stepped out from the desk with a newspaper in his hand. "What I hold here is proven evidence that the recovery from lunacy is less than one percent. One percent!" He slapped the paper on his hand, and people jumped. "The late Alfred Plugg, God rest his soul, who has always withheld judgment from the less fortunate, was told by Mrs. Gibbs' own stepfather," he pointed a long finger at Anna, "that she *had* recovered from her mental affliction." He stared her down. "I dare say, not!" He shook his head, scowling. "Less than one percent."

A low murmur trickled across the crowd, and Will looked around. "What kind of horse and pony show was this man after?" he said, never turning to the reverend.

"These two concerned brothers recall their father refusing to allow her to live at Flora, their large plantation home. Mr. Plugg feared she would repeat her dreadful pattern of hurting others."

Anna leaned toward her lawyer and mouthed. 'That's not true.' Mr. Flanders patted her on the arm.

"You see this woman before you," he swung his arm wide at Anna, "had been institutionalized for killing her own brother!"

The gasps from the crowd brought Will to his feet. The reverend grabbed his arm and pulled him down.

"Mr. Plugg kept her at the pond house, isolated and away from where she could do harm." The man walked back to his desk, shaking his head at Bernard and Floyd. "But alas, in all his attempts to protect others, one cold morning, she turned on the only one true benevolent heart that cared for her and pushed him into an icy pond and held him under until his life was no more." His voice dropped, and he shook his head. An eerie silence hung in the old grange hall.

"But why?" The man suddenly came alive, flinging his hands to the side. "Why would she kill the hand that fed her and cared for her?" The Plugg's lawyer shook his head with a dramatic frown.

"Besides being without sound mind," he raised his voice dramatically, and pointed accusingly directly at Charity, "the *baby* sitting on its mother's lap this very moment was on its way." He glowered at Anna, "And it was not, I repeat not, Mr. Plugg's baby."

"It's that half-breed's," Floyd sneered pointing to Will across the room.

Will felt someone grip his shoulder to keep him in his seat. More gasps ricocheted through the crowd, and a woman from the outside the window yelled, "Jezebel! Ingin' lover!"

Mr. Flanders stood, putting his hand up to quiet the crowd. "Your Honor, I have done my best to put some of these details in my report before you. I find it very disturbing that this fragile woman had to sit through such a public scorning."

"Mr. Grubber," the judge said, "I think I've heard enough. Please call your eyewitness."

"I'd like to call Mr. Milton Topper to the witness chair," Mr. Grubber nodded.

A bent over man with dirty black hair came forward. He never looked up from the ground.

"Mr. Topper, will you please recount what you saw the morning of Alfred Plugg's murder?"

He glanced up at the Plugg brothers and back to his feet. "I, harrumphggg." He noisily cleared his throat. "I…was lookin' fur my dog." He scratched his head. "By the pond." He scratched his chin. "And I saw that woman push him on the ice." He balled up his hands, pulling apart his old hat. "Oh, and then I saw her hold him under." He nodded to the Plugg brothers and turned and went back to his seat.

The judge fingered through the papers again and looked at Mr. Flanders, "Your witness."

Mr. Flanders shrugged.

The judge took a deep breath. "Is there a Mr. Holden in the courtroom?" He searched until a man in the back stood.

"That's me, your Honor, sir."

"Sir, I have your account here in front of me," the judge said. But could you tell us again about that morning."

Mr. Holden stepped forward. "I was havin' my eggs and heard a pounding at the door. The Missus called me from the table, sayin' our neighbor, Mrs. Plugg was a needin' help. I noticed the woman's hem and feet were wet, and I grabbed my coat. Just a few feet from the bank, there was Mr. Plugg, lying face down, blood on the corners of the ice, but his head and torso were under the water. There weren't no movement. This one," he pointed at Anna, "was huffing and puffing that he'd a sezi—"

"Did you find the man dead?" Mr. Flanders cut him off.

"Yes, sir. He was already dead. Took about four of us, Ned, Gus, Thomas, and his horse from the livery to pull him out. Cold day that one was."

"Thank you," Mr. Flanders said and sat down. Charity squirmed in Anna's arms and let out a squeal.

"I'd like to take a moment to speak to the sheriff," the judge said. He motioned for the sheriff to come near his table. They talked, and Will wanted to close his eyes. They were talking about the baby. The sheriff nodded and pointed to Anna. The judge looked long and troubled at her and shook his head.

"All right, I will recess to make my decision." He gathered his papers.

"Excuse me!" Will turned to see Mrs. Hart standing, hands on her hips. "Mr. Grubber has already repeated hideous things about this poor woman, and since I am not confident in Mr. Flanders' investigation, I would like to speak."

"No Negro or woman is allowed to speak in a court of law," Mr. Grubber whined his boorish, arrogant voice. "For obvious reasons."

Mrs. Hart rose taller. "I am a businesswoman who can run a store, and if you're interested in the truth today, your honor, I *am* qualified to speak."

Both lawyers stood to quiet her as she started to testify.

"First, Mrs. Gibbs is one of my vendors and customers. I can testify, no matter her past, she is not insane."

"Enough, please." Mr. Grubber put his hand up.

"Number two, since I do business with this woman on a regular basis, I will testify on the Holy Bible, she has not and never has been pregnant."

The crowd turned to each other and whispered.

"Sit down, madam!" Mr. Flanders turned daggers on her.

"None of that don't matter!" Bernard jumped up, eyes ablaze. "We got a witness. She held him under and killed him!" Floyd jumped up next to him.

Anna stood with Charity on her hip. "And that would be a lie."

The crowd resounded in chatter, and the judge pounded his gavel on the table.

Mr. Flanders grabbed Anna's arm and roughly pulled her and Charity into her seat. Will jumped up in a flash, pushing the rows aside in front of him. He was going to take that lawyer by the neck. No one was going to treat his wife and baby like—

Others stood blocking his path.

"Sit down, sit down, everyone!" The judge stood pounding his gavel. Pointing to the sheriff, he said, "Take care of this crowd while I take a recess."

44

WILL FELT REVEREND Horworth's hand pulling him back. He was going to hurt someone if he didn't get some air. How could her lawyer just sit there like a mute? The Plugg's lawyer sounded like he came right from the snake oil sideshow, and Anna's lawyer looked like he was in a hurry to get back to supper. He tried to move around the people getting out of his row. Mrs. Horworth was suddenly next to him.

"Mr. Gibbs," her firm tone stopped him. "Why do they want her put away so bad? It's obvious to anyone with a brain they are lying." Her eyes narrowed.

Will shook his head as people moved by them. "I…I guess they just want to make her pay for the death."

"Speaking of pay, did she ever say her stepfather married her with a dowry? Did her parents have money? Did Mr. Plugg get anything at the wedding?"

"I don't know." Will looked past her. The sheriff had taken Anna and Charity to another room. "She never said anything about that."

"As his widow, she should have been entitled to part of his large estate." Mrs. Horworth let out a long sigh, and her eyes narrowed in suspicion. "How would we possibly find out about that?" She shook her head.

"She did tell me in her mother's last letter, her mother implied that one day, in the event of his death, she would be well taken care of."

"Just as I thought. There *was* a dowry." She blew out a small huff. "Maybe those Plugg brothers aren't as stupid as they look," Mrs. Horworth mumbled, letting him pass.

FIFTEEN MINUTES LATER, Will sat like a caged animal back in his seat. When the door opened, and Anna came out, it looked like Charity had fallen asleep. She gracefully sat in her chair and turned to face him. He froze. Her expression was like a stake impaling his heart. Her distant watery stare meant all hope had left her being.

The judge sat and hit his gavel. Charity flinched off her shoulder "The court is now back in session." He cleared his throat and piled his papers. "Upon review of the testimonies and eyewitnesses, I am prepared to make my verdict."

"Mrs. Gibbs, please rise."

Will held his breath as she rose, holding the baby. He caught movement out of the corner of his eye.

"Please excuse the interruption, your honor." Reverend Horworth and his wife stood. We don't believe our testimony was ever taken. We've never spoken to Mr. Flanders."

The judge nodded to him. "You can have five minutes, Reverend."

"We met Mrs. Gibbs the day after Mr. Plugg's death." She had been thrown from her home by these two men." He pointed at the Plugg brothers. "Without a coat or any money, she showed up on our step, and we allowed her to sleep in our church. If Mr. Gibbs was her lover, don't you think she would've run to him?" His shoulders rolled up with a wide-eyed expression. "One night, Mr. Gibbs did come to our door, but he was looking for a family member that had run away. They had *never* met before, and it was at my wife's suggestion they marry. Anna, Mrs. Plugg, had no home, and Mr. Gibbs needed help with the care of his siblings."

Mr. Grubber stood, "This is a lovely tale straight from a storybook."

"My husband lives by the Word of God and does not lie!" Mrs. Horworth nostril's flared. "But you, sir, are the one who lives in a fairy tale." Her eyes narrowed on the man and the room stilled. "My second cousin was the first Mrs. Plugg." Her face glowed red. "She was a soft and gentle woman who was shamed, isolated, and fettered by the ruthless Mr. Plugg. The man you paint as benevolent and kind was the reason her life was cut short by a weak heart. Far happier in glory, I assure you. Half this room knows Mr. Plugg as a cruel slave owner, who, in spite of the Emancipation Proclamation, has yet to free one slave from bondage!"

"I beg you, your honor," Mr. Grubber drawled, "this is *not* a Freeman's Bureau meeting. We all know Kentucky is allowed to be neutral on the subject, and I believe their five minutes is up."

"Then I have one last question for you," she pointed her finger at him. "As the Plugg's lawyer, how much inheritance is this woman losing by going to prison?"

He shook his head, frowning at the judge. "I'm not privy to that information. I was only retained to represent the murder of their father."

"Without an heir, I've understood common law says it's up to half of the estate," her voice rang strong through the packed building. "With these two living, she would be entitled to a third. As long as she doesn't know of her dowry at the wedding and is accused of a crime, she did *not* commit, she can be put away and no one the wiser?" Mrs. Horworth slammed her fists on her hip, "Eh, boys?"

Now the reverend had to grip his wife by the elbow. As the Plugg brothers rose, shouting and cursing at her, she leaned forward willing to take them on nose to nose.

Will's mind whirred as the judge pounded his gavel yelling. "Everyone, settle down!"

With the last pound of the gavel, Charity woke up screaming. Anna held her close and tried to comfort her. The crowd hissed and booed at the vile things the Plugg brothers yelled. Will watched the look on the judge's face. It was getting redder and redder. Then, for a strange moment, all the baby's crying and the people's shouts seemed to go silent. *'The battle belongs to Me.'*

Something deep and comforting settled into Will's being, and he closed his eyes and sat down. The rattled crowd finally settled and sat.

The judge called the two lawyers to the front. "Mrs. Gibbs, if you could rise again."

As she stood and bounced Charity, the baby's cries settled down.

"The reverend's wife has brought up an interesting point I cannot address at this time. But to the crime of murder, Mrs. William Gibbs, I here do find you *not guilty."*

The crowd jumped to their feet again, cheering. Will rose slowly as people around him patted him and shook him with their congratulations. All of their responses were like unwanted distractions. He just needed to see her. She turned to him, dazed her eyes filled and overflowed. Finally, a small smile rose on her pale lips.

Will pushed the chairs aside in the two rows in front of him and took two long strides until she was in his arms. He embraced the two clutching them tightly, Charity let out a squeal, and Will loosed his hold. Grasping's Anna's face, he kissed her wet cheeks, whispering, "Thank God, thank God," over and over.

"WE GOT US a church to burn!" Floyd yelled over the crowd. The sheriff shook his head and escorted the Plugg brothers from the hall.

"And we will just rebuild it!" Mrs. Horworth hollered back.

Anna handed the baby to Will and walked to where the woman stood with the Reverend and the Harts.

"Your fortitude astounds me," Anna choked out. "How can I thank you?" Shock and recognition covered Anna's face. "And you." Anna squeezed Mrs. Hart's arm.

"You already have," The staunch preacher's wife nodded with a creased smile. "When Reginald told me your past, I knew you were just another victim of Alfred Pluggs'. Then he showed me the scripture in Isaiah about the barren widow."

Anna nodded. "Those words seemed to come alive today."

"Stay a strong, caring woman. Love this man." Mrs. Horworth nodded to Will, standing next to her. "Take care of all that God gives you." She touched the baby's head as the Horworths, and the Harts smiled and turned to leave.

"And come to church." She said, winking over her shoulder.

45

A NNA STRADDLED THE horse behind Will with Charity tucked in her cradleboard. Holding him tight, she thought to tease him about forgetting the wagon, but the idea of not expecting her to return with him, held no humor—maybe it would one day when they could look back. For today, the sun on her face and the sounds of birds and the fresh spring air were enough to repel what she'd been through.

The gate to their land appeared, and her throat tightened. She was so close now, only a hug away from her family. Will swung his leg over the horse's head and jumped down. Goosebumps tingled over her in expectation as he pulled the horse forward by the reins. Will smiled back at her; he must have known the family would be watching. First, the moppy-haired Nathan appeared from the cabin. Anna covered her mouth, but a squeal still escaped. Behind him came wide-eyed Milo and Maribelle waving and shrieking their joy; her eyes filled with tears. Will came to the side of the horse and helped her off. Pulling the cradleboard from her shoulders, she handed the baby over and took off running across the field to the happy faces coming toward her.

"Anna!" Maribelle screamed with joy. Milo collided with her legs first, almost knocking her over. Before she could reach down to hold him, Maribelle came flying up into her arms.

"You're home!" Milo cried, jumping up and down as he clung to her, jiggling the two of them and adding thrill and mayhem to Anna's homecoming.

Maribelle snuggled her face in Anna's shoulder. "I thought I'd never see you again." Her arms squeezed her neck. Nathan wrapped his long arms around all of them. "Anna, we are so glad you are home. Are you home for good?"

She nodded up and down, trying to hold back her sobs. They all stood crying and holding each other. Will and Charity caught up with the joyful reunion, and they finally pulled their clinging arms apart. Della stood a few feet away, and Anna felt her heart break in two. The young woman was pale with tears streaking down her face.

"It's okay," Anna signed, "I'm home. Everything's going to be okay." Anna closed the gap and held the young woman in her arms. Della wept as Anna had never heard before, deep long sobs shaking the teen to her core. Will motioned, and the others followed him to the cabin. Holding Della, she stroked her hair and rubbed her back for a long time until the girl's sobs subsided. Anna backed away. "I love you and will always be here for you," she signed and wrapped her arm around her. Della clung to Anna as they walked back to the cabin.

Later, after everyone was done chattering on about their time apart, Will rose and leaned into her ear. "I have to meet with my grandfather. I should only be gone an hour or so." He rose and looked at his brother. "I know the Plugg brothers will retaliate, but Nathan is here. He knows what to do."

Anna rose and placed Charity against her shoulder. Their jubilance over her freedom was tempered by the fact the Plugg brothers' vengeance could be close. "Do you think they will harm Tallie and Otis?" Anna touched Will's sleeve before he opened the door.

"I can't say." He squeezed her hand. "But we will protect our family."

Nathan nodded his agreement at his brother's words.

MILO AND MARIBELLE were bathed and ready for bed. Anna opened a picture book on the table for Milo to read and Maribelle hung on Anna's arm as she tried to balance Charity in her lap. Della dried the last dish and turned to the table. Anna pointed at Charity, and Della looked to the ground. Milo began to read, and Della looked around the cabin.

Chin down, Della took a careful step forward, holding her hands out. Anna lifted Charity over to her and pulled Maribelle up on her lap. Trying to focus on Milo's story, Anna looked up to see Charity giving Della wide-eyes. Charity's little hand came up and grabbed Della's nose, making Della smile. Walking the baby around the table, Della gave her a little friendly bounce.

Being home in the small space made Anna's heart melt anew—the smells, the sounds, this miracle of Della holding the baby. An hour past dark, Anna kissed the children good night and walked to the window over the kitchen counter. Nathan's low lit lantern sat on a stump as he and Will talked outside with rifles over their shoulders. She wanted to relish her return home, but the dark cloud of retaliation loomed. In their room, Anna carefully scooped the children's bath water out, then filled the tub with fresh warm water for her own bath. The thought of being finally clean again was enticing. With Charity asleep in her drawer, she was only going to wash and then soak for an extra moment. Something touched her hand, and her eyes flew open. Will looked down at her, smiling.

"Enjoying a nap?"

Anna sat forward. "Oh, I didn't mean to fall asleep. Goodness, the water has gone cold. Will grabbed the towel off the chair and held it out for her. She stood as he wrapped her in the warm fabric, and his arms held her snug as he whispered in her ear, "I knew I missed you, but I can say, I really, really did miss you?"

Anna smiled up at those dark, hungry eyes. "And I missed you." She teased his lips with a kiss. She pulled back and murmured, "I don't think I told you—"

He kissed her, stopping her words.

After a blissful moment, she spoke against his warm lips, "But last night, you coming in that cell to stay with me…" She shook her head and exhaled. "I was so scared and hopeless."

Will rubbed her back and arms, bringing the warmth back to her skin. She relished his touch and continued, "Neither of us got much sleep." She gazed up at him. "I don't think I have words to tell you how much it meant to my heart. You do take my heart and…" He dropped little kisses up her neck. "…My body, my, ah, being, ah." She softly groaned and savored another important moment where her husband didn't need a lot of words. His touch and her desire were enough said.

AN HOUR LATER, Anna felt Will leave the bed and begin to dress. "Where are you going?" She sat up, whispering in the dark.

"Nathan and I are taking turns watching." He pulled his suspenders up over his shoulders.

Anna sighed and laid back on her pillow. "How long?" She smoothed her hand over his side of the sheet. "How long do you think we are in danger?"

"I don't know." He chewed on his lip, "Getting a different judge than usual; the way the women spoke up and swayed him." He shook his head. "I doubt the sheriff is going to do any extra watch on the church or the mercantile, and certainly not this place." He sat on the corner of the bed and pulled his boots on. "I wish I could just watch the barn and fields, but I worry about the cabin and the children."

Anna found her nightgown and slipped it over her head. "I can help."

"No." He twisted to face her. "You need rest."

With her back against the log wall, she pulled her knees up to her chest. "Will, I've felt the relief and joy all day. But now a kind of anger is surging through my blood. I don't think I can sleep. They're used to controlling their slaves with fear and intimidation. I lived with it for years. Now, they are allowed to do the same to the decent folks of this town. How will justice be served?"

"Or *when* is the question." He stood. "For now, this is what I know to do. Any man who comes to this land to harm person or crop, I will shoot."

"You said your grandfather knew I would bring trouble to this land." She pulled the blanket to her chin. "If anything happens, I will blame myself."

Will put his knee on the bed and leaned forward to clutch her chin. "God went before us, Anna. Didn't He?" Her eyes dropped away, and he waited until she looked back. "We have no guarantees about tomorrow. We only know God said he would always be with us and whatever we have to face He'll work it out for our good." Releasing her face, he ran his fingers lightly through her hair. "Rest, please, and if you can't, praying is good, too."

46

THE SUMMER HEAT stifled any cool breeze as Will talked with a group of men after church. Anna had visited with Mrs. Horworth and Mrs. Hart, but now the balmy summer sun beat down on her as she waited next to the wagon. A squirmy Charity on her hip didn't help, and perspiration formed on her brow. Blowing out a breath, she'd wished she'd remembered to bring her fan. Milo and Maribelle ran past her playing chase with the other children. Della stood close chewing on her fingernails and watching people out of the corner of her downcast eyes. Anna fanned her face with her hand and pulled Charity's bonnet forward. Shade and a glass of lemonade were in order.

Lemonade. She bit back her demure smile. Hadn't that been the drink she'd brought her husband one night in the barn? Watching him now, she felt even more attraction toward him than she knew was possible. Tall, strong, lean, and handsome. She had trouble not watching his every move as he nodded and spoke among the other men. His best shirt, which she had made him, stretched across his chest and shoulders.

Charity leaned forward and grabbed the wood side of the wagon. The busy baby was never still for one moment. Everything within reach of her hands was hers to pull and put in her mouth.

Ann had never brought up the discussion with Will that she was *not* pregnant. Every day was full to the brim with the baby's care and the others. Glancing up at the simple cross on the church, she wasn't surprised barrenness didn't hurt her heart like it once had. Will's reasoning for the changes in her body were possible, but just like everything else, she never felt any disappointment from him about her barrenness. His only needs were to see her cared for and protected.

No doubt the usual news of Kentucky following the thirteenth amendment was what held them all in deep conversation. Would the slaves ever be free to come and go as they wished without constant fear? So many opinions and yet so much bondage remained.

Will had hired four teens and a Negro couple from the Freedman's Bureau for help in the first leg of the harvest. She knew by their rations of food, money was tight. She reminded him they'd done it before, and they could hold on again. Needing a fresh breeze from somewhere, she turned her attention to the edge of town.

Will's grandfather stood, with a cross expression creasing the line between his eyebrows. His lips pressed into a straight line. Before true terror could set in about whatever had caused the man to show up outside the church, her eyes rose above Will's grandfather. Dark smoke. Instantly she knew it was from their property. Weeks of silence from the Pluggs, and now they strike, today? *Nathan, oh dear Jesus, had they got to Nathan?*

Her heart froze in fear, and she turned a haunted gaze on her husband. Their eyes met for a split second before Will called for two of the men to help. As the men jumped on their wagon, she'd the good sense to move away as he snapped the reins and the horse bolted down the road dragging the bouncing, rumbling wagon behind them.

Charity fussed, as Anna ran in a circle gathering all the children. Mrs. Horworth helped her and the children into a neighbor's wagon. She huddled the others in her arms as Charity wailed.

The dark smoke of the barn burning was a sight straight from hell. They could see sparks and embers floating like black feathers high into the air. After the rough ride, the gate was ajar as the wagon came to a stop. Anna pressed Milo and Maribelle to her skirts as they approached the cabin. Still standing, thank God.

Without waiting for help, they all jumped from the wagon, and Anna rushed them into the cabin. "Do not leave this cabin door!" She pointed, needing them in one place. Handing Della the baby, she turned to look for Nathan.

Other horses and riders were pulling into their yard, and still more drove their wagons across the brown grass out to the burning barn. Fearful and teary-eyed, she dodged the horses, looking side to side. Was he out near the barn? Had Will already— She slid to a stop seeing the Negro teens and the couple huddled in a pile under a group of trees to the left. Anna ran to where they were but didn't see Nathan. Wide-eyed and mouth hanging open, she tried to breathe. A rope dangled from the tree above, and she finally noticed they had bruises and bloody burns around their necks.

"Oh, dear God." She covered a moan with her hand. "What happened? Are you all right?" They stood on shaking legs, and all gaped wide-eyed at the burning barn. Anna followed their stares and stepped back as the enormous black and burning structure collapsed like sticks in the fireplace. Men pulled their wagons back, and others ran. Even at this distance, the group under the tree could feel the wind of heat hit them.

"We'z get the shovel's and put out any fire trails," one of the workers said.

"No, you must let me tend to those rope burns." Anna looked back at all of them. "Did you see Nathan?" Her tone sagged with pain. "Did you see him?"

They nodded their heads. "He done cut us down."

"Had the fire already started? Did you see who started it?" Anna tried unsuccessfully to steady her breathing.

One of the teen workers shook his head, looking at the ground. "Ones whose strung us up. Big men wid hoods over their head and eye holes cut out. They's done got us and started that big barn to blaze at the same time. Masta Nathan didn't know which way to shoot." Her face flinched. "But he came after us, cut us down and they done run off."

Anna felt the constricting pain relax to normal in her chest. Nathan had to save the workers from hanging. He couldn't protect the barn and crop and them at the same time. He'd done the right thing.

She looked out to the town folk gathering. Some were already getting water from the creek to protect the property from the sparks. Surely Will and Nathan were helping somewhere in the mix. She had to blink and look again. The entire landscape had changed into smoldering smoke, the massive barn missing from its rightful place. A dark cloud across the land, isn't that what Will's grandfather had predicted?

"Come, come to the cabin." Anna straightened, filling her lungs with air and resolve. "Let's tend to those wounds."

ANNA SAT CURLED up on her bed, nursing Charity. The cabin hummed with people going in and out, someone brought a pot of beans, and she was thankful for all the care and concern. She'd seen Will, and finally caught sight of Nathan, from afar but they had yet to come home.

Was it Will's Indian grandfather drawing her attention like she thought? But when they rode out of town, there had been no sight of him. Her eyes wearily dropped to where Charity suckled on and off, dozing. *Trouble to the land.* The man *had* warned them. If Will had never married her, none of this would've happened. She heard others outside saying they could rebuild the barn.

But everyone knew the first large harvest had been hanging from those rafters. All that the Gibbs family had worked for was burnt and gone. The bank loans would come due, and what would they do then? Lumber to rebuild cost money. She sighed and pulled her fingers across Charity's wispy little strands. The Plugg brothers had waited and schemed. They knew when to start the fire. They knew when Will would be gone. Poor Nathan, she rested her head back against the log wall. She hadn't just brought trouble to this land. Now he had every right to blame her, too. The workers had probably already packed their things and left. They could've harvested what was left, but there was nowhere to hang the tobacco leaves.

Weeks ago, they had laid in bed and talked about leaving. Will didn't want Anna and the family to live in constant fear. He was willing to take them away, saying he could find another trade. She exhaled, remembering their words. Anna lifted the sleeping baby over her shoulder; Charity let loose a burp.

What did God want?

They had prayed that night. Should fear be a reason to leave?

And then life just kicked back in, and they'd gotten lax in thinking the Plugg brothers would just forget everything. Were they naive in their simple faith? Was the rescue from her murder charge as much as God wanted to do? Something from the reverend's words tried to surface. He made God sound loving and benevolent.

Would *she* ever pick and choose when to be good to her children? No, as a good parent, you would always want to protect them. What had Will said that first night at home? The two constants, God was always with them and would always use their circumstances for good. Wrapping Charity tightly, she gently laid her in the bed and stood to look out the window. She drew her hand down her face. A small plume of smoke still rose in the distance. Closing her eyes, she felt her body and faith sag—she couldn't see how losing months of their labor, their ability to feed the family would possibly work for any good.

47

A S THE WIND lightly shifted back and forth, Anna could smell smoke on and off most of the night. Just before dawn, she realized Will slept like a fallen tree next to her. As the sun began to peek over the land, she noticed his clothes and face still had the black soot from yesterday's ordeal. He must have collapsed into bed exhausted.

She laid still, ruminating on her worries, yet she could not begin to imagine how he felt as he watched all his months of toil and sweat go up in flames. He stirred and cracked a tired glance at her.

"I'm sorry I didn't get back here sooner," his voice cracked with fatigue. "Others told me you were tending to the workers." He groaned, turning to his side. Anna took his hand. It was rough with calluses.

"No, Will, *I'm* sorry." She caressed his rough, stubbled cheek. Brushing some dirt with her thumb, she leaned forward and kissed him softly. "I've brought this disaster upon you and your family. You should have never agreed to marry me."

"Yes, I should have." He pushed his arm underneath her and pulled her close.

"You tried to warn me," she said. "You said there is no blessing. Do you remember that?"

"Um hum," he said sleepily, closing his eyes.

"I should have known to tell you. There will be no blessing *from me*. Your grandfather was right all along," her tone weakened.

"No." He gathered her tighter. "Look at all you've overcome in your life. Whatever the challenge, you are the one who rises above it all."

She brushed her face against his chest. Listening to his breathing deepen into sleep, she murmured, "While I drag everyone else through hell."

REALIZING LATER IN the day how much she'd lived her life in isolation, she greeted another wagon as it rolled into the yard. People from the church and town folk she'd never met came in a steady flow to bring a wagon load of lumber or a pie. To her surprise, the Freedman workers had stayed and went to work framing up lumber in the distance. Milo and Maribelle had loaded up the old wheelbarrow and kept water and food going back and forth. With Della's cooperation to help with Charity, Anna was able to be hostess and direct help from the cabin.

Wiping her hands on her apron, she looked up to see a finely dressed man at the open cabin door.

"Good day, sir," she nodded, quickly eyeing the man as he pulled his derby into his hands.

"I'm Mr. Frost from the bank."

Anna felt her stomach drop. So soon?

"I would be off to speak to Mr. Gibbs, but it is a hot day today and—"

Anna noticed the man was dripping with sweat. "Please come in, sir, let me get you some water."

"Thank you, ma'am."

His eyes glanced at the small surroundings. "Do you mind if I take a sit for a spell?"

"No, please," Anna held her hand out toward one of the chairs.

"I was at the trial a few weeks back," he said, reaching for the water.

Anna tried to lift a quick smile. Her notoriety could go away at any time, and it would not hurt her one bit.

"Some things got me to thinkin'." He took a drink. "I always felt for your husband. I was the oldest when we lost our dear mother."

"I'm sorry," Anna nodded, refilling the glass.

"It was long ago." He lifted a sad smile. "But your man has done right by everyone, and I hope he's told you—this land is not his."

Anna sighed. "Yes, he told me it was left to Nathan by his step-father."

"And I have respect for someone who works as hard as he does, for little possible gain." Mr. Frost took another drink. "So just on a whim, I looked into some accounts at the bank. Mr. Plugg did receive a large dowry, deposited in his account the week of your wedding." He took a long pull from the glass of water, then delicately patted his mouth with a snowy handkerchief.

"I never knew about it." Anna turned away, wanting to lock those memories as far away as possible. She'd rather not talk about the Pluggs.

"But you are entitled to it as his widow."

Anna slowly turned back to him. "Sir, I appreciate you seeing what I see in Will Gibbs, but if you think I would be able to get money from the Plugg brothers, you are misleading yourself."

"I've already ordered the transfer into your name. Women don't have their own account, so I assumed you wouldn't mind if I put the money in with Mr. Gibb's account."

Anna froze; several emotions conflicting within her. She sat down hard. "And they know about this transfer?" She could feel her face reddening. Della walked in bouncing Charity, looked at them and turned around and walked out.

"You, sir, can now see why I'm not happy." She moved to the open door then and pointed out at the pile of black rubble. "That is what they do if you cross them!" She twisted her hands in her apron. "My brother-in-law and five workers were almost killed!"

Mr. Frost stood, holding his derby in his hands. "I have made the sheriff aware of what they've done." He rolled his lips, squinting. "I've been to the courthouse and filed a lean on the plantation until they pay for these damages and for pain and suffering, and I requested that the pond house should be yours."

Anna felt her body sway back. "That's—I—don't—I" she sputtered. Sighing softly, she said, "I don't want you to think your efforts are not appreciated. But how many years are we to stay awake at night wondering if this is the night they burn the cabin with all of us in it? Leans and dowries…" she gripped her forehead. "Pond houses and new barns are for nothing if we are all dead."

He walked to the door and looked out. "The mayor is aware of the leniency and tolerance the sheriff displays towards certain groups that, apparently, he is a part of. He was told to hand in his badge if he didn't stay clear of the raiding going on, and represent protection to all in our county—that's everyone living here, including the Negroes." He took a breath and tilted his head to the side. "I've been told he chose his job. The mayor was embarrassed by your imprisonment. I'd like to believe the sheriff will protect and serve *all* of Centerville as he has been ordered to do."

Anna followed him out to his fancy, black buggy. Scratching her head, she felt guilty for belittling his apparent help. "I'm sorry if I came across ungrateful."

"No, no. You've been through a lot, and I know Will is busy. Will you tell him of what we talked about, and be sure to tell him the bank is here to help him."

"Yes, sir," she stood back as the buggy left the yard.

Della and Charity came around the side of the cabin, and Anna signed, 'thank you' to Della as she reached for Charity. Blowing out a breath, she balanced the baby on her hip. Raising a hand to block the sun, she watched and listened to hammers pounding nails in the distance. Would Will see the banker's interference as worsening the contention, just as she had?

48

THE EVENING AIR finally cooled. After the children had gone to bed, Will and Anna stood outside by the black pot talking of the banker's visit.

"I know you fear the retaliation," Will raked his fingers through his hair. "And I have been hesitant to tell you this, but my grandfather shot at two of the largest men."

Anna's chin tics showed him how much turmoil she carried. He swung her around to nestle against his chest and hold her. "They had on hoods, but word about town is Bernard and Floyd were hit," he said next to her ear. "One with an arrow in the leg, the other with an arrow through the shoulder."

Anna dropped her head back against his chest. "Oh, Will, it only keeps getting worse."

"My grandfather has been to the sheriff, which is unheard of for him. But what better proof to hooded men being on our property than arrow holes in shoulders and legs?"

She turned and clasped her hands behind his neck. "What do you want to do?"

He watched her for a long moment. He was to lead this family. God knows he'd felt a failure a hundred times. He weighed her question, knowing the answer would be whatever she needed, he would do.

"I want you safe and protected. I want Nathan and Della, Milo and Maribelle and even Charity to grow up without fear and torment. I want to see that free, black men have a chance. They're good workers. They should have their own land, their own crops. They should work hard and prosper, just as we hope to do."

Anna nodded in agreement. She ran her hands along his broad shoulders and embraced his thick upper arms.

"I want to stay here and rebuild." He looked out to the darkened landscape. "With the help from the others, I'll have a temporary barn up for the last of the harvest." He looked back at her. "Nathan and I have talked at length about what to do. He finally opened up about a secret he's been carrying."

Anna stilled, squinting.

"He wants to go to college." Will shrugged, "I think it's a good idea." He rubbed her back. "He's felt guilty for even saying it. He thought he would let me down."

"What would he do there?"

Will smiled, wide-eyed. "I really don't know." The cooler night air felt good on his skin or maybe finally talking this out brought more relief to his burdens. "Maybe because I remember when it was just me and my mother. People always looked at me funny, and we had to move here or there. Until I married you, I felt pulled by my grandfather, and yet I knew his life wasn't my future. Even though it's been hard, every moment here with you on this land has felt right. Right for me." He swept a loose strand of hair behind her ear. "If Nathan has a desire to go, he has my blessing." He nodded. "But what's most important to me is you. I want to make you happy, Anna, so what do you want?"

She pulled in a deep breath and exhaled. "You have given me more than I knew I should have wanted." She chuckled at her own words. "You do make me feel safe and protected—not because you can control everything that happens." She dipped her chin and eyed him. "But because you have filled my heart with love and helped me to have faith." Her fingers played with the hair on his collar. "Your acceptance of me has made every day new and hopeful. Your kindness has made me feel beautiful and wanted. Sooo…" she smiled up at him, and he smiled back.

"You are all I want. And if you are here, then I am here, and I believe God is with us." She barely finished before he touched her lips with his. Soft and tender kisses increased in desire as he gripped her body against his. "Dear heavens." She pulled away, searching his eyes. "Whatever else the future holds," she feathered her fingers through his hair, "I hope these flutters in my stomach never go away."

THE FOLLOWING WEEK, Will broke away from the barn framing to take her to the mercantile to see Mrs. Hart. After a quick stop at the bank, he entered the store as she visited with her friend. Her face warmed as he walked up to her. Reaching out to take Charity from her arms, he looked down at the table.

"These are yours," he fingered the newest baby gowns that Mrs. Hart had just tagged and put on the table.

"They are." She smiled shyly.

"Very nice." He looked around the store. "I don't see any baby beds." He kissed Charity's sweet cheek. "This one no longer fits in a drawer."

"That's true." Anna smiled at Mrs. Hart.

"We have some in the catalog you could order," Mrs. Hart said. "In only a couple of weeks, we could have it from Lexington."

"Ahh…" Anna hesitated, they'd no extra money. "Let's talk about it first." She nodded to Will.

They both thanked Mrs. Hart and left the store.

"Can we walk a moment?" Will asked as he held her hand down the step. "This is where I first met you." He smiled. "Milo loved you before I did."

"Socks, the boy loved those silly socks," she said as they walked down the block and turned right. Far ahead, she could make out the pond, and soon they walked up to the two-story, brown house.

Anna felt her breezy countenance fade. Like a haunted nightmare, this house made her head tics go off.

"They arrested the Plugg brothers," Will said out of the blue.

"What? How?" Her whole body froze.

"My grandfather's arrows. Floyd can't use his left arm, and Bernard's leg grew infected. They are in a bad way. They agreed to sign over the pond house and two slaves of your picking if we agree to drop the charges of attempted murder of our field workers. They are charged for arson and have to pay for the barn and loss of the tobacco from their harvest."

Anna didn't think she could possibly have heard that right. "Two slaves, like Tallie and Otis?"

Will nodded, wide-eyed, "Yep."

"Please tell me this is no joke, Will." She clutched her hands together. "They could be freed!"

"I just spoke with the bank. He has a wonderful price for the sale of this house. I assumed you would want to sell it and maybe use the money for a bigger house on our land."

Anna knew her mouth still hung open. "Now *that* would be a blessing!" She laughed, wrapping her arms around him and Charity.

One year later

"MARIBELLE, COULD YOU please follow Charity?" Anna shook her head. The toddler was fast on her feet and out the door before Anna could dry her hands. The new house had rows of windows facing the front and Anna smiled as Charity tried to dodge Maribelle's hand holding.

"I'm done." Milo slammed his school book closed. "Can I go help Otis in the barn?"

"I'll check your work later. Yes, you *may* go." Anna piled his book and slate next to Maribelle's books. They both had been excelling at the Centerville school.

Tallie came in from the back door. "That plum tree done bout broke my apron strings right off me." She laid the fruit on the table and pulled her apron loose.

"Mmm, preserves and jam would be wonderful." Anna squeezed one. "They look perfect." She raised the fruit to her nose and enjoyed the sweet, fruity scent, "Mmmm."

Tallie ran her hand over the school books. "Besides Otis's church group, I started helpin' on Wednesday nights teaching readin' and writin' at the sharecroppers meetin' house."

"Wonderful," Anna said. "I can get paper or slates or whatever you need." Anna glanced out the window as the girls chased chickens around the yard.

"I often did think you's was still sum crazy girl from dat crazy house teaching an old Negro like me to read and write. Mmm-humm, sho' crazy."

"And I thought it was crazy you wrote a letter to the judge the day of the trial. If you would've given it to my lawyer, he never would have read your account of the morning of the death." Anna shook her head and placed the fruit in a large bowl. "And neither of us knew the replacement judge was an abolitionist." Anna still held the awe in her voice.

"Whoo-wee," Tallie sang. "The good Lord know how'da match socks in a row, don't He?"

"And now our Nathan wants to be a politician so that he can help people." Anna loved having him home for the summer—working hard alongside Will and the other sharecroppers till sundown.

"What else you needin' done for supper?" Tallie asked, looking at the stove. "You expectin' that old Injin back tonight?"

Anna smiled. "I make a helping for him every night. We can't predict what he needs. But he sat at the table four nights last week, I think."

Della walked down the broad wooden staircase signing to Anna.

"What's she wantin' now?" Tallie asked.

"She's out of thread. She's been doing some beautiful pieces of tatting." She nodded to Tallie. "The little drawstring bags she makes are perfect for the flavored tobacco."

"Who done think some man wants all those purdy collars around his pouch?" Tallie took the loaf of fresh bread and began to slice it.

"Collars?" Anna laughed. "I just know they sell for twice as much as the regular tobacco."

Maribelle herded the busy toddler into the house and closed the door quickly. Anna stopped what she was doing and swooped her big baby up into her arms and kissed her cheek. "Now you smell like the chicken coop." Charity rocked in Anna's arms, and Anna set her down. "That child never walks anymore." Anna laughed, watching the short, fat legs churn across the floor and flop on the settee. "Little peanut tries to climb everything now."

Anna couldn't help but watch her little darling, Charity's little legs didn't meet the edge of the brown seat, but she sat straight and tall smiling proudly. The living room still amazed her; big windows on one side, a large rock fireplace on the other. It didn't seem like a year ago, seven of them crammed into a cabin now the size of her upstairs bedroom. A lovely room with a wonderful addition called a door.

"Charity," Maribelle whined, jumping on the settee beside her. "You're going to get dirty feet on all Anna's nice furniture."

Anna handed Della the thread, and she sat and worked on her pieces at the table. "Beautiful," Anna signed, touching the little tobacco pouches. A thought occurred to Anna as her mind flitted to her days at Lennhurst Asylum. Here sat Della, in her smartly fitted new dress, her hair up in a twisted bun. She'd bloomed and changed so much. Many at Lennhurst Asslym were unable to function, but then many were capable of doing things.

A powerful thought coursed through her. Maybe it was from reading Patience's latest letter. The garden retreat of rest and solitude Patience and her husband had built on their land in Pennsylvania sounded wonderful. Maybe it was Will in the jailhouse assuring her her life was just beginning.

She grinned and looked out the big window. Will was washing up with Nathan and the other sharecroppers. So much hustle and bustle to keep her occupied here. But she couldn't ignore how her heart sped up at the idea. Soon, she would take it to Will and then to God in prayer.

Epilogue

IT WAS EARLY Christmas morning, 1868, when Anna brushed a lone tear away. Will had found the reverend's scriptures and taken the paper from her Bible. The churchman had carefully handwritten each meaningful word for her in her cell, her state of hopelessness. Will gifted her and built an oak wood frame, cutting the glass to fit the paper. Sitting it proudly on the mantel above the large rock fireplace, he squeezed her hand and winked at Anna's moment of emotion. Now the words from Isaiah 54, "*Sing, O barren, thou that didst not bear; break forth into singing...*" stood above the mantel, a testimony to the goodness of God. In the years that followed, the words would often make Anna shake her head and smile up at God. "*...for more are the children of the desolate than the children of the married wife, saith the Lord.*"

After a year of prayer, the reverend's wife introduced Anna to young Camila Dixon. The ten-year-old from Centerville was defective and unreachable, her discouraged parents claimed. With Della by her side, they started to meet with her on Thursday afternoons and then slowly more came. By the end of the year, Camila and two other disabled students were using sign language, writing, and sewing.

In 1873, the doors opened to the Mercy School for Disabled Children. Dispirited parents brought their children from all over the county to the Gibb land. A year later, simple dorms were built to house those who came from far away, and some, unfortunately, were abandoned at the school's doorstep. Tallie, who they insisted take days off, but rarely would, oversaw the hiring of the sharecropper's wives as they took shifts cooking and caring for all the children God brought. Tallie was often heard saying, "keepin' busy," kept her old callused foot from steppin' into heaven.' Camila Dixon was the first hired teacher.

With Nathan's prompting, Della, at thirty-one, left home and took a job at the Georgia School for the Deaf. There, she met and married her husband, Ronald. Though they'd dedicated their lives to helping the deaf, they were blessed with two sons of their own—neither born deaf.

Nathan had married Josephine Balkner, whom he met at Berea College. The first college in the Southern United States to be co-educational and racially integrated. Making their home outside of Frankfort, Nathan rose through the ranks, becoming a representative in the House of Representatives, where he fought for the welfare of the freedman and enslaved in Kentucky. They were blessed with four sons and two daughters.

After college, Milo came back to the land to help Will. He enjoyed the business and sales side and brought the flavored tobacco into the prosperous new market. He married Rosalie McClung, his childhood sweetheart from Centerville school. They had three daughters.

Maribelle followed Nathan's advice to attend Berea College and soon returned to teach at the Mercy School. Lucas Pearce, a gentlemen friend from her college, had heard Maribelle talk of the school for the incapacitated. After coming to see Maribelle and the school, he wrote an article for the Kentucky Gazette recounting the hope and gentle family-like rehabilitation the school offered, and the word spread.

A year later, Congress voted to support the work of Mrs. Gibbs with a ten thousand dollar grant. Later that year, Lucas Pearce stood with Maribelle at the altar, under the canopy of thick tree branches. The same area the hanging of five people almost took place. With all the family in attendance, Lucas wed the beautiful young woman while the family and residents cheered them on. With the expansion of the school and grounds, he stayed on to be the first administrator. They grew their family of three boys and one daughter east of Centerville.

As the reverend and Mrs. Horworth aged, they took on a new young preacher, named Charles Sandavol. His fiery messages of God's grace and forgiveness caught more than the congregation off guard. One muggy evening while Will and Anna rocked on the front porch, he came to humbly ask for Charity's hand in marriage. Will and Anna looked at each other, dabbing the tears away, their baby who started life in a wardrobe drawer was all grown up and going to be a wife—and a preacher's wife at that.

At Charity's bridal shower, Anna gave her her mother's spoons from her large buffet. Will had built a thin display box for them years earlier with red velvet backing. Anna remembered the day he set the spoons in the buffet—setting to the side her large stack of letters from Elias and Patience. She wanted to be thankful for his kindness, but something different must have shown on her face. He'd said, "The past is important, Anna, it's okay to put it on display." He pinched her chin, smiling. "It reveals the faithfulness of God who never leaves us and uses all things for our good and His glory."

Of course, when she thought of it that way, he was absolutely right.

"Behold, I have created the smith that bloweth the coals in the fire, and that bringeth forth an instrument for His work; and I have created the waster to destroy.

No weapon that is formed against thee shall prosper, and every tongue that shall rise against thee in judgment thou shalt condemn. This is the heritage of the servants of the Lord, and their righteousness is on Me, saith the Lord." Isaiah 54:16-17

Who Would I Be
Inspired Me
By Erin Jamieson

There's vision you've placed inside of me waiting to be seen
Epiphanies locked inside my mouth asking me to speak

But I've lived in fear for quite some time
I have boxed you in I've drawn the line
There's a gap between who I now see
And who I thought you were making me

Who would I be if I could sing without reservation
Where would I go if I could run unhindered
What would I do if I could take off all this fear and hesitation
Would I even know myself if I could see
Who would I be

These walls that I've built around myself have locked my
freedom out
I've walked around my own Jericho and I'll shout 'til the
walls come down

'Cause I've lived in fear for quite some time
But I'll claim the place you've sealed as mine
There's a bridge between who I now see
And who I know you are making me

Who would I be if I could sing without reservation
Where would I go if I could run unhindered
What would I do if I could take off all this fear and hesitation

Would I even know myself if I could see
Who would I be

I'm tired of saying no and thinking it's impossible
Remove the line I drew with fear
I want my dreams to match the magnitude
Of the God who called the stone to move
No dream is too big for you

There's vision you've placed inside of me waiting to be seen

"Who Would I Be" Copyright 2014 Erin Jamieson. Written by Erin Jamieson and Calah Caballero.
https://open.spotify.com/track/0GIJkVjDDjktWZoURIoGF2?si=E6h5IUTBRJaLpu-K64hhkA

https://itunes.apple.com/us/album/who-would-i-be/1355593654?i=1355593657

Author's Note

One of the hardest things about the walk of faith is when things don't turn out as we think they should. Maybe I'm the only one who struggles with this, but I don't like it when bad things happened to good people. I know God's promises are true and for me, but many a depressed day I have spent questioning and rethinking what I believe. Our faith is the substance of things we hope for (good outcomes) but we do not always see. Aren't you glad God called us believers? I would have called us all controllers. When I curb my own expectations and fully focus on divine faith, something shifts in me. I can believe unknown purposes are happening from God's hand—so many I will never see. And because He is a good Father, I can trust beyond my limits of understanding.

Anna is a lovely example of someone who has little hope her heart that her circumstances would ever change.

Ohhhh grace of God for what we cannot see.

YOU are the believer for *your* generations! Well done beloved, stay strong and Trust beyond what you see!

Believing with you—

Julia

Jesus said, "So, you believe because you've seen with your own eyes. Even better blessings are in store for those who believe without seeing."

John 20:29 MSG

Please come find me at www.Juliadwrites.com.

Sign up for my inconsistent newsletter and be entered in all my fun giveaways.

www.ingramcontent.com/pod-product-compliance
Lightning Source LLC
Chambersburg PA
CBHW030330200626
46816CB00006BA/1991